*On the Sabbath
we went outside the
city gate to the river,
where we expected to find a
place of prayer. We sat down and
began to speak to the women who had
gathered there. One of those listening was
a woman from the city of Thyatira named
Lydia, a dealer in purple cloth. She was a
worshiper of God. The Lord opened her
heart to respond to Paul's message. When
she and the members of her household were
baptized, she invited us to her home. "If
you consider me a believer in the Lord,"
she said, "come and stay at my house."*

And she persuaded us.

—ACTS 16:13–15 (NIV)

Ordinary Women of the BIBLE

Ordinary Women of the BIBLE

BEFITTING ROYALTY
LYDIA'S STORY

ELIZABETH ADAMS

Guideposts
Danbury, Connecticut

Ordinary Women of the Bible is a trademark of Guideposts.

Published by Guideposts Books & Inspirational Media
100 Reserve Road, Suite E200
Danbury, CT 06810
Guideposts.org

This is a work of fiction. While the characters and settings are drawn from scripture
references and historical accounts, apart from the actual people, events, and locales
that figure into the fiction narrative, all other names, characters, places, and events
are the creation of the author's imagination or are used fictitiously.

Every attempt has been made to credit the sources of copyrighted material used
in this book. If any such acknowledgment has been inadvertently omitted or
miscredited, receipt of such information would be appreciated.

Scripture references are from the following sources: *New American Standard Bible (NASB)*.
Copyright © 1960, 1962, 1963, 1968, 1971, 1972, 1973, 1975, 1977, 1995 by the
Lockman Foundation. Used by permission. *The Holy Bible, New International Version
(NIV)*. Copyright © 1973, 1978, 1984, 2011 by Biblica, Inc. Used by permission
of Zondervan. All rights reserved worldwide. www.zondervan.com. *Holy Bible, New
Living Translation (NLT)*. Copyright © 1996. Used by permission of Tyndale House
Publishers, Inc., Wheaton, Illinois 60189. All rights reserved. *Contemporary English
Version (CEV)*. Copyright © 1991, 1992, 1995 by American Bible Society. Used
by permission. *Complete Jewish Bible (CJB)*, copyright © 1998 by David H. Stern.
Published by Jewish New Testament Publications, Inc. www.messianicjewish.net/
jntp. Distributed by Messianic Jewish Resources Int'l. www.messianicjewish.net.
All rights reserved. Used by permission. *The Holy Bible, King James Version (KJV)*. *The
Holy Bible, New Century Version®. (NCV)* Copyright © 2005 by Thomas Nelson, Inc.

Cover and interior design by Müllerhaus

Cover illustration by Brian Call and nonfiction illustrations by Nathalie Beauvois,
both represented by Deborah Wolfe, LTD.

Typeset by Aptara, Inc.

Printed and bound in the United States of America

10 9 8 7 6 5 4 3 2 1

Ordinary Women of the BIBLE

❖

BEFITTING ROYALTY
LYDIA'S STORY

CHAPTER ONE

Lydia pushed on as the crowds pressed close. The streets were filled with merrymakers, already celebrating, as well as women leading donkeys pulling carts laden down with supplies. She waved at Leia and Asuman, indicating for them to stay near. She probably did not need to fuss at them, as they knew these streets as well as she did. But the parcel they transported today was irreplaceable, and she would not be at ease until they had delivered it safely.

"Some people must not realize the festival does not start until tomorrow." Leia ducked her head as a man, already stinking of much drink, leered at her as he passed by. She moved closer to the wagon, protecting the parcel inside. Asuman nodded and spoke softly to the donkey, urging it on.

Tomorrow already. They were late making this delivery. She had hoped to get the cloth—possibly the finest cloth her workshop had ever created—to Felix last week, but the special weave on the fine-spun wool had proven trickier than she'd expected. His seamstress would have to work quickly to turn it into a robe. But it would be worth it when he saw how it shimmered in the sun.

"We will be there soon." Lydia pushed through the crowd and soon emerged into the agora teeming with people.

Vendors selling fish, fruit, or spices called out from their stalls, and the tables where men gambled were full. The fortune-teller called out from her regular booth, trying to lure customers to hear her predict the future. To the left, the municipal building stood. It was imposing, made of marble blocks and fluted columns. A statue of the emperor guarded the steps. To the right was the library, which the magistrates sent from Rome had filled with books and manuscripts of all kinds. Crowds spilled out of the temple to Saturn, making their offerings for the holiday. Saturn was said to be the god of crops and growing, and many in the area believed they depended on his mercy. Lydia knew better and tried her best to guide the cart through the crowd. A woman, laden down with baskets of meats and vegetables, pressed into Asuman, who stumbled against the wagon.

"Sorry," Asuman said, ducking her head. The woman stormed off as if she had not heard.

"It is just up ahead," Lydia said, pointing to the far side of the agora. She was grateful it had not been Leia. Leia was loyal and dedicated, and she was a master crafter at the loom, but she had a sharp tongue and was quick to pick a fight. Lydia just wanted to make this delivery without incident.

They finally made it past the square and entered a side street lined with large homes. This was the part of the city where the government officials preferred to live, with its hilly streets that gave them the best views over the city. "It is just up there," Lydia said. The donkey's hooves clapped along the stones.

Lydia had supervised deliveries to this house before. Felix, a high-ranking magistrate, liked to be well dressed and was one of her most loyal customers. The house did not look like much from the outside—just blocks of cut stone pressed up against its neighbors—but Lydia knew better. While Asuman tied up the donkey, Leia knocked on the door, a heavy wooden slab carved with intricate scrollwork. Lydia hoisted out the heavy bundle of fabric.

"I can help with that," Asuman said, coming up next to Lydia, but Lydia shook her head.

"I do not need help," Lydia said, balancing the heavy parcel in her arms. Asuman knew better than to argue.

They were quickly ushered inside the house by a servant girl with glossy black hair and high cheekbones. The late-afternoon sun filled the central courtyard with light. They were ushered upstairs to Felix's private chambers at the top of the house. As soon as the three women were inside the room, the servant stepped out and closed the door.

"Lydia." Felix sat behind a wooden table, writing on a strip of parchment. He set his quill down and pushed back from the desk. Light streamed in through the arched windows that showed a dramatic sweep of the town. "It is good to see you again."

"It is good to see you too. You look well." Felix wore linen robes of a deep indigo, and his beard was neatly trimmed and oiled. She had learned that it was wise to flatter Felix, who liked to be admired. "That color looks very good on you."

"It is a beautiful color, isn't it?" Felix laughed as he stood. Behind him, an open door led into his sleeping quarters and revealed his bed, beautifully carved and layered in deep purple coverings. "I got the fabric from a beautiful woman. One who makes the finest cloth in Macedonia."

Lydia forced herself to keep the smile on her face from faltering as she shifted the parcel into Leia's arms. She had learned to ignore the way he studied her form whenever she saw him. He was a powerful man in the city, she reminded herself, and one of her best customers.

"I would like to meet this woman who is my competitor," Lydia said, keeping her voice light. Of course she recognized the fabric as one of her own, but she knew better than to fall for his flattery.

Felix laughed again. "See? That is why I like you, Lydia. Clever and funny as well as beautiful." He gave her one more appraising look and nodded, and then he stepped forward. "Let us see this cloth you have kept me waiting so long for."

He crossed the stone floor, inlaid with strips of marble, and indicated that Leia should set the parcel down on the table in the corner of the room. Lydia moved toward the table, positioned next to an arched window that looked out over the theater and the aqueduct. Leia set the package down, and she and Asuman stepped back while Lydia unwrapped the heavy cloth covering that protected the fabric within. She gently pulled out the finely woven wool. It was the color of ripe eggplants, and it was shot through with threads the color of gold. Her team had rarely worked so hard on a piece, and she was pleased with the result. She lifted the bolt of fabric and unwrapped a section, letting it hang free. The golden threads gleamed in the sunlight that streamed in through the windows.

"I don't know how you do it, Lydia, but every time, you make me something more beautiful." Felix stepped forward and ran his fingers over the wool, nodding at its smooth touch. "It was very clever the way you wove that gold thread in."

"My weavers are the best in Philippi." She was not bragging. It was true, and everyone knew it. While it was quicker and easier to purchase and dye whole strips of cloth, Lydia's team had dyed this wool in its raw form and had it spun and then woven it after the color was fast. This meant they were able to weave the shimmering golden thread in with it. "Leia worked on this piece." She nodded at Leia, who kept her eyes on the ground.

"You are very talented," Felix said. He trailed his fingers along the fabric one more time and then moved his hand and placed it on Lydia's arm. She forced herself to not flinch. She was mindful of Leia and Asuman standing just behind her. "You have handled the business admirably since Andreas passed."

"My husband built up a strong business, and I am doing my best to honor him." Lydia had largely run the business herself while Andreas had been alive, but she could not say so.

"It has been, what, two years now?"

"It will be two in Martius."

The way Felix looked at her, she felt as if she were a goat being appraised at auction. "You are a beautiful woman. You would make a fine wife for the right man."

"I am focused solely on my business at the moment." His hand felt heavy on her arm.

"You would not have to run a business if you married me. You could spend your days as you wished, sitting in the shade and talking with the other women. Your every need would be met, and you would attend all the best gatherings and be much admired in the province." It was hardly a declaration of love. She took in a deep breath and let it out slowly.

Felix trailed his hand down her arm. "You are still young. We would have many fine sons. Surely you want sons."

Lydia would not let her face betray her emotion. "I am focused on my business at the moment," she repeated.

"I am a Roman citizen," Felix said. "You would be protected."

Protected from the laws that Felix and the men he worked with enacted, he meant. After Caesar's armies had conquered the whole Hellenic region and installed their own system of government, the officials had begun to bestow special privileges on residents who bore Roman citizenship. These citizens had freedom from many taxes and had special status within the colonies. If Andreas had been a Roman citizen, they would not have had to pay many of the local taxes that had saddled their business, and the dye works would have been even more profitable. Felix, a Roman patrician, would need to obtain special permission to marry her, a citizen of Macedonia, but she had no doubt a man in his position could obtain whatever he needed. And yet Lydia could not imagine marriage to Felix being worth the gains.

"I am afraid I must focus all of my energies on my business for now." Lydia stepped back, pulling her arm away.

Felix's brow creased, and he continued to watch her.

"Come here tomorrow for the feast," he said. "Celebrate with us. We will have much food and wine and dancing, and all the best people in Philippi will be there. You will see."

"That's very kind." Lydia tried to keep her voice even and steady. "But I do not celebrate."

His gaze did not falter. "That is right. I had forgotten. You worship with the Hebrews."

"I worship Adonai."

The quiet stretched out just a moment too long before he spoke again. "Even still, you would make a fine wife."

"I thank you, truly," she said. "But I must be going now." She gestured for Leia and Asuman to follow her, and she started for the door. "You may send payment for the material."

"It came quite late," Felix said as she walked away. "My seamstress will have to work very quickly to finish the robe before the festival begins. Because of that, I will not be able to pay the full amount, you understand."

Lydia understood that he was punishing her for her refusal. A part of her wanted to insist that he could and should pay the agreed-upon price for the fabric he had already told her was her finest. But she was more concerned with getting out of here with her dignity intact.

"I am sure you will pay what is fair," she said, and then she pulled open the door and walked out into the hallway. The same servant girl who had led them upstairs stood outside the door and now ushered them downstairs.

As soon as they were out onto the streets again, Leia burst out, "That man is insufferable."

"Please do not let him bother you, Leia," Lydia said. "We cannot let him worry us. He is one of our best customers, and we must speak of him with respect."

"Not such a great customer if he doesn't pay," Leia said, but a look from Lydia silenced her.

Asuman untied the donkey and they started back toward the agora. The crowds were thicker now, and the women were pressed together as they walked.

"I don't know," Asuman said. "He is not bad looking. He is rich. And if you married him, you would be one of the finest couples in town. Would you not consider it?"

"No, I would not." Lydia's voice was firm. For so many reasons, she would not. "Now let us forget about that man. We must get back to the workshop. There is still much to do."

After they passed through the city gates, the crowds thinned, and they had more space to walk. The stones were hard beneath their feet, but there was a breeze, and it carried the scent of eucalyptus and jasmine. The workshop was housed in a stone building not far off the *Via Egnatia*, the Egnatian Way, the road that linked the western sea to Byzantium, far to the east. Andreas had taken great pride in the construction of the new workshop building when he had taken the business over from his father many years before. Andreas had never had much interest in the actual work of dyeing, spinning, and weaving cloth, but he had enjoyed the prestige that came with the lucrative trade, and had spent far more than he should have on making sure the building was the largest and finest of the dye works in the area. Lydia supposed she should be grateful. While he had lacked business sense, he had left her with a strong, well-built workshop, the envy of other owners of local dye works.

"Leia, would you please check the loom room?" Lydia asked as they neared the workshop. "Please make sure they are close to finishing that linen I promised Miklos. Asuman, will you make sure all is in order with the thread?"

Both women nodded, and after she opened the heavy wooden door, they scurried off. They were good workers, and loyal. Giorgio stepped in from the storage room and greeted Lydia as she crossed the small front space where she handled her business dealings. The room was cool and well lit from narrow openings Andreas had wanted built into the top of the walls. They were meant for ventilation, to let the stench of the dyes out, but they also brought in sunlight.

"Was Felix pleased with the fabric?" Giorgio asked. His gray hair was matted to his head, wet from the heat of the vat room.

"He was," Lydia said, settling onto the stool. After the long walk, it felt good to rest. "Though he threatened to withhold part of the payment because it was late in coming."

"That man would take a denarius from a starving child if he could get away with it," Giorgio said.

Lydia shook her head, stifling a smile. It was dangerous to say such things about the magistrate—there was no telling who might overhear and report the words—but Lydia had long ago stopped trying to tell Giorgio what he could and could not say. Lydia did not know how old he was, but he had deep wrinkles and his hair and beard were gray. He had worked here at the dye works, supervising the boiling of the dyes, since Andreas had been a child. He did as he pleased, and as long as he continued to make the most stunning dyes in the region, Lydia would not complain.

"You had a visitor," Giorgio said. "Damon came by to collect payment for the latest shipment of wool. I told him you would return shortly. He will come back after he visits the other workshops." Giorgio winked. "Wants to get paid before the holiday, no doubt. Saturnalia is not much fun without some coins in your pocket."

"Thank you, Giorgio." Giorgio had been one of Andreas's most loyal workers, and while he had always treated her with respect during her husband's lifetime, he had not been pleased when Lydia took over after Andreas's passing. It had taken many months before he would look her in the eye, and many more before he started to accept her orders as valid. But over the months, he had come to tolerate working for a woman and had even begun to chastise other workers who defied her. He even tried to joke with her from time to time. "If you could start to clean out the vats, I would appreciate it," Lydia continued. "It is almost time to close."

Giorgio often stayed here overnight when there was a dye on boil, but because of the holiday, the vat room was empty.

Giorgio nodded and then turned and walked back through the doorway toward the storage room.

Lydia sat at the table and pulled out the strip of vellum she used to track her costs and income. Andreas had not been much for numbers, so early in their marriage Lydia had taken on the task herself, taught at a young age by an indulgent father who let her look in on his own business dealings while she was a girl. She marked that she had made the delivery to Felix, and that payment was still due. She added up the amounts due to her various suppliers. The largest payment, as always, was due to the man from Neapolis who supplied the seashells used to make the costly purple dye. Then she counted out the coins she owed to Damon, who sold the finest wool. She became so absorbed in her calculations that she didn't hear the door open again or notice that Damon had entered the workshop until he stood in front of her. She saw his frame before her, started, and then laughed.

"Damon. Goodness. I didn't see you." He was a tall man, solidly built. How had she missed him come in?

"You were concentrating hard on something." Damon smiled. He had supplied wool to Andreas for many years, and she had gotten to know him since she had taken over the business. He was a kind man who charged fair prices.

"I was looking over the accounts," Lydia said. "I guess I was more wrapped up in the numbers than I realized."

Damon shook his head. "I have never met a woman who found business accounts so intriguing." He was teasing her.

"You must not have met too many women responsible for making sure they can pay their workers, then." She set her quill down and sighed. It had grown darker as the sun slipped lower in the sky.

"No, I suppose that is true." Damon tilted his head just a little. "There are not many women who are brave enough to take charge of a business."

"I am not sure whether it was brave or stupid." Many had urged her to let Andreas's brother, Tobias, take over. Tobias would have gladly stepped into running the profitable workshop, but Lydia had fought to keep hold of the business she herself had helped build. She had grown up learning this trade, and she did not need anyone to help her run the dye works. She had held firm to the business, even though many would have liked to strip her of it.

"Perhaps a little of both." Damon laughed. "But you have proven that you are better than most men at this."

"You flatter me. You must want your money quite badly."

"I do want the money. I have my own workers to pay." Damon stepped closer. "But that is not why I flatter you. I do that because I like to see you smile."

Coming from another man, it might have sounded disingenuous. But there was something about Damon that made her trust him. She reached for the coins and held them out. The face of Caesar Augustus glinted in the soft light. "Flirting with me will not make me pay you more."

"See? I told you that you are better at business than most." Damon took the coins and counted them before slipping them in the leather bag at his waist. He smiled at her again and then turned back toward the door. "Have a nice holiday, Lydia."

"You as well." There was no need to tell him that she had no intention of joining in the raucous debauchery that Saturnalia inevitably became. Damon cast one last look back at Lydia and then pushed open the door and walked out into the early evening light.

Good. That was one account settled, Lydia thought, marking the payment on her vellum. But somehow, she still felt a twinge of disappointment that he was gone.

CHAPTER TWO

Few of Lydia's workers came to the workshop over the next three days. As Saturnalia was an official Roman holiday, they were entitled to the days off, and Lydia spent much of the latter part of the week alone, experimenting with the dried pigments stored in heavy earthen jars. This was what Lydia loved best—measuring out small amounts of the costly powders, their jewel-like colors arrayed before her, and adding water and olive oil, then slipping a fresh, clean cloth into the mixture. Lydia would never tire of seeing the way the fibers soaked in the pigment, turning first a light hue and darkening with time. In these quiet days, Lydia was experimenting with madder, a root vegetable that could be used to produce dye some said could replace murex shells for making purple cloth. Some workshops, she knew, had started to mix madder in with the pigment made from the shells to save costs, but though madder was far cheaper, Lydia was unhappy with the resulting color. Each batch of mixed dye she tried created an inferior color—a reddish magenta, a pale lavender, a sickly orange color. None of the batches made with madder produced the vibrant, deep purple hue that was so desired. After three days of tests, Lydia had decided that while the madder might be cheaper, she would stick to the more costly but more beautiful murex shells.

On the Sabbath, she did not go to the workshop. Instead, she made her way out of the city gates and down to the banks of the river Gangites. There were but a small number of followers of Adonai in Philippi, and they had no synagogue in which to gather. Andreas had been working for many years to receive permission from the magistrates to have one built, but he had not gotten far, and so they continued to gather each week along the banks of the muddy river to offer worship to the one true God.

Lydia made her way to the river that Sabbath morning, along with her servants Danae, Iduma, and Elodie, as well as Leon, the man who kept her garden and cared for the animals. It was especially important to gather with fellow Jews now, when most of the town was united in offering sacrifices to the Roman god Saturn. Lydia joined the small group of Jewish worshippers. First she greeted Andreas's mother, Dorit, kissing her on each cheek. The woman had grown frailer since Andreas passed, and many weeks she could not make it to the Sabbath gathering, but she enjoyed seeing the other members of their small community.

"Shalom, *Imma*," Lydia said, bowing her head. She knew the term made the older woman happy, though she had never tried too hard to make Lydia feel like a daughter.

"Shalom, Lydia." Dorit nodded. "You look well."

"You as well."

Dorit had made it clear over the years that she had hoped for many grandchildren, and she did not hide her disappointment that Lydia had only delivered one daughter. Andreas's brother, Tobias, had given her four grandchildren, and that had softened the blow some.

Dorit turned away to greet one of Tobias's daughters now, and Lydia turned and greeted her friend Agata and sister-in-law, Sara, but then she quickly made her way across the muddy bank to greet Anna.

"Shabbat shalom." Lydia leaned in and pulled her daughter close for a hug. "It is good to see you."

"Shabbat shalom." Anna returned the greeting and pulled back. "You look tired. You have been working too hard."

Lydia did not want to discuss this again. "You look well yourself."

"I am serious, Imma. You do not have to spend every day at that stinky workshop. You could relax and rest. Enjoy your later years. Let someone else handle the work."

Lydia bit her tongue, ignoring the familiar refrain. For one thing, she was still several years from turning forty—she was hardly in her last days. But also, Anna had never understood her taking over the dye works. As a girl she had never failed to comment on the smell that clung to Andreas whenever he returned to the house, and she had shown no interest in the business as she grew.

"How is Daniel?" Lydia changed the subject. She had already spotted her son-in-law, along with her three-year-old grandson, Eli, on the men's side of the gathering. Daniel was speaking intently with several of the other men of the congregation. No doubt deciding which man would lead which portions of the service, Lydia assumed.

"Much better. He still has a cough, but it is improving. The doctor said he must rest, but it is so difficult. You know how hard he always works. So many people depend on him."

Lydia nodded. Her son-in-law was in the building trade, working alongside his father and brothers, and there was much work in the rapidly growing city. He also took great pride in his own importance—but Lydia stopped herself. There was no need to be uncharitable. Daniel provided very well for his household and loved Anna. Andreas had arranged the match, and Anna had been pleased. That was what mattered to Lydia.

"And how is Eli?" Lydia watched her grandson tossing rocks into the river with another small boy. He seemed to have grown since she had seen him last.

"He is starting to learn his letters. Arina believes he is even more advanced than his father was at that age."

"That is very good." Lydia had already spotted Daniel's mother talking with the wife of Daniel's youngest brother. She had nodded, and Arina had nodded in return.

Anna continued to talk about Eli until Daniel stood on the tall rock at the side of the river and began to chant in Hebrew. He had been chosen to recite the prayers this week, then. Lydia joined in, repeating the familiar words of the benediction, and then they repeated the *shema,* or creed. Lydia found herself soothed by the recitation of the familiar words from the Torah and the prayers to Adonai.

Lydia had only begun to worship Adonai when she had come to Philippi to marry Andreas. His family—like Daniel's— was one of the few devout Jewish families in Philippi, and

17

Andreas's father would not allow the match unless she converted to the Hebrew faith. Lydia's father, eager to establish an alliance with the rival dye-maker's family, had agreed, and Lydia had converted to Judaism shortly before her marriage. At first, she had missed the variety of having so many gods to pray to. She could not understand why she must be limited to offering prayers and sacrifices only to Adonai. But over the years, she had come to love the rhythms and the rituals and the language of her adopted faith and had come to fear and respect the God of Abraham, Isaac, and David.

After the reading of the Law and the Prophets, Ephrath moved to the great stone and turned to face the small gathering. Lydia was grateful to see that he had been selected to speak. A dealer in animal skins, he often had more insightful observations about the ancient texts than the men in the congregation with more formal education.

Daniel did his best to keep Eli seated and focused while Ephrath spoke, but the boy wiggled and flopped down and tried to wrench his way out of his father's grasp. Lydia did not see why the child could not sit with his mother and grandmothers. He was small yet, and he would be still in Lydia's lap. But Daniel would not allow it, did not want his child, who would one day be a man, to get confused. Anna did not argue with her husband's word, and Lydia knew better than to voice her thoughts on the matter.

While Ephrath spoke, Lydia noticed a group of men gathering a short distance down the riverbank. They were unkempt— she could see that from here. Their robes were filthy, and their hair and beards grew untrimmed. Lydia tried to focus her attention on Ephrath's words, but her gaze was pulled to the gathering down the bank. Who were these men, and why were they here? Sometimes women came out here to wash clothes, but it was rare to see men gather here. And they did not seem like revelers enjoying the holiday. There was none of the whooping and shouting that usually accompanied the drunkenness and debauchery of the festival of Saturn. Lydia continued to watch as Ephrath droned on. They also did not appear to be Druids or to be from one of the small sects that worshipped Dionysus or any of the other false gods. Their cults were not sanctioned by the Roman government, and their worshippers were usually not so bold as to gather in public.

Lydia watched as the smallest one, who appeared to be their leader, sat on the riverbank and opened a satchel. He pulled out what looked to be bread and shared it around with the three men who also sat around him.

"They are now calling themselves followers of the Way," Anna whispered. And then, with derision in her voice, "Christians."

"Christians?" Lydia did not know the word.

"Followers of that zealot Jesus down in Galilee. They believe he is the Christ." Anna could not hold back a smirk. "Daniel says they arrived from Neapolis yesterday."

Lydia nodded. She had heard about the political squabble that had flared up over the man who claimed to be the long-promised Messiah, the Christ—*the anointed one*, in Hebrew.

He had ended up hanging from a Roman cross, dying alongside common thieves, though not before leading thousands astray. Another false prophet.

Lydia still observed the men while Ephrath continued to speak and throughout the final benediction. The men ate their meal quietly, watching the water flow past.

"I must go," Anna said as soon as the final prayer was done. "It is time for Eli to rest."

Lydia nodded, watching her daughter march to the side of the gathering where the men were. Now that the service was over, it was allowed. Lydia followed a few steps behind and scooped up the wiggling child, who threw his arms around her and relaxed against her.

"How are you?" she asked the little boy. He had the same round cheeks and brown eyes flecked with gold that Anna had had as a child.

"Bored. Why is it so long?"

Lydia had to laugh. It was a long time for a child to sit.

"You will come to appreciate the service as you grow older," Lydia said.

Anna was already reaching out for her son, trying to take him into her arms.

"We must go, Imma," Anna said. "Daniel says it is time to leave."

Reluctantly, Lydia released her grandson. "You must join me for supper," she said.

"Daniel has much work to do. He will be busy all day," Anna said. "But soon." Then she turned toward her husband, who was already starting to walk away from the river and back toward the city gates.

It was the Sabbath. The day of rest observed by Jews the world over. Besides that, it was still a Roman holiday. What houses would he be building today? What work would he do? But Anna was already gone, scurrying after her husband with her son in tow.

Lydia watched them go, and then she turned back and walked over to where Agata and Sara were waiting. Sara wore a gold choker around her neck, as well as a jeweled ring on every finger. Sara was married to Andreas's brother, Tobias, who worked as a tax collector, while Agata was a widow, like Lydia. Both had been lifelong followers of Adonai.

"It is hard when they are so young," Agata said.

"I suppose it is." Lydia remembered Anna's childhood as a joyous time, full of wonder and excitement and tender hugs, but maybe time had erased the hard edges.

"You must go to visit her this week," Sara said. "While Daniel is at work."

Lydia nodded. It was hard to find the time when she spent so many long days at the workshop. But Sara was right. She would go visit Anna and Eli this week.

Sara began to talk about the new grandchild she was expecting and the gown she was having made, and Lydia half listened. Lydia really should pay better attention. Sara's daughter was married to a devout man in Corinth, and Lydia would be expected to produce a gift for the new child. But her attention was caught by the men who had been sitting farther down the riverbank—the Christians. They had finished their meal and were now walking toward their group.

"Who are those men?" Agata asked as soon as Sara paused. She nodded toward the approaching group. The short one was at the front, along with a taller, thicker man. Behind them were the two others.

"Anna says they are followers of Jesus," Lydia answered. "They call themselves followers of the Way, she says."

"What do they want?" Agata asked, her eyebrows rising. "Why would they come here?"

"I do not know," Lydia said. They didn't appear threatening. None carried a weapon, and their stance was not menacing. But there could be no good reason for them to approach this gathering now.

"I have no use for false prophets or those who follow them." Sara sniffed, and she started to turn away. But the men were almost upon them now. Lydia could not think how to turn and leave them now without upsetting the men. And who could know what these foreigners might do when upset?

"Shabbat shalom!" the shorter one called out. "Good morning to you."

Neither of her friends gave an answer, so, after an awkward pause, Lydia called out, "Shalom."

The men stopped when they were just in front of the women. "We do not mean to interrupt," the leader said. "It seems you have just finished your Sabbath service."

"That is correct." There was no warmth in Agata's voice.

"I am a Jew myself," the short man continued. "I have studied with the finest teachers of the Torah and been educated among the best scribes."

Lydia listened. Why was he telling them all this? Up close, she could see scars on his cheeks from long-ago acne and dark brown eyes. Curls of dark hair cascaded from under his hood.

"I am Paul," he said. "This is my friend Silas." He gestured at the taller, larger one. Up close, she saw that he was much bigger than his friend. "And these are our friends Timothy and Luke." He gestured to the two behind him. Timothy was pale and lanky and young, not much more than a boy, really. Luke was darker, with fine, handsome features. He was not as disheveled as the others and wore a cleaner robe of delicate blue linen. "We are traveling around the world to spread the Good News about the Christ," Paul continued.

"The good news is that the troublemaker is no longer among us," Agata said.

"You have heard of Him, then?" Paul asked, his voice losing none of its warmth despite his frosty reception. "Perhaps you did not hear that after He died and was laid in the tomb, on the third day He rose again."

Agata shifted on her feet. "You are telling us He came back from the dead?"

Lydia had not heard this claim about the man Jesus. It was ludicrous. She studied Paul's face. He seemed to truly believe what he was telling them. She sensed no falsehood in him. What he was saying was ridiculous, of course, but she got the sense that he was not some huckster out to trick them. He was sincere, though misguided.

"Exactly," Paul continued. "And after He rose again, He walked among men for another forty days before He went to be with His Father again."

Sara snorted. But though Lydia knew it was ridiculous and understood that none of it could be true, there was still something inside of her that wanted to hear what else they had to say.

"If this man could bring people back from the dead, why would He not bring my Jacob back from the dead?" Agata asked.

Paul looked at each of the women, really looked at their faces, and in that moment he looked at Lydia, she felt as if he could see inside her very self. Then, gently, he said, "Why don't we have a seat by the river, and I will tell you what I believe."

Sara and Agata both hesitated and looked at Lydia. Lydia was not sure what to do. The servants had already gone back to prepare the midday meal, save for little Elodie, who waited under a grove of poplars to accompany Lydia home. They would be waiting for her, and Iduma did not like her cooking to sit. And these men were clearly nothing but misguided fools. No good could come of sitting down with them now. And yet Lydia felt herself start to move toward the rocks, as if controlled by something outside of herself. Agata and Sara did not move at first, but soon she heard footsteps behind her, and she realized they were coming with her. It took a moment for the four men to settle in on the rocks around them, close enough that they could speak and hear but not so close as to feel like a threat.

"I am sorry for your loss," Paul said, looking at Agata. "We know that before his own death, Jesus brought a few people back from the grave. That is one of the many ways we are sure He was from Adonai. But He did not come to earth to bring back the dead. Instead, He came to free us from the power of death entirely. He was the long-promised Messiah."

Once again the women looked at one another. What this man said made no sense. The Messiah foretold in the scriptures would free the chosen people from bondage of Roman oppression and give His faithful peace and security. Jesus had not done that. And what did he mean, free them from death entirely? It was nonsense.

And yet...

There was some silent hum within Lydia while these men spoke. She would not be able to put it in words if asked, but it was there, opening her ears to the possibility within the impossibility.

"I myself found this hard to believe," Paul continued. "I had ideas about what the Messiah would be, and Jesus did not fulfill my expectations. I was a faithful Jew, and I believed His messengers were speaking blasphemy. I made it my job to persecute them, to wipe their heresy out of the land. I gathered up as many followers of Jesus as I could so they could be put to death. And let me tell you, I was thorough. I was ruthless. If it had been up to me, all the disciples would have been put to death."

"But here you are," Sara said dryly.

"But here I am, telling you that I had it all wrong. That Jesus was the long-promised One. Listen."

And then he proceeded to tell them an impossible story. He told them that as he had been walking along a road outside Damascus, he had seen a light that fell from heaven. He talked about being blinded, being able to neither eat nor drink. He spoke of a man named Ananias, a follower of Jesus, who came to his home, trembling because he knew of Saul's reputation for persecuting believers, and how Ananias gave Saul a message from Christ himself, that God had chosen Paul to carry His message to the Gentiles and their kings and to all the people of Israel.

Sara cleared her throat and shifted on the rock.

And now, Paul continued, here he was, obediently sharing the truth that Jesus was the Son of God, the Christ.

While Paul spoke, Lydia watched the one called Silas. He was a large man, muscled from much labor, with coarse skin and wiry hair. He could have been a guard or a member of the Roman army, except that she saw the traces of ink tattooed into his arm, just visible under the edge of his robe. He had spent time as a prisoner or slave, then. And yet as he listened to the words of Paul—words he had no doubt heard many times before—tears rose up in his eyes.

"The prophecies about the coming Messiah—they are all fulfilled in Jesus Christ," Paul continued.

Sara let out a sigh. "I will not listen to any more of this nonsense." She pushed herself up. "Tobias is waiting."

She stood, waiting for the others to follow her. Slowly, after a moment's hesitation, Agata rose too.

"Lydia?" Agata held out her hand, offering to help Lydia to her feet. But Lydia did not move. She could not have said why she did not get up and walk away as her friends did. It defied all logic and reason for her to remain here. And yet there was that hum. It had not been silenced as Paul told his impossible tale. It had grown louder, as if all the parts inside of her were strumming the chords of some imperceptible song.

"I will stay," she heard herself say. She saw her friends start, saw them look at one another and then gaze down at her.

"Come, Lydia," Sara said. "We have heard enough of this nonsense. It is time to go." Agata leaned down, offering her hand again.

"I will stay," Lydia repeated, louder this time.

Again her friends hesitated. They were not worried for her safety, Lydia knew. Lydia ran a business. She often spent time in the company of men, and she did not shrink from them. No, Lydia knew that they feared she had lost her wits.

"I want to hear more. I will stay," Lydia repeated. "Go if you choose, but I am staying."

After another glance at each other, Sara and Agata both turned to go. She saw Agata look back at her as she walked away, but she did not stop.

"What did you mean, Jesus came to free us from death?" Lydia asked.

"Ah." Paul nodded. "We know that death entered the world through Adam. Because of his sin, we were all condemned to die. Death was the result of sin." Paul turned to the one with fine features, the one called Luke. "My friend Luke is a doctor. Luke, tell us what happens when life leaves a body."

Lydia did not need a doctor to explain the process to her. She had seen it herself—first, her mother, while she was still a child, and then her father. She had seen their bodies slowly shut down. Heard the rattle in their breath as death neared. She had seen the moment the life went out of their eyes and their breath slowed to nothing.

"The human body is carefully designed," the one called Luke began. "Its systems and organs all work together to keep a person alive. But when a person dies, the systems cease, and the body begins to rot. It is just a shell left behind. It is nothing."

"But it is not the same for those who believe in the truth," Paul said. "Just as sin entered the world through one man, Adam, we are freed from sin by the death of one man, the man we call the Christ. Those of us who believe in Him, we are dead to sin, and we are alive in Christ. We who are baptized into Christ Jesus are baptized into His death; therefore, we are buried with him through the baptism in death. In the same way, just as Christ was raised from the dead, through the glory of the Father, we too may live a new life."

Lydia heard the words, but they did not make sense to her. What was Luke talking about? What did Paul mean, going on about sin and baptism? What did he mean, Jesus's followers would have a new life? It did not make sense. None of it made any sense.

But she could not deny that hum that was growing louder within her every moment. She could not understand the mystery of Paul's words, but something within some part of her she'd never known before responded to them anyway.

"I know that these words are hard to understand," Paul said. "I myself thought it was all nonsense. For the message of the cross is foolishness to those who are perishing. But to us who are being saved, it is the power of God."

It did sound like foolishness. If she was as smart as others said she was, she would get up and go right now and leave these men and their empty words behind.

But she did not.

Instead, she sat still. She let the words fill her. And she felt, in some way she would never understand and could never begin to explain, her heart being opened. The words these men spoke did not make sense, but at that moment, nothing in her life had ever made more sense. It was as though she had been waiting her whole life to hear what they had to say, only she hadn't known it until now. Before she could stop them, tears stung her eyes, and though she tried to contain them, they soon spilled down her cheeks. Lydia was more confused than she had ever been, and yet at the same time, she felt the most incredible peace. Like she could finally let go of a burden she hadn't known she'd been carrying. She did not know what she was feeling, knew she would never be able to explain it, but it also felt like home.

Luke, the doctor, handed her a clean cloth he'd pulled from his robe. Timothy, the one who had not yet spoken, moved toward her and put his hand gently on her arm. Under normal circumstances, she would have moved away from a strange man's touch, but this was anything but normal. His touch steadied her, and she gave in to the feelings that overwhelmed her—confusion and doubt and, despite it all, that overwhelming peace. The humming inside of her was finding resonance.

How many years had she stood here on this dirty riverbank, praying for the Messiah to come and free His people from their suffering and oppression? This Jesus—He was nothing like what they had been expecting. The Jewish people were waiting for a king. A ruler who would establish his dominion and set them free from oppression, not a carpenter from some backwater in Galilee. They were waiting for a nation, a holy land promised to their ancestors, a place where the Hebrews would be free from foreign rule. Jesus had brought none of that.

And yet these men claimed that He had brought freedom from sin and death instead. That in dying, He had given them life. Lydia did not understand it, but in that moment, she had never felt more free.

Could it really be true? Could this Jesus really be the Son of God? Could He really be the Messiah they had been waiting for so long?

As tears spilled down her cheeks, she realized the answer. Despite all the reasons it seemed impossible, she believed. She could not explain it, but she knew by the way the hum within her had turned into the most beautiful melody she had ever heard.

No one said anything as she continued to weep. She did not understand why she was crying, but in those tears she felt clean. And then, when she had spent them all, she gathered her words, cleared her throat, and asked, "What must I do to be saved?"

Paul gave a small smile. "You do not have to do anything. The work has already been done. All you must do is believe."

Lydia considered this. Could it really be that simple? "I believe."

Then Paul nodded, as if he'd already known the answer. "You are blessed and highly favored, Lydia."

In that moment, she knew it was true.

"May we pray for you?" Paul asked.

Lydia suddenly wanted nothing more.

"Lord, we are Your humble servants, and we thank You for opening the eyes of Your daughter Lydia. Bless her and make her grow in knowledge and understanding."

"May it be so," the others said quietly.

Lydia sat and waited. What was she to do now?

The men were smiling, but none seemed ready to move.

"What now?" she asked. She was not used to simply sitting around, as she was a woman of action.

"Now you are a follower of Jesus Christ, a fellow laborer in the Gospel," Silas said quietly.

Lydia nodded. She understood that. "But what do I *do*?"

Luke laughed but not unkindly.

Paul smiled. "Would you like to be baptized?"

"Baptism." Lydia remembered Paul had mentioned this earlier. "This is like the *tevilah*?"

"It is like the tevilah," Paul said. "In that you are bathed in water. But it is not a purification ritual. You do not need to be purified, Lydia. You are already made clean. Baptism is a symbol that you have been changed."

Paul explained that John, the cousin of Jesus, had used the practice in preparation for the coming of the Lord, and after Jesus Himself had been baptized, now His followers and disciples did the same as a symbol that they had been changed. "You go under the water, like the three days the Christ spent in the tomb, and then emerge changed, just as He did."

"Then I will be baptized," Lydia said. Suddenly, she had never wanted anything more. She had tasted of the goodness of the Lord, and she longed for all of it. She wanted the whole world to know the truth of what these men were saying. "Myself and my whole household."

Luke laughed again, but Paul simply nodded. "Have your household come here at once."

Lydia turned toward Elodie, who was now standing alone under the grove of poplars. She was watching Lydia uncertainly. Elodie was the niece of one of the women who cleaned the dye jars at the workshop. Elodie's parents had more children than they could afford to feed, and her aunt had promised Lydia that the girl could cook and clean and sew. Lydia had taken her more out of pity than need, and the girl had proven to be as inept with a needle as she was in the kitchen, but Lydia liked her gentle spirit, and she kept her around anyway. Now Lydia gestured for the girl to come to her, and she began to walk toward the group gathered by the riverbank.

"Elodie, run back to the house and fetch Danae, Iduma, and Leon," Lydia said. "Have them come back here right away, please."

"Back here?" Elodie eyed the gathering warily. She had to have seen what had happened. She had to know that something had changed in a big way. "They will be preparing for the noonday meal."

"I understand," Lydia said. "But this is more important. Tell them to come at once, for we will all be baptized. We are now followers of Jesus, the Christ."

Elodie did not move for a moment, but her eyes widened. She took a long, slow breath, and then nodded. "Yes, miss." And then the girl turned and started back toward the road, in the direction of the city gates.

"Tell me more about Jesus," Lydia said.

Paul nodded, and while they waited for Elodie to return, the men told her about how Jesus had been born to a virgin, a woman who was engaged to a man descended from the line of King David himself, as Isaiah had prophesied. They told her the Christ had been born in Bethlehem, the City of David, as Micah had predicted. They told her how, when the baby Jesus was presented at the temple, the holy man Simeon had recognized the long-awaited Savior. With each fresh revelation from the men, Lydia was filled with wonder. How could she not have known? All she had heard about the man they called Christos was that He was a zealot and a troublemaker, a false prophet who had claimed, like so many before Him, to be the Messiah and ended up dead. But she had not heard that He was also a fulfillment of the prophecies the Jewish people had clung to for so many centuries. She had not realized that He had performed signs and wonders no one could explain— multiplying loaves and fishes, walking on water, raising the dead. How could she not have known? She would have believed long before now if only she had known.

"We must tell others," Lydia said. "They have to know."

"That is what we have dedicated our lives to," Paul said, nodding. "It does not matter how many rulers are upset or how many times I am imprisoned for it. I will not stop sharing the Good News until it has spread throughout the world."

Lydia nodded. Now that she knew, she would share that saving knowledge wherever she could.

It seemed like no time has passed before Elodie came back, leading Iduma, Danae, and Leon. The older servants approached warily, confused. Elodie had no doubt told them what had happened and why they were here.

"These men have taught me a great truth," Lydia said. Her knees groaned as she rose to her feet. "I believe that Jesus is the Christ, and I have decided I and my whole household will be baptized."

She watched as Iduma took a small step back. Leon took in a deep breath.

Danae spoke first. "Of course, mistress. If you think it is best."

"Let us all be covered by the blood of Jesus Christ."

Lydia was not blind. She could see their hesitation, their fear. She knew it was a dangerous thing she was asking them to do. There were not many Jews in Philippi, but at least Judaism was tolerated by Rome. The followers of Jesus, these Christians—well, that was a whole different story. But now that Lydia knew the truth, she could not pretend otherwise.

Paul, seeing their hesitation, quickly began to speak, telling them the same thing he had told Lydia, about how he knew Jesus was the Redeemer they had waited for. After he finished speaking, Lydia could see that Iduma and Leon were still skeptical. Well, her servants may not understand yet, but they would someday.

Paul led Lydia to the river and instructed her to take off her sandals. Then Paul stepped into the river, walking carefully until the water lapped at his waist, and gestured for her to follow him. Silas held on to her arm, supporting her as she stepped into the icy water. The cold bit into her, and she slipped on a smooth stone, sending up a splash. The water moved much faster than she'd realized, and it pulled at her long robes. An image flashed into her mind—as a child, she had nearly drowned in the river Lycus when she'd waded too far in after a storm. She remembered the feeling of being pulled under, fearing that she would never come up again. Her father had rescued her from the waters that day, clutching her to his chest and dragging her back to the riverbank. The fear and hopelessness of those brief moments still haunted her in her dreams sometimes and returned to her now, but Silas had stepped into the water next to her, and his strong arms kept her upright as she walked carefully across the rocky riverbed. He did not let go of her until she stood facing Paul in the middle of the river, foamy water flowing around them in whirls and eddies. For a moment, the sound of the rushing water drowned out all else, but then Paul spoke.

"Lydia of Philippi, do you believe that Jesus is the Christ, the Redeemer of Israel?"

"I do." And though just hours before, she had thought it ridiculous, now as she spoke the words, she had never meant anything more in her life.

"Then I baptize you in the name of Jesus Christ." Paul touched her arm and gestured for her to move closer to him, and Silas held her up as she stepped closer to Paul. Paul lowered her gently backward toward the water. Fear gripped her for the briefest moment, but then she remembered that she could trust these men. She closed her eyes and held her hand to her nose as the cold water closed over her, and then, quickly, she was lifted up and out of the water. Her hood slipped back, heavy with river water.

And when she opened her eyes again, she laughed. She did not feel any different inside, but somehow everything was different.

"Thank you," she said, as tears filled her eyes again. Paul nodded, pressing his lips together, and then Silas grasped her again and held her upright as she made her way across the swirling water back to the riverbank. Silas did not let her go until she was steady on the rocky bank. Whoever he was, whatever his past included, she was grateful for his strong presence.

The day had not felt cold when they were sitting on the bank, but now, with her clothing and hair soaked, Lydia felt the chill. Luke, the one with the handsome features, removed his own fine cloak and wrapped it around Lydia's shoulders.

"Danae?"

Danae did not move for a moment, but then she took in a breath, removed her outer cloak—thinking ahead in a way Lydia had not—and handed it to Elodie before she stepped toward Lydia. She was younger than Lydia and had served as her personal maid since her wedding, when she had been a gift from Andreas. She was thorough in her cleaning, and she knew about many herbs and poultices. She had made special teas for Lydia during her pregnancies and special tinctures for her after she had lost one baby after another. Lydia knew she could trust Danae and was not surprised to see her obey now. Danae walked uncertainly. Silas held out his hand and she took it, hesitantly. She glanced back at Lydia. Lydia smiled, trying to encourage her, before Danae stepped into the river. Paul held her tightly and lowered her into the water, and she came up sputtering, her eyes wide. Paul held her while she regained control over herself, and then Silas led her back to the riverbank and waited while Elodie handed Danae's cloak to her. Danae wrapped it quickly around herself and then held her arm out for Elodie's own cloak. Elodie took her cloak off and walked into the river. Once she had been baptized and returned safely to shore, Lydia instructed Leon that it was his turn.

Leon glanced at Danae, who nodded, almost impercepti- bly. Leon sighed, and then he moved toward the bank. None of Lydia's servants said a word. None of them met her eye.

Lydia knew they did not comprehend why she was making them do this. Their hearts had not been opened as hers had—yet. But they would know the truth soon enough, and they would be glad.

When Leon was back on the bank, wrapped again in his dry cloak, Lydia turned to Iduma, the oldest of her servants. Iduma had served in her father's house and had come with Lydia from Thyatira when she had married. She had been a faithful cook and manager over the years.

"Iduma, it is your turn," Lydia said gently.

"It does not hurt," Elodie said softly. Kind Elodie.

Iduma hesitated. Then, taking in a deep breath, she said, "I will not."

Lydia felt as though she had been slapped. Iduma was strong willed and had chosen to ignore Lydia's directions a few times over the years, instead doing tasks in her own way, but she had never shown outright defiance.

"You must," Lydia said, fighting to keep her voice calm. "I and my household now serve Jesus Christ."

She did not want to lose Iduma. She was a wonderful cook, and she was shrewd enough to get the best deals in the marketplace. In addition, Lydia knew that Iduma had few options if she left Lydia's house. She was not young, and she had no husband and no family to care for her. But Lydia could not waver on this.

Still Iduma kept her feet firmly planted. Lydia felt the gazes of the men in the river behind her, and shame now mixed with the frustration she felt. Why could Iduma not trust her?

Danae said something to Iduma, though Lydia could not hear what was said. But slowly, Iduma peeled off her cloak. She shot Lydia a look of pure anger, and then she kept her gaze on the ground. No one said a word while she was baptized in the river, and then Silas led her back to the bank and Elodie clutched her. Iduma would not look in Lydia's direction. She stood the bank, dripping, seething.

She might not understand now, Lydia thought, but she would see. She would believe, and she would know why Lydia had done this someday.

For now, seeing her household gathered around her on the riverbank, Lydia was filled with joy. She and her household now served the Anointed One.

"You may head home," Lydia said to the servants, and they did not waste time starting toward the road. Then she turned back to the men. Paul had made his way out of the river and now stood with the other men.

"How long will you stay in Philippi?" Lydia asked. She hoped they would not leave soon. She had so much to learn. They had so much to teach her.

"We will stay as long as the Lord wants us," Paul said. His clothes were sopping, his skin covered in gooseflesh. He seemed even smaller now that he was soaked. But he did not appear to mind. Instead, he wore a wide grin.

Lydia took his answer to mean they did not have firm plans.

"Where are you staying while you're in town?" Lydia asked. Perhaps she could meet with them before she went to the workshop some days, to hear more about the mighty things Christ had done.

Paul chuckled and gestured toward the grove of trees on the far side of the river, away from the Via Egnatia.

"Last night we slept over there. Tonight?" He shrugged. "The Lord always provides."

"You slept outside? On the ground?" This would not do. These men were messengers spreading the Good News. They deserved to sleep in a palace, not a hard patch of ground.

"We sleep where we can," Timothy said. "Our comfort is not of the utmost importance."

No, this would not do at all.

"You must stay with me," Lydia said. "There is plenty of space. You will be able to come and go as the Lord directs."

There was not much discussion between the men before they accepted. They did not know that her home was large and comfortable, and she supposed it did not matter. Surely any home was better than sleeping on the ground.

"We would be very grateful," Paul said.

"Then come." Lydia gestured for them to follow her. "It is well past time for the noonday meal. Come eat."

There was no argument from the men as they followed her to the road, where the Krenides Gate loomed ahead. The servants were some distance ahead of them, walking resolutely back toward the city.

When Lydia had come down this road to gather for the Sabbath service this morning, she'd had no idea how many things would be different before she returned. She'd had no thought that she would meet followers of Christ, let alone believe them and join them or invite them into her home. Now that she had, she did not know what the future held. All she knew, as she led Paul and Timothy and Luke and Silas toward her home, was that God had opened her heart, and because of that, everything was about to change.

CHAPTER THREE

L ydia slept well and deeply, and when she awoke, the winter sun was already above the horizon. She washed and dressed and went down the stairs to break her fast, and she found Paul and Silas and Luke already at the table.

"Good morning," Luke said as she came into the room. They had all bathed when they had arrived at Lydia's house the day before—Iduma, holding her nose, had insisted— and their robes were clean. They had laughed when they were shown to the tub of heated water, claiming they had not bathed in warm water for many months. Paul's beard had been trimmed, and Luke's olive skin was set off by the light blue color of his robe.

"Good morning." Lydia saw that Iduma had brought them fresh bread and yogurt and cheese and oranges, and the men were all enjoying healthy portions. "Did you sleep well?" Danae had been to the cistern, and there was fresh water in earthen-ware cups, brought through the Roman aqueduct.

"I have not slept so well in many months," Paul said. He was peeling the rind off an orange in a strip, and the sweet scent of citrus filled the air.

"It is the first time we have slept in beds in quite some time," Luke said. "It is wonderful."

"Your generosity is very much appreciated," Silas added. His beard had also been trimmed, and in his simple linen robe, his size was even more apparent.

As Lydia sat, Elodie emerged from the next room, carrying dishes and a linen napkin for Lydia. She set them down and then vanished back into the cooking room.

"I am glad to offer hospitality," Lydia said. "It is nice to have the rooms be full again." Though she had left the men to settle into the two rooms she mostly used for storage last night, she had heard them moving around and talking in low voices, and it had filled her with a kind of peace. "Where is Timothy?" He was not with the others.

"He has gone for a walk," Paul said. "He likes to get exercise each morning."

"He likes the silence," Luke said, smiling. "Which is sometimes hard to get." He nodded toward Paul, who was sitting in the seat where Andreas had liked to sit.

"I cannot help that the Lord has given me a voice to use in His service," Paul said, setting the citrus peel down. He had managed to pull it off in one long piece, and it spilled out in a coil on the table. He laughed softly, and it was clear he was used to their good-natured ribbing. "If our Lord had wanted peace and quiet, He should have chosen someone with less to say to spread His Gospel."

"You will notice that Paul writes many letters," Silas said. "We encourage that."

"When he is writing, it is the only time he is not talking," Luke added, laughing.

Paul shook his head and put a spoonful of yogurt in his mouth.

Lydia reached for the loaf of crusty bread and sliced off a piece with the knife. It was a beautiful golden brown, and the inside was soft and white. She also poured a bit of olive oil onto her plate, the golden liquid spreading into a pool. "So." Lydia dipped the bread into the oil. "What will we do today?"

There was a pause. Luke and Silas both looked toward Paul. He set down his spoon.

"*We* are going into the city to preach the Gospel." Paul gestured at Silas and Luke. "You should plan to do whatever it is you normally do on the first day of the week."

Lydia felt her stomach twist, but she willed herself not to show it. "This is hardly a normal first day of the week."

"Of course, you are right," Paul said smoothly. "Once you have believed the truth, it is impossible for things to return to normal. That is why we have dedicated our lives to spreading the Gospel." He broke off a piece of the crusty bread on his plate. "Each of us has felt exactly the feeling you are feeling now."

"So then you see. I also want to dedicate my life to spreading the Gospel." He also had felt what she said she wanted. Why, then, was he not meeting her eye?

"Each of us is called to do just that," Paul continued. "But not all of us are called to do it in the same way."

"I see." All the warmth that had filled her when she had woken was slowly ebbing away. "You do not…" She didn't even know what she was trying to say. "You will not want me to come with you."

Suddenly she felt silly. Who was she? She had not believed in Jesus a day before. What did she know about preaching? And she was a woman. She would not be seen in the same way as these men. Men would not listen to her or believe her word. Had she not had enough experience in business to understand that?

It was just that...well, everything was different now. She'd assumed that meant *everything*. She had planned then to dedicate her whole life to sharing the truth she had found.

"It is not that," Silas said softly.

"Of course we want you to join us," Luke said. "It is just..."

"You are needed in other ways," Paul said. "Think of a body. There are many parts, are there not?"

"Of course."

"If the whole body were an eye, how would we hear?" Paul said. "If the whole body were an ear, how could it smell?"

Lydia watched the oil on her plate push slowly out toward the edges of the dish.

"In the same way, we are all parts of the body. God has placed each part in the body just as He wanted it to be." Paul spoke with confidence, as though the words he was speaking were evident, though Lydia struggled to understand. "And we, as followers of the Way, are part of one body. We each have a job within the body of Christ."

"I see," she said, although she did not.

"Our job—" Paul gestured around at the men. "We have been called to go out into the streets and preach the Good News. That is our role within the body."

"And you are saying it is not mine," Lydia said. Something within her smarted, and she hated herself for it. What did she know about sharing the Good News? But despite that, she still felt the sting. She had been told so many times throughout her whole life that she was not enough. That she should step aside and let someone else do the job she believed was hers. That she could not manage the household accounts, because she would be too busy raising children.

That she could not run a dye works, being but a woman.

"I am saying your role is even *more* important," Paul said. "It is a special part of the body, one that is given special treatment."

"And what is that?" Lydia was not sure she wanted to hear whatever it was Paul was going to tell her. Was she meant to clean up after the men? To prepare food for them? To be a helper, the one who made the men look good? That was what Andreas had believed her role to be. To support him while he received the praise for her hard work. If that was to be her role in the body of Christ, Lydia would struggle, but she could accept it. It was worth it, if that was her job. She would do whatever she was called for in the service of the Christ. But she could not deny that it stung. She would once again be relegated to the jobs the men did not want for themselves.

Paul gestured around at the walls of the room. Sunlight streamed in from the open central courtyard, where Leon was hunched over a plot of herbs.

"You have a beautiful home," he said. "It is large and well kept."

"Thank you," Lydia said.

"We spoke about this last night," Paul said. "Timothy and Silas and Luke and I. About what a lovely home it was. About how many people could gather here."

"Yes…?" Was that what she had heard them murmuring about? It was not something spiritual in nature, but instead about the size of her home?

"We wondered." Paul cleared his throat. "Well, the converts we make this week. They are going to need somewhere to worship."

She had not considered this. She was used to worshipping on the riverbank. "Will we not gather by the river?"

"It…" Paul seemed to not know what to say. That was when Lydia realized they were speaking about something serious.

"Rome has not recognized Christianity yet," Silas said simply.

"We pray that it will, soon," Paul said. "Our numbers are growing by the day. But for now, it can be…" Paul took in a breath. "Well, not everyone sees what we do with the same eyes."

Then Lydia understood what the men had been trying not to say. "You are telling me that it is dangerous to be a Christian." They had not wanted their newest convert to be scared away by the danger, she understood.

But this danger was no news to Lydia. She had known that the religion was forbidden by Rome, and that it was seen as a cult, an offshoot of Judaism. She had known that, and still she had joined.

"There are many who do not like what we believe," Paul said.

"That is true," Lydia said, thinking back to the comments Sara and Agata had made yesterday. Until she had believed herself, Lydia had felt the same way.

"We cannot worship in the open," Luke said. "Is it not safe. We need a place to gather, where our members can be hidden from those who do not understand."

"I see." Lydia began to understand what these men were asking.

"Lydia," Paul said, "how would you feel about hosting the first church in Philippi here in your home?"

After she had eaten and the men had gone out to preach throughout the city, Lydia spent the morning in her workshop. But at the noonday meal, she walked back into town and to the home Anna and Daniel shared. It was a large home in the area where Daniel's family lived, with heavy stone and decorative scrollwork around the few windows. There was a heavy wooden door protected by a wrought-iron fence. Lydia put her hand through the gate and knocked on the door, which was opened a moment later by Emira, who had come to Daniel's home with Anna as part of her bride price.

"Good afternoon, mistress," Emira said, ducking her head. Then she pulled the door back and unlocked the gate to allow Lydia to step inside. "It is good to see you."

"It is good to see you as well." Lydia had always appreciated Emira's sweet spirit and gentle nature. She had always cared for Anna tenderly, and from the time she was a small child, Emira had been Anna's special favorite. Lydia had hesitated to let Emira go and would not mind some of her even-tempered obedience in her home now, but Anna had begged, and Andreas had never been able to say no to his daughter. Emira's hair was streaked with gray now, and she was thicker in the middle than she had been, but she was happy to see Lydia and ushered her inside the home. It was cool inside, and the polished stone floors gleamed. "Is Anna at home?"

"I will go see if she is available." Emira ducked her head and disappeared down the corridor. Lydia gazed around at the tall ceilings, the fine furnishings, the cushions embroidered in gold thread. When Lydia had first seen the house, she'd been surprised that Daniel could afford such a large home in the wealthiest section of the city. But then she'd realized that the fast growth of the city was the very reason Daniel could afford it. Being a builder was surely a rewarding trade these days.

She heard little Eli playing and was pleased when Emira came back and ushered her into the open courtyard at the center of the home. Anna had planted and carefully tended a garden, and the space was filled with colorful flowers arranged around walkways and benches. When Lydia stepped into the yard, Eli looked up from the pile of sticks he had been playing with and ran toward her.

"Yia-Yia!" The little boy wrapped his arms around her legs. She bent down and lifted him up, pulling his little body close. She buried her nose in his hair and took in his smell.

"Hello, Imma." Anna was crouched in front of a rosebush, pruning its branches with metal shears. Pink blossoms brought color to the lush greenery of the garden. The scent of jasmine perfumed the air, and the green stalks of creeping phlox and bougainvillea, still in their winter barrenness, grew lush and thick. "Has something happened?"

Lydia did not often come to visit at this time of day. No wonder Anna was worried. *Yes,* she wanted to answer. *I have heard the truth about Jesus, and my life will never be the same.* But instead, she answered, "You have roses, even at this time of year."

"There are varieties that bloom all through the year. All you must do is plant the right ones."

All you must do was to spend a small fortune having plants sent from all over the world, Lydia thought. But if it brought Anna joy, she could hardly complain.

Eli wiggled to be set down, and Lydia put his feet on the ground again. He ran off and went back to his pile of sticks.

"Mother." Anna sat back on her heels and looked up at Lydia. "What is going on?"

"I—" Lydia was not sure how to begin. She reminded herself of what Paul had told her, that she had God's spirit within her, and that He would give her the words to speak. "I wanted to tell you about something."

Anna was watching her, her forehead creased. There were dark circles under her eyes, and she looked pale.

"After the Sabbath service, I started talking to those men who were down by the river."

"The followers of that heretic who claimed to be God's son?"

"Yes." Lydia understood Anna's reaction. It was the same as hers had been before she understood. "The thing is, when they started talking, something within me told me to listen. So I did, and they told me incredible things."

"Oh Mother, please do not tell me you listened to their lies," Anna said. "It only encourages them. They feed on people like you."

"People like me?"

Anna shrugged. "Lonely widows. They also favor the young, the poor, the infirm—anyone who is likely to believe that there is something wrong with the life they lead now. You were the perfect target."

Lydia tried not to let the words sting. Was this how Anna saw her?

But she would not let herself get distracted.

"Well, I listened, and I understood. Anna, the Messiah we have been waiting for all these years? He has come. It is Jesus."

Anna was staring at her, her eyes wide, her mouth open. "You don't really believe that. Please tell me you don't really believe that. This is some kind of terrible joke. It is not funny."

"It is not a joke. Anna, please listen to me. All of the prophecies about the Messiah? They are all true of Jesus. He comes from the House of David. He was born of a virgin, and He was from Bethlehem. He—"

"You're serious, aren't you?" Anna set down the shears.

"I have never been more serious. This news has changed my life. Just listen, Anna. Jesus performed miracles. He healed lepers, He fed thousands on a few loaves of bread. He raised the dead. And He died to free us from sin and death."

"He was a zealot who was executed for telling lies. He was a deceiver, and Adonai will not be mocked."

"I understand why you think that, but if you would just listen—"

"I will not. I do not have to sit here and listen to more of these lies." Anna pushed herself to her feet. "I cannot believe that you, the woman who taught me the importance of holding fast to the truth of the scriptures, are now spilling out these heresies, one after another. But I do not have to listen to them."

"Anna. Please don't get angry. This is good news. The best news."

"It is 'news' that will not enter my home again," Anna said. "I do not know what happened to you, Imma, but perhaps you need to see a doctor. These lies that are coming out of your mouth are not at all like the mother I know. Your words are heresy, and I will not hear any more of them in my home."

"But if you would just listen—"

"I will not." She turned, her robes swishing. "Eli, it is time for us to go inside."

The little boy, perhaps sensing the urgency in her voice, hopped up and trotted over to her.

"You may see yourself out," Anna said over her shoulder before she vanished inside.

The men returned to the house triumphant that evening. "Seventeen believed in Christ today," Paul said. He was laughing as he removed his cloak.

"And all of them were baptized," Silas added. "This city is hungry for the saving grace of Jesus."

"Praise God," Lydia said, and she meant it with every part of her. She knew that these men were doing good work and that she was blessed to be counted among their number. "It is amazing that you were able to speak to that many."

"Paul did not simply speak today," Luke said. "He preached. From the raised dais in the agora."

Lydia knew where they meant. It was where slaves and animals were auctioned off.

"And seventeen stopped to listen?" Lydia found it hard to imagine anyone hearing much of anything in that crowded square.

"Many more stopped to listen," Paul said. "And these seventeen believed."

"That is wonderful news." Lydia gestured at Elodie, who had been hovering in the corner of the room, and asked her to bring a bowl and pitcher to the rooms where the men were staying. Elodie nodded, and all four men trooped up the stairs to wash, laughing and praising God the whole way.

After they had vanished upstairs, Lydia crossed the courtyard and went into the cooking room to check on the evening meal. She found Iduma hunched over, stirring some sort of stew in a heavy earthenware pot. She was flushed from the heat of the open flame.

"It smells wonderful," Lydia said as she stepped inside. Lydia smelled meat and roasting onions, and there was a plate of greens laid out, as well as more bread.

"It was the best I could do with what I had." Iduma tossed in a pinch of sea salt from the pile on the plate next to the stove, and then she straightened up and turned toward Lydia. "Cooking for so many is much different than cooking for one. It was hard to find enough with the budget I was given." She used the edge of her robe to wipe away a sheen of sweat from her forehead. "I had to use lentils to bulk it up, as there was not enough goat."

Iduma had mentioned often that she missed cooking for larger groups, so Lydia suspected this was not truly the source of her concern.

"Then you must have more money for your trips to the market," Lydia said. "You must have what you need. Will five denarii more per week be sufficient?"

It was a large amount, more than most households would spend on food in a week. But Lydia was willing to stretch if it meant feeding her guests well and keeping her servants happy.

"That would help," Iduma said.

"I understand that it is much more work for you," Lydia said. "So I will increase your weekly pay as long as the men are here."

Iduma nodded, and Lydia could see that she was pleased, but she did not say so.

"How long *will* the men be here?" Iduma asked.

"I do not know," Lydia answered.

Iduma gave an answer that was somewhere between a grunt and a sigh, and Lydia thanked her again before she turned and walked to the dining room, where Danae was setting out dishes for their meal. When the food was ready, Elodie was sent to call the men downstairs, and while they ate the stew, they told Lydia about the people who had mocked Paul as he preached in the square and about the converts who had heard the message and believed.

"Tell her about the young girl," Timothy said to Paul. "And how the spirit in her recognized the truth."

Paul nodded. He did not need much encouragement.

"It was incredible," Paul said. He took a sip of Lydia's favorite good sweet wine and set his cup down. "There is a girl who predicts the future in the square."

"Yes, I know of her. She is said to have the Python spirit," Lydia said.

Paul nodded, understanding, but Timothy's brow wrinkled.

"It is said she speaks from the knowledge of the Oracle at Delphi," Lydia explained. Timothy then nodded, understanding. A python was said to guard the Oracle until Apollo slew him. Many therefore connected the god Apollo with a python, and when he spoke from site of the Oracle, it was through the fumes of the burning python. The girl sat behind a table in the market, and it was said she channeled messages directly from the Oracle, so people paid money for her to tell them their future. Lydia knew she was a slave because she had seen the numbers inked on her arm, but she did not know who owned her or where she lived. She spent most of each day predicting the future, and no doubt making a large sum for her owners in the process.

"Many people pay good money to hear her lies," Lydia continued. "She tells them what they want to hear, and they reward her richly for it."

"That is the one," Paul said. "We did not notice her at first as we were walking through the square, looking for a place to stand, but as we walked near to her table, she stood and called out, 'These men are servants of the Most High God, who are telling you the way to be saved!'"

"Truly?" Lydia had never heard the girl speak, and she was not one of the group that gathered to worship Adonai. How had she even known of the Most High God? And how had she recognized the truth of what these men proclaimed?

"It caused quite a stir, as you might imagine," Paul said. "Her handlers pulled her back into her chair and hushed her, but she kept shouting that we were servants of the one true God as we walked away."

"Naturally, this one took it as an invitation," Luke said, pointing his thumb toward Paul.

"How could I not? I wanted to know how she knew, and I wanted to know if she wanted to be baptized. But we could not get close enough to speak with her," Paul said. "She is guarded by many large men, who encouraged us to move along." He scooped up a bit of the stew.

"The men made Silas look small," Timothy said. Lydia was glad to see him speaking, opening up a little more. She had noticed that though he was quiet and often seemed overshadowed by the large personalities of those around him, he seemed to genuinely enjoy the company of the others and sometimes had a wry comment to add.

"She must make a great deal of money for her owners to be so well protected," Silas said.

"I believe that is true." Lydia had never given much thought to how the operation worked, only felt sorry for the girl, whose eyes seemed lifeless as she met one customer after another.

After a few moments of quiet, Luke nodded at Paul. The leader was sipping his wine, staring at some point far off in the distance.

"What is it?" Luke asked. "What has got you so quiet?"

"Please, keep at it, whatever it is," Timothy said, garnering a laugh from Silas.

"I'm still wondering how she knew," Paul said.

"The Lord will show us," Luke said, and Paul nodded. The conversation moved along, and after they had finished the meal, the men returned upstairs, and Lydia settled the household accounts, adding extra money to the budget for Iduma to use in the market. That would help alleviate her frustration. Though in truth, Lydia knew that the cost wasn't what was really behind Iduma's huffing. She would see, in time, Lydia thought.

Before Lydia retired, she climbed the stairs to the spare rooms to make sure the men had everything they needed. She heard quiet voices in the first room, and she knocked gently.

"Come in," Paul called. Lydia pushed open the door and found him sitting with Silas, who was using a sharp knife to whittle away at a piece of wood, and Timothy, reclining on cushions. The sky had darkened, and the light from an oil lamp splashed dancing shadows across their faces.

"We are making plans for our Lord's Day gathering," Paul explained, and Lydia nodded.

"I would very much like to know more about that," Lydia said.

"We will know more as the day gets closer," Paul said, and she understood that they did not wish to discuss it now. Lydia nodded and closed the door gently, and she stepped toward the other door but heard only silence behind it. She thought Luke must be asleep or otherwise did not want to be disturbed, so she began to turn back when she heard a voice inside call out, "You may come in."

Lydia hesitated but then put her hand on the door and pushed it open. She found Luke sitting at a small table, hunched over a parchment, writing. The light of the oil lamp danced across his features.

"I heard you outside," Luke explained. "I did not want you to think I could not be disturbed."

He gestured for her to step into the room. She saw that the men had moved all four of the beds into this room and were using the other for gathering.

"What are you writing?" Lydia asked.

"At the moment?" A jeweled ring on Luke's hand caught the light. "A letter. To my wife."

Lydia could not contain the surprise she felt. "You are married?" She had assumed—well, she had not given much thought to the lives these men must have lived before they appeared at the river, she realized. But given how they lived and how they traveled, she had assumed they were all free from family obligations.

"For over fifteen years." Luke indicated the chair across the table, and she sat down uncertainly. "We have two daughters."

"Your wife does not mind you leaving?"

"She believed when I did. She understands the importance of this work."

"That is good," Lydia said.

"It would be impossible if she had not also become a convert," Luke said. "If she did not believe in the importance of my work, she would mind very much. This is why it is so good when an entire household embraces the Way together, as you have done. It cannot work when some in a family believe one thing and others believe another."

Lydia nodded. She had converted to Judaism at her marriage for this very reason.

"In any case, my wife is used to me traveling for my work," Luke explained. "This is different, of course, but it is not the first time I have left."

Lydia thought for a moment. "You are a doctor." Paul had mentioned that in their first meeting.

"That is right. I actually trained at the medical school here in Philippi," he said.

There was a large and well-respected training school for doctors here in the city, and many came from all over the region to train.

"You are from Macedonia, then?"

Luke shook his head. "Antioch. That is where I first heard Paul teaching, and I believed. There is a large church there." He set down his quill. "I joined them when they set sail from Antioch. I spent many years here in Philippi when I trained to become a doctor, which is why I agreed to come with the others on this journey. Paul hoped it would help to have someone who is familiar with the area."

Lydia took all this in. "So you have not been with the others the whole time?" That explained why his clothing did not have the same ragged appearance as the others.

"No." Luke shook his head. "And I do not know how long I will stay with them. I must get back to my practice at some point." And then, after a pause, "And my family."

Lydia had many questions but did not want to probe too deeply.

"It must be hard, to pick up and leave everything to travel like this."

"In some ways, yes," Luke conceded. "It is hard to take time away from my work, and I miss my children. It is hard to sleep on the ground when I am used to my thick bed, and to not know where our next meal will come from. But those things pale in comparison to the incredible privilege of sharing the message of the Christ. It is the salvation of the whole world. How will they know truth if we do not go and tell them?"

As Luke spoke, the shadows cast by the oil lamp danced across has face. He had fine, even features and eyes an unusual shade of green.

"I am grateful you have made the journey," Lydia said, and he smiled.

"You have been most generous to us," Luke said. "We know the Lord's plans are perfect, but it is still hard to believe that the first person to believe here in Philippi was someone as gracious as you."

"I am glad to share what I have," Lydia said. "It is too much for one anyway." Anna expected her wealth would all pass to Eli someday, and many in Andreas's family believed she should have already passed along her grandson's inheritance, but Lydia saw no reason to part with the money she was largely responsible for earning.

"We are grateful." Luke sighed and began to roll up the parchment he had been writing on. She noticed a stack of parchments on the edge of the table.

"You are writing more than a letter, it seems."

"I am always writing," Luke said. "In the same way that Paul is always talking."

Lydia laughed. The man could go on.

"It helps me make sense of my thoughts."

Another indication that Luke was a man of means, Lydia noted. Parchment and ink were costly.

"I am keeping notes of our time together. Someday, when the message of Christ has spread across the whole world, people will want to know how it happened. I will write that book, someday." He cocked an eyebrow. "Who knows? Maybe you will even be a character in the story."

Lydia smiled. It was a fanciful thought. He was kind. But something he'd said struck her. "Do you really think it will spread across the world?"

Luke leaned back on his stool and considered before he answered. "If you had the cure to leprosy, would you keep it to yourself?"

Lydia tried to make sense of his answer. Hadn't Paul told her Jesus had healed a leper? Couldn't He have ended the disease altogether, then? And where did Luke, the doctor, fit into this example? She was not sure what to make of his question, but she answered, "No, I would not. Leprosy is a terrible thing. I would do whatever I could to end it."

Luke nodded, the light casting shadows on his cheeks. "The message of Jesus Christ has the power to save. It is the answer to sin and death. I will spend my life making sure as many hear the message as possible. The others with me—they feel the same. Any setback, any imprisonment or beatings we face are all worth it to see the message of Jesus spread around the world. We will not rest until every soul knows the name of Jesus Christ."

His words stirred something in her, and listening to him speak, she felt a sense of peace settle over her. Perhaps Luke had been right when he'd said God had known what He was doing letting them meet Lydia first. She may not be particularly useful at preaching or standing on street corners gathering souls, and she could not imagine traveling around by boat, living meal-to-meal and sleeping wherever she could, as these men did. But she had one thing they desperately needed. She had money, more than she needed. She could help fund their church and their future journeys. She could make sure they could afford to carry this news to the four corners of the world.

"I will not rest either," Lydia said. "I will give my life to the Good News too."

CHAPTER FOUR

A few days later, as Lydia was preparing for bed, Danae cleared her throat and hovered by the doorway. She had brought Lydia a pitcher of water for her bedside, as was her custom, and had pulled the heavy embroidered curtains closed.

"Yes?" Lydia had just pulled the bedcovers back.

"I...I thought there was something you should know." Danae held a lamp in one hand, and Lydia would extinguish the one by her bed when she left.

"What is it?"

"Iduma is..." Danae's voice faltered. "Well, she is saying that we do not have to be followers of the Way ourselves, no matter what you say. She is trying to convince the rest of us to flout the decision you have made and to privately keep our own worship."

Lydia cocked her head. Iduma had never seemed particularly devout to her, so she found it surprising that Iduma would now be so insistent on devoting herself to Jewish practices. "She wishes to continue to worship Adonai but not Jesus?"

"Not exactly." Danae hesitated again.

"It is okay, Danae. Please, tell me what is happening."

"You see, Iduma never did fully accept the idea that Adonai is the one true God. She did not grow up with the idea, and so it has always seemed strange to her."

Lydia nodded, dreading what she feared was coming next. "So she had been praying to idols this whole time?"

Danae nodded. "She has."

Lydia felt anger flare within her. Her servant had been praying to idols in this home? For a moment, Lydia was glad Andreas was not here to know this truth. He would have had her fired immediately, set out on the street this very night. Lydia would not act so rashly. Not yet, anyway. But still, she felt deeply betrayed.

"And now, she is worshipping them more openly," Danae continued. "And trying to convince the rest of us that it is all right."

"She is?"

"She has told Leon that since you are now worshipping a false god, there is no reason we should not worship as we see fit. And I...well, I thought you should know."

"Thank you, Danae." Lydia could see that it did not give Danae pleasure to share this news, yet Lydia was glad she had. "I will talk to her."

"You will not..."

Lydia shook her head. "I will not tell her how I know."

Danae's face betrayed her relief.

"Thank you for telling me."

Danae nodded and went out the door, closing it softly behind her.

Lydia considered how to respond to this news. Andreas would not have hesitated to expel the traitor. But Lydia thought there must be another way. She would need to think and pray on it.

Lydia was going over the household accounts again the next night when Paul sat down at the table across from her.

"We are costing you much by our presence," he said, nodding at the sheet of parchment. "I am sorry." He carried a cup of wine, and he set it down on the table. The others were still upstairs, Lydia supposed.

"You have no need to be sorry," Lydia said. "You are welcome here."

"We are thankful," Paul said. "How can we help? We can try to use less oil. Drink less wine." He touched his cup gently.

"You do not need to change your behavior. It is an honor to serve God by hosting His servants."

Paul watched her a moment longer, and then he nodded. "Thank you."

Lydia turned back to her parchment, but Paul did not leave as she had expected. She realized he had not said all he had come to say, and she set her quill down.

"You are not married," Paul said.

For a moment, Lydia was taken aback by the direct nature of his statement, but then she realized he intended it as a question.

"My husband passed almost two years ago," she said. "His chest began to ache, and then not long later, he fell down and was no longer breathing. It was very sudden."

"I am sorry. It must have been difficult."

Lydia did not know what to say. "It was hard on all of us, my daughter especially. He always spoiled her so."

"You have but the one daughter?"

Lydia nodded again. "We wanted more, but...we were only blessed with one."

"That is good." Paul took another sip from his wine.

Lydia started. She must not have heard him right.

"What?"

He set his cup down and shook his head. "I am sorry. That must have sounded terrible."

Lydia waited for him to go on.

"What I mean is, it is hard on a family when one member accepts Christ if the others do not believe."

"My whole household was baptized."

"Yes, and that is wonderful. But if you had a husband, would he have been baptized along with them?"

Lydia saw what he was saying. "No, I doubt he would have. Not unless he too had his heart opened."

"And we would not have been able to stay here, if he had not believed too."

Lydia contemplated his words. "Are you saying that it is good that my husband died because it gave you a place to stay?"

"No, I did not mean that. I am sorry." Paul let out a breath. "I have a way of saying things poorly. I often make people misunderstand things I say." He took another sip. "What I meant was that God works out His plans for us, even in things that seem terrible or that we do not understand. I mean that there is still good in them anyway, if God uses them."

Lydia did not know how to respond, but Paul continued. "I was supposed to marry a girl by the name of Eugenia. She was quiet and kind and pretty. But before our wedding, she was found to be with child. I was not the child's father. Her father tried to have me fulfill my promise and marry her anyway, but I could not."

"It sounds much like the story of how our Lord was born," Lydia said.

Paul nodded. "Except that in this case, the baby's father was an attractive servant in her father's house and not God Himself. And no angels came to persuade me to marry her anyway."

"I am sorry. That must have been terrible for you."

"It was, at the time. But this is my point. It seemed impossible that I would ever see good in the terrible situation, but God knew what He had planned. If I had been married to Eugenia, I could not have left to travel the world and spread the Gospel. I would have been committed to caring for her and our children and not free to be used by the Lord."

"So you are saying it was a good thing she had a child by her father's servant?" Lydia struggled to accept what he was saying.

"I am saying that God uses all circumstances, even the terrible ones, for His glory." Paul now stretched out his hand, hovering his fingers over the flame of the lamp. "I could have made my family convert and be baptized, but you know as well as I do that there is a difference when one truly believes in their heart."

He had seen Iduma's attitude then, and how Leon resisted prayers as well. She thought, too, about when she had married Andreas. She had converted to please his parents. But once she had believed that Adonai was the one true God, it had changed everything about her posture toward the faith and her worship. "That is true."

"I do not know if Eugenia would have believed in her heart the truth of Christ."

Lydia leaned back. "You do not think she would have believed, even after the dramatic experiences of your encounter with the Christ?"

Paul shrugged. "I cannot say. All I can say for sure is that I feel certain that I could not have been used by God in this way if I had been married to someone who did not believe."

Lydia considered this. "Surely He would have used you otherwise."

"I suppose." He now moved his hand back and forth across the flame, as if daring it to burn him. "But not in this way."

"And you are saying that because I am unmarried, God is using that as well?"

"I believe He is. He would have provided for us in another way, I am certain, but because of your circumstances, He is using you powerfully. You did not have to ask anyone whether you could help us or host the church. You did not have to navigate a marriage where one believed and the other did not. And because of that, the church will flourish."

Lydia was not sure what to think. It was hard to imagine how things would have been different if Andreas had lived. But if God wanted to use her circumstances for the spread of the Gospel, she could do nothing but offer herself willingly.

CHAPTER FIVE

When Lydia was summoned from her workshop to the home of Felix the magistrate once again, she took Leia with her. Leia chattered the whole way through the city. Lydia had been called plenty of times before when Felix wanted a new piece of cloth, as he would not come near the stench of the dye works himself. As they walked, Lydia saw Paul standing on the dais in the agora, preaching to the crowd, most of whom ignored him, and she said a prayer that God would open the ears of many just as He had opened her own.

When she arrived at Felix's home, she was ushered up to his rooms, as usual, but this time, Leia was made to stay below with the servants.

"She is not a servant," Lydia insisted. "She is in charge of the loom. She is an integral part of weaving the right fabric for Felix."

But Felix's servants, though apologetic, were insistent. Felix had asked to see Lydia on her own and had left orders for only her to be admitted to his chambers.

Lydia followed the maid up the stairs, hesitant. She did not relish the idea of being alone with Felix, and yet she did not know what to do. She did not see how she could say no to a man who represented such a large part of her sales. The maid pushed open the door, and Felix called for Lydia to come inside. She stepped into the room and saw that he was standing by the window, gazing out over the city.

"Lydia." He turned and smiled, and he gestured for her to come toward him. "You are so good to come."

"It is good to see you." Lydia walked toward him as the maid closed the door.

"Come, look," Felix said, turning back toward the window.

Lydia walked toward the window and stopped a short distance from it.

"Isn't it beautiful?" Felix asked. There was something hopeful in his voice, as if he wanted the view to please her.

"It truly is a beautiful city," Lydia said. The buildings were spread out before them, houses running down the hills, the tan and white stone glowing with warmth in the afternoon sunlight. The people walking along the narrow streets looked so small. From this height, one could see the aqueduct, its arches silhouetted against the hazy blue sky, as well as the theater, just beyond the wall, and beyond that, the Egnatian Way, stretching out to the end of the world.

"I am glad you think so," Felix said. He sighed and then turned and walked away from the window. "Come." He stopped in front of a round table pressed up against a wall. On it was placed a decanter and two cups. "Celebrate with me." He picked up the decanter and poured red wine into each of the cups.

"Celebrate what?" Lydia stayed by the window, but he gestured for her to step closer.

"The news has just come down from Rome. I am to be named the new praetor in Philippi." Felix held out the glass.

"That is wonderful news." The praetor was the lead magistrate, which in effect, would make him the most powerful man in the city. "Congratulations."

"You must have some wine and celebrate with me," Felix said, again indicating the cup. Lydia did not know how to refuse, so she stepped forward and took it.

"It is truly wonderful." The wine was sweet and very strong, no doubt fortified. "It is quite an honor."

"It is." Felix took a long drink of his wine, keeping his eyes locked on Lydia as he drank it down. "It is something I have wanted for quite some time."

"Then I am even more glad for you." She took another small sip and then put the wine down. It was not to her taste.

"There is something else I have wanted for a very long time." Felix took a step closer to her. The way he was looking at her made the hairs on her arms stand up.

"When will you be installed?" Lydia asked, hoping to distract him. "I assume that is why you have called me here. You will need to have fine new robes, of course. We'll make them out of the grandest fabric ever. We will have to make a special weave, more beautiful even than the Saturnalia fabric." Something in her told her to keep talking,

"Of course," Felix said. "I will want the most glorious robes anyone in this town has ever seen for the ceremony." He drained the last of his wine and then set the cup down. "But there is something else I want that day as well." He stepped

73

forward and placed his hand on Lydia's waist, and when she pulled back, he used the strength of his arm to pull her in closer and then to press her back against the wall. "I want the most beautiful woman in Philippi by my side on that day as well."

He pressed her close to him.

"I do hope you will find her." Lydia's mind raced, and she felt panic rising, but she forced herself to take deep breaths and to think. She knew she could not overpower him. She would have to convince him to let her go with her wits.

"You are funny," he said. His breath smelled sour, with the sickening tinge of the sweet wine. "And you have such spirit. I have always liked that about you. I cannot bear boring women."

"I suppose all women have their virtues." She pushed back against him with all her strength, but he was like a mountain of muscle. He did not even appear to feel it. "The quiet ones are so often the sweetest tempered."

Felix laughed, running one hand along the edge of her robe. "The sweet-tempered ones are no fun."

Lydia shoved against him. "Let me go."

"You are the only woman I want," he said, as if he hadn't heard.

"You flatter me." Lydia leaned back, but she could not escape his grip. In response, his fingers began to work their way to the tie of her robe.

"Say you will marry me, Lydia," he said. "You will become a citizen and be protected. You will be the most powerful woman in Macedonia, with all the rights and privileges my wife deserves."

"Your offer is very kind, Praetor." Many women would be flattered by his offer, but she was not one of them. She tried once again to free herself from his grip, but he continued tugging at the tie of her robe with one hand, while he pressed harder against her. The rough plaster of the wall dug into her back. "But I am afraid I cannot accept."

"You must," he said, and leaned in to plant a messy kiss on her lips.

"No, I do not. Let me go." She pushed against him again, and once again, he did not seem to even feel it.

"You must, or I will put a stop to all of it," Felix said.

"All of what?" She struggled again, but he held her tight.

"I know that you have gotten involved with those men who go around teaching about Jesus," Felix said. "I know they are living with you. I know you are supporting them. I do not care what you do with so many young men in your own home. But I—"

"What I *do* with the men?" Lydia shoved him again and stomped on his foot as hard as she could, and this time it seemed to startle him. A flash of anger registered in his eyes. "I assure you, there is nothing untoward—"

"Like I said, I do not mind," Felix said. "But I know as well as you do that those men who are living with you are practicing a religion that is forbidden by Rome. I could have them all arrested and thrown into prison. I have heard that you too count yourself among their number. I could have you arrested as well." At this, he leaned in to nuzzle her neck, as if this were a stimulating thing to contemplate. "But if you marry me, you will be safe."

"Are you saying that if I don't marry you, you intend to throw me in jail?"

"Perhaps. I intend to do many things to you," Felix said. "But it will be more enjoyable for you if you are my wife before I do them." He leaned in again and tried to plant another kiss on her lips, but she ducked, and summoning all the strength she had inside of her, she brought her knee up sharply and hit him as hard as she could. He cried out and stumbled back, clutching himself. As soon as he was off of her, Lydia rushed across the room and to the doorway. She yanked on the door, flinging it open. She glanced back at Felix, who was writhing on the ground and moaning. Good, she thought. He deserved far more than that.

"I am afraid I will not be able to make the cloth for you after all," she said before she gathered her strength as best she could, adjusted her robe, held her head high, and walked out the door.

The next morning Paul and the others were up before dawn, directing Leon and Iduma and Milena to clear the furniture out of the room with the dining table, the largest room on the first floor. The men worked together to push the table into the courtyard, and then they dusted and swept the cleared space. Lydia caught more than one frustrated glance between Iduma and Leon, but they did as Paul instructed. When the room was cleared and ready, Paul asked them all to gather for prayer.

"God, Father of our Lord Jesus Christ, Father of mercies and God of all comfort, give us the spirit of revelation in knowledge of You," Paul began. "Enlighten the eyes of our heart and strengthen us in power through Your Spirit." Paul continued to pray for some time, until the first tentative knock on the door indicated the first worshipper had arrived.

Luke was sent to answer the door. Each of the believers had been instructed to draw the sign of the fish—the *ichthus,* whose letters were an acrostic for Jesus Christ, Son of God, Savior—with their finger at the door. Luke now led the convert inside. It was a woman Lydia had seen in the market. She sold vegetables and greens grown on her land outside the city. Lydia nodded, smiled, and welcomed her, and the woman nodded, polite but distant. She was as nervous as Lydia was about what was to happen here today, she guessed.

"I am Lydia. You are welcome here."

The woman nodded. "Callista." And then, almost as an afterthought, "Thank you."

More guests began arriving, some in groups, some on their own. Each was welcomed and ushered into the open room. They came in ragged robes and in pressed linen, some with braided hair and oiled beards and some with simple head coverings. Lydia pushed herself to overcome her hesitations and did her best to greet each one. Though she could be bold in business, she had a natural reticence when it came to meeting new people, and now there were dozens of people she did not know gathering in her dining room. She recognized a few but not many. She would meet them now, she decided as she began introductions. There was Claes, a player in the theater whose garrulous nature became clear immediately, and he conversed and made friends easily among the group. There was Charis, a servant in the house of a family Lydia's husband had known. She had risked much to be here, Lydia knew. The family was of high standing and would not stand for a member of their household attaching herself to this forbidden faith. There was Daphne, who begged by the city gates. Lydia had seen her many times and never thought to wonder what her name was. Daphne. She would never forget it now, Lydia knew. There was Euodia, and her husband, Eneas. Each hand she clasped was precious. These were her brothers and sisters in Christ. This was her new Christian family.

Lydia had expected that she would miss gathering by the river with the Jewish community. For so many years—since she had first come to this city—she had gathered each week to worship Adonai. And yet, once Paul called this gathering to attention and started to pray, she realized that her spirit responded in a way that she had never experienced on that muddy riverbank. It was as if everything inside of her had been thirsty for something, and the words Paul spoke about the Savior filled her parched soul with cool, refreshing water. For so many years, she had prayed, along with the others on that riverbank, for the Messiah to come liberate His people, and now, as the gathered group listened as Paul spoke about the saving grace of Jesus, about His life, death, and resurrection, she knew, in the very depth of her bones, that He had come at last.

Lydia had not known what to expect, but the church service followed closely the rhythms and structure of a Jewish worship ceremony—prayer, readings from scripture, a message—and it felt familiar to her. Though none of the others in the gathering came from the small group of Jews in Philippi and therefore had likely never gathered in a communal worship service like this one, they followed along easily enough. Lydia considered as she looked around—she believed Christ was the promised Redeemer of Israel. But the others in this room had likely previously worshipped a pantheon of other gods or had reserved reverence for the emperor himself. What had brought them to this saving knowledge of Jesus Christ? How had they seen the truth in the story of this carpenter who had given His life to redeem them all?

Paul exhorted them to hold fast to the faith they proclaimed and to speak the truth in love, knowing the message of Christ was the truth of salvation. And then they prayed together, each person echoing in their hearts the words Paul proclaimed from the front of the room.

Lydia did not know most of the others gathered in this room. She did not understand the monumental change that had happened in her heart over the past week, nor did she understand what would happen next with this mismatched group of people who had gathered in her dining room. She did not know what the future held for any of them.

But as she looked around at the people who had gathered here to worship a God very few of them understood, she felt more certain than ever that this was right, and she committed in her heart to do whatever it took to see the church in Philippi flourish.

CHAPTER SIX

Lydia was in the dye room, standing with Giorgio over the vat of boiling dye. Filip, the apprentice who had worked with Giorgio for many years, stood nearby, watching. The mixture had been cooking for the past ten days, boiling in a huge, heavy copper pot. The room had thick walls and became stiflingly hot in the summer, but in winter, the heat and moisture in the air was not as unbearable. Giorgio never complained even during the worst of it. He patiently tended the fire beneath the dye vat, watching as the crushed murex shells and the water turned into a thick stew, and then, as it bubbled and boiled, the mixture in the vat turned from white to yellow, and finally, to the deep, rich eggplant color her cloth was known for. Now Giorgio was ready to decide whether the dye was properly saturated.

"Do you think it is ready?" Lydia asked. It looked right to her, the color somewhere between crimson and dried blood. But Giorgio knew best. He had been with Andreas for many decades, and he understood the process of drawing color out of the shells as no one else. She relied on his judgment.

"We will only know once we try it," Giorgio said.

It was likely the truth, but it was not what she wanted to hear. It took more than ten thousand shells to make a small amount of the pigment needed for the dye. The cost of the ingredients in that vat was more than most men would make in a lifetime. Wasting even the small portion it would take to test its color on a fleece was unthinkable.

"I believe it is ready," Giorgio continued, giving her a smile.

"All right," she said and pulled off a small portion of the fleece the women who worked with Asuman had cleaned. Its soft tufts left an oily feeling on her fingers. Giorgio took the bit of fleece and grasped it in his tongs. Then, slowly, he lowered the bit of wool into the bubbling dye, and the fibers began to absorb the color. She loved to watch the bit of fluff transform from something plain and common—though Damon's wool was nothing but the best, it was still wool from the many thousands of sheep in the area—into something extraordinary. Lydia held her breath as he kept the ball of wool under the surface, and after some interval only Giorgio could mark, he raised it slowly, revealing a deep bruised scarlet color.

"It is ready," he said.

Lydia nodded. It was the right shade. They would add the rest of the wool and leave it to boil for many days before it would be dried, carded, and added back into the dye a second time. After that, it would be finely spun and then woven by hand. It was a costly, labor-intensive process, but that was how she produced the best purple cloth in Greece.

"All right," Lydia said. "Let us add the remainder of the fleece."

She watched as Giorgio lowered the rest of the soft woolen fleeces from Damon's latest batch to the pot and held her breath as the dark liquid closed over it, instantly turning the fibers to a deep eggplant. It was a relief to see the latest lot was on its way.

"Lydia?"

She turned to see Asuman standing in the doorway. The long skirt of her robe was dotted with woolen fibers, a natural result of carding wool for so many hours each day.

"You have a visitor," Asuman said. Lydia nodded and turned, and she followed Asuman back through the spinning room, where women hunched over wheels, turning various shades of plain and dyed wool into thread, and then through the loom room, where the thread was carefully and swiftly woven into fine linen and wool. She went through the storage room, where racks with dozens of earthenware jars held costly pigments and bases for dyes, and then into the front room, where she found Sara waiting, a sour look on her face.

Lydia started. She was not used to seeing anyone but business associates here. Few people came out this way unless they had to. "Hello, Sara."

"Goodness, Lydia. I do not know how you can stand it," Sara said, pulling the edge of her cloak up over her nose. A ruby ring Lydia had not seen before gleamed on her finger.

"The smell?"

"Of course the smell." Sara coughed. "It is enough to make one choke."

"It is strong," Lydia admitted. "You don't notice it so much after a while."

It wasn't that she didn't smell the putrid stench of the decaying sea snails as they boiled. It was that she had trained herself to not mind it. There was nothing that could be done about it, not if she wanted to continue to create colored cloth.

"Let us go outside," Sara said, turning toward the door. Lydia nodded and followed her friend out into the bright winter afternoon. The sunshine brightened the beige bricks of her workshop and the trees that grew along the side of the road. They stood in the shade of a stand of eucalyptus trees. The smell of the dye works still hung in the air, but it was less noticeable, masked by the earthy scent of the leaves. "That is better." Sara let the cloak slip down from her face.

"What brought you out this way this afternoon?" Lydia asked her sister-in-law. Sara spent most days at home, sewing or mending, or else at the market. It must have been something important to bring her out here beyond the city gates.

"You were not at the Sabbath service yesterday."

Naturally, some had noticed. Lydia should have been prepared for this.

"I...I'm afraid I could not make it." It sounded ridiculous, even to her ears.

"Then, I was in the market this morning, searching for fresh fish for Tobias's dinner tonight," Sara said. "You know how hard it can be to find good fresh fish at this time of year. Anyway, I was walking around looking at the different stalls when I ran into Agata. And she told me the strangest thing."

Lydia nodded. She had not spent as much time at the market as her friends, but she knew it was a notorious place for sharing gossip.

"Agata told me that those strange men are staying in your house," Sara said. "Those Christians from the river the other day. I told her it could not be true. I said it was not possible. But she insisted that Cosmo had seen them leaving in the morning and then returning later that night—and not just one day but every day this week. And he also says there were quite a few strangers coming to your door yesterday morning."

Cosmo lived down the street and worked in the municipal buildings. He had no doubt told his wife, Cybill, who talked to everyone.

"Some have speculated that instead of joining our Sabbath service, you held some sort of gathering of your own, with these Christian men involved. Well, obviously you don't want rumors like that flying around, so I thought I would ask. You can tell me it's not true and I could put a stop to it now, before things get out of hand."

Sara watched Lydia expectantly.

"I am afraid I cannot," Lydia said.

"You cannot what?"

"I cannot put an end to the rumor. It is true. The men are staying with me. And I did host a church service."

"You cannot—" Sara's hand flew to her mouth, and she froze. "What?"

"I mean that I invited them to stay with me." Lydia had not intended to keep the news a secret, but she had also suspected that the news would not be well received by her friends and, especially, members of Andreas's family, like Sara. "And that we had a gathering of believers."

"What do you mean?" Sara was shaking her head. "Why would you do such a thing? Do you not know who they are?"

"I do know." Lydia steeled herself, trying to keep her voice calm and level. She had known this was coming, she reminded herself. She did not need anyone's permission to worship as she liked. "I know that they are disciples of Jesus Christ, the Son of God. I know that they are spreading the Good News that Christ has died and was resurrected for our sins, and that He is the Messiah we have been waiting for."

Sara's mouth hung open. Lydia had rarely seen her friend dumbstruck, as now.

Lydia tried to remind herself how shocked she herself would have been to hear such news just two weeks past. Her life had changed completely and in a very short space of time. She could not be surprised that Sara needed time to accept the news.

"You don't mean that," Sara finally sputtered.

"I do." Lydia nodded. "I cannot explain why, but I do. I believe God opened my heart, and I sensed the truth of the men's words. I was baptized in the river that day. I and my whole household."

"But…" Sara was shaking her head.

"I know it is unexpected—" Lydia began, but Sarah cut her off.

"It is not only unexpected, it is heresy. Adonai did not send that ruffian, that carpenter, to be the Messiah." Sara practically spat the words. "Where is his kingdom? Where is the land of peace and prosperity for our people, if he is the Messiah?"

"Jesus did not bring a kingdom like we were expecting," Lydia tried to explain, though truthfully she was far from understanding it well herself. "His kingdom is not of this earth."

"Can you really believe this?" Sara asked. "Can you believe that while we, His Chosen People, have been longing for the Promised Land of safety and security for the Hebrews, Adonai would change His mind? That He would deny us what He has promised for so long?" And then, after she took in a long, slow breath, she let it out. "I sometimes forget that you are not truly one of us."

Lydia flinched as if Sara had slapped her. She might not have been born a Jew, but she had been a faithful follower of Adonai since the day she married Andreas. She had never doubted, never worshipped the gods of her homeland or of this place. She had become, as deeply as she could, one of God's people. And yet she had never been fully embraced as a full-fledged member of the faith because she did not have Jewish blood in her veins.

"What does Anna say?" Sara asked.

"That is between me and Anna—"

"She was horrified, wasn't she? As she should be. What madness made you listen to those men? Please, tell me it is not too late to undo it."

"I cannot tell you what it was they said that caused me to believe," Lydia said calmly. "But I can tell you that it is the truth. If you go into the agora and listen to the men preach—"

"Oh, I have heard them in the agora," Sara said. "I have seen the short one standing on the stage, shouting about Jesus to any and all. I have seen many poor, insipid fools stop and listen, even seen some be swayed by his fine words and promises of an eternal life." She practically spat the words. "I just did not expect that you would be among those who were taken in by this foolishness."

Lydia did not know what to say. She could see that she would not sway Sara, and so she stood and let her speak.

"And you say these men are staying in your home?"

Lydia nodded.

"Lydia, even if you believe their nonsense, you cannot let them stay. You are a single woman. It is not appropriate to allow these strange men to live in your home."

"There is plenty of space," Lydia said. "They stay in the spare rooms far from mine. There is nothing untoward."

"But what will people say?" Sara's voice had taken on a higher pitch. "Think about your business, Lydia. Will people want to do business with the woman who is housing the zealots harassing people in the square?"

"They are not zealots."

"They are saying that Jesus is greater than Caesar. Tobias has told me that those in government have certainly noticed that, and zealots is what the magistrates are calling them. And not only that, they are heretics. They are saying that Jesus is the Son of God. They need to stop harassing people, or Tobias says there will be consequences."

"They are not harassing people. They are sharing the Good News."

"That may be how you see it. Not everyone sees it that way."

"I am sorry to hear that."

"Lydia, you must distance yourself from these men now, or it will have serious consequences for you."

Lydia took in a deep breath. "I suppose that is a risk I will have to take," she said.

She had not intended to cause strife. She had not meant to do anything. All she had done was believe what she knew to be the truth. That Jesus was indeed the Son of God.

"Lydia, please. For the sake of your family, if not for yourself. Stop this nonsense. Or at least, if you must believe it, do it privately. Do not allow your family and your business to be tainted by the stain of what these men are doing."

Lydia understood then. She finally realized what Sara had been truly getting at. Sara did not want to be associated with the Christians in any way. If Lydia had to follow them, couldn't she do it quietly, so it didn't impact Sara?

"I cannot deny who I am or what has happened to me," Lydia said calmly. "I will not deny the name of Jesus Christ."

"I am very sorry to hear that."

Sara said nothing for a moment. Then slowly she turned and, without another word, began to walk back toward the gate.

Lydia tried to put it out of her head, but she could not. Of course she could not. Sara was no doubt saying what everyone was thinking. But that did not make it easier to hear. Lydia's husband's family would not understand. They could not—not yet, anyway.

Lydia spent much of the rest of the afternoon in the weaving room, working next to Leia on the spare loom. It was an intricate process, taking the thread that had been spun from the dyed wool and weaving it, strand by careful strand, on the upright loom. The weights tied to the warp threads kept the vertical fibers taut, and it took a fine hand to make sure the wool threads were aligned perfectly and smoothly. The weave was fine, the thread very costly, and mistakes or distraction could ruin the fabric and many months of work.

In spite of that, or perhaps because of it, Lydia found the work soothing. She did not often have time to spend at the loom, not when she was usually occupied with making payments and managing the sales of the finished material, but when she could, she liked to put her hands on the raw materials and create. She had always loved watching fabric emerge, one row at a time. It seemed almost like magic to see a spool of thread turn into a piece of cloth, and her mind loved the symmetry of it, the simple repetitive motions that created something extraordinary. It took her back to the simple days of her childhood.

Lydia had learned to weave long ago in her father's workshop. Her mother and older sister had stayed away, preferring to spend their days at home and gossiping in the marketplace, and Lydia knew her mother had not thought it appropriate for the owner's daughter to be toiling alongside the paid help. But Lydia had loved the work, and her father had indulged her. He always had. He had allowed her to sit at the side of Mariah, a small, hunched woman with a fiery spirit who had been weaving for her father for many decades. Mariah had patiently taught Lydia to string the machine, to tie the weights, and to use the shuttle to build the fabric strand by strand.

More importantly, Mariah had taught her to feel the story inside the thread. She had shown her how to listen to the soft sighs of the sheep who had grown the wool and to smell the grass beneath their feet. Mariah taught her to feel the soft pressure of the ocean on the murex shells and to taste the sharp tang of the seawater. Mariah believed she had to listen to the thread and it would tell her how to weave it into the finest version of the cloth. The other workers had laughed at her and thought she was daft, but over time, Lydia began to understand what Mariah meant. And now, all these years later, she heard Mariah's raspy laugh and her soft songs play in her head as she worked the fabric, row by row.

The light was nearly gone from the room before Lydia realized it. Leia was still working, though she had to lean very close to the thread to see it.

"I am sorry," Lydia said, stepping back. It was past time for Leia to leave, but she could hardly do so while Lydia was still here. "I have kept you working far too long."

"It is all right," Leia said. "I wanted to finish this piece anyway."

She was being kind. Lydia thanked her again and told her to go home. The spinning room was empty, though Giorgio was still here. When there was dye on to boil, he stayed through the night to tend to it. Filip had offered to stay, many times, so that Giorgio could rest at home, but Giorgio always refused. He needed to supervise the dye himself, he insisted, and Lydia had long since given up trying to argue with him. Lydia gathered her things and readied herself for the journey home. But when she stepped into the front room of the workshop, she found Damon waiting, a large bundle in his arms.

"Oh." Lydia stepped back, but she felt a smile curving on her lips. "Hello. I did not expect to see you today."

"You are a hard woman to get ahold of." The way he was looking at her made her stomach warm.

"I was at the loom. Have you been waiting long?" Someone had lit a lamp in this room, and the soft light illuminated his even features, his straight teeth. He was more handsome than Lydia had noticed before.

"Seeing you now makes it worth every moment." He stepped forward and jostled the package in his arms. "I wanted to show you something."

"What is it?" She cleared off a space on the table and indicated that he should set the parcel down. He gently lowered it to the wooden surface and began to undo the rope tied around the thick burlap covering. His hands moved slowly and deliberately, every motion controlled. He almost seemed to be teasing her, drawing out the anticipation. Finally, he loosened the knots and pulled back the outer covering. Lydia leaned forward to see the snow-white fabric folded neatly inside. The weave was very fine, and there was a slight sheen to the surface.

Lydia gasped. "Is that—"

"Silk." Damon smiled. "I worked for many months to get my hands on it, and it just arrived. I knew you were the right person for it."

"May I?" She dared not touch the precious fabric without asking.

"Of course." She reached out her hand. It was as soft as a baby's cheek, smoother than a rose petal. "But how did you get it?"

Lydia had only seen silk a few times in her life. It was costly—much more costly than the wool and linen she worked with. It was made from the vomit of worms, she had been told, and was spun only on the far side of the world. It was an expensive and dangerous journey to bring it along the trading route from Serica, and however Damon had gotten this much of it— far more than she had ever seen in one place—Lydia was grateful.

"I have trading partners with connections all over the world," Damon said. "When I was asked whether I wanted it, I did not hesitate. I knew fabric this fine could only be meant for someone as talented as you."

"You are trying to flatter me into buying this." Lydia eyed him. "What is the price?"

Lydia wanted this silk. She would pay whatever it cost. But she could not let Damon know that.

"I am only speaking the truth. Do you think Hektor would know what to do with fabric this fine?" He inclined his head toward the door, in the direction of Hektor's workshop down the road. He made linen so rough a carpenter could use it to sand wood. "There is only one person I would trust with fabric this fine."

"You did not tell me the price."

Damon laughed and leaned forward to unfold another section of the fine fabric. When he straightened, he stood closer to Lydia. "Are you really thinking about money at this moment? You should be dreaming about what you intend to create from fabric this beautiful. It would make a wonderful robe for a nobleman. Or perhaps a gown for a wedding for some rich young bride."

"What is the cost?" She could not let herself dream until she knew the price. She had many ideas for this fabric, but she knew the cost would be exorbitant.

Damon smiled. "Five hundred denarii."

It was a fair price. More than fair. Lydia would not let her face betray her delight. "Two hundred."

"You are trying to steal it from me."

"Three hundred."

Damon pressed his lips together, and then he let out a sigh. "Two hundred fifty. That is my cost. I will not make anything on the sale, but it will be worth it to see you create the most beautiful gown ever seen in Philippi."

Lydia pretended to consider. She knew he was giving her a good deal. He was watching her. His eyes were smiling, though his mouth was not.

"All right," she finally said. "I will pay you two hundred and fifty denarii, far more than it's worth, because I cannot believe I will ever see this much silk in one place ever again in my life."

"And I will sell it to you for that price, far less than it's worth, because of the way your face lights up when you look at it."

He was flattering her again, but this time, she let herself wonder if flattery was all it was. Did he mean what he was saying? As much as she hated to admit it, there was a small part of her that hoped it was the case.

"I will need to go to Caesar's temple. I do not have that much money here." The imperial temple was considered the safest place in Philippi, and the city leaders allowed residents to hold their money there, under heavy guard, for a fee. "I will go tomorrow. Will you bring the fabric back then?"

"I will leave it with you now. I trust that you will pay what you owe."

Lydia ran her fingers over the smooth weave again. It was luxurious. She would dye it the richest purple she had ever made, and it would make a stunning gown. "Thank you."

Lydia folded the fabric back up and wrapped it in the burlap once more. She hated to cover it, but it would be safer to store it this way. Damon stepped back to allow her to work and then moved to the side so she could hoist the bundle. It was heavier than she thought, and when she struggled, Damon reached out and steadied her arms with his own.

"Thank you." Her skin was warm beneath her robes where he touched her. "I have it now."

Damon nodded and stepped back. Lydia intended to store the fabric in the locked box that held the coins she kept on hand, but she was not sure it would fit. The key was in a hidden pocket of her robe. She shifted the bundle to one arm and propped it against the wall then pulled the key from the pocket. She fitted it into the lock on the face of the cabinet. The box was made of iron, and the lock the strongest they could get. Andreas had assured her that nothing could break into this box. She adjusted the bags of coins that sat inside, and she tried to fit the bundle in, but it was too large.

"May I?" Damon had appeared to the side of her, and he reached out his hands. She heard Andreas's voice in her head saying she should not allow anyone so close to the open box. But she did not fear Damon had the wrong motives. She handed him the fabric and he set it on the table again. He unwrapped the burlap and refolded the fabric, this time folding it over once more, and then he wrapped it up again. "Try it now."

Damon handed her the bundle, and this time it fit within the box.

"Thank you." She closed the door of the box and locked it again and then straightened up and tucked the key into her pocket once more. "It will be safe there."

She smiled at Damon, who did not seem to be in any hurry to leave.

"Are you returning to the city?" Damon asked.

"I was planning to go home now. It is late." The shadows cast by the light from the lamp had lengthened, and the sounds of people outside on the road had quieted.

"It is late indeed. I have kept you too long." Damon pointed to the high windows. "The sun is gone from the sky. It is not safe for a woman to walk alone now. You must let me escort you."

"I walk home alone most days," Lydia said. Andreas had not liked it when she had walked by herself, had said it was not safe or dignified. Now that she did not answer to him, she did as she pleased.

"That does not mean you should. I will walk with you."

Lydia hated the way her heart beat faster at his words. She was not a young girl, her head full of fancies. She was a grandmother. A business owner. But she did not argue.

"I must do one thing first."

Damon nodded, and he stepped back to wait by the door. Lydia walked through the storage room and past the looms and the spinning rooms and found Giorgio sitting on his chair in the dye room. He was eating a strip of dried meat, watching the flames dance.

"Please get some sleep," Lydia said.

He nodded and held up his hand, indicating that he had heard, but continued to gaze at the fire. Lydia hesitated in the doorway. It did not seem right that an old man should sleep on a bundle on the hard floor in this hot, smelly room. But Giorgio would not have it any other way, she knew. She had wasted her breath arguing with him many times over the years and knew it would get her nowhere, so she said good night, turned, and walked back to the front of the workshop, where Damon was waiting. She gathered her things and blew out the lamp, and they walked out together.

The street was quiet, most of the other workshops dark. Lydia realized that they would need to hurry if they were to make it inside the city walls before the gates closed. This time of year, the guards locked the gates so early. A soft breeze rustled the trees above them, and the sky was a deep indigo, pricked with tiny twinkling stars. As they began to walk, the hard soles of the sandals striking against the stones, Lydia glanced over at Damon. Milky light from a crescent moon spilled down, making his features appear even more handsome. Lydia looked away quickly, before he could see her drinking him in.

"What will you make from the silk?" Damon asked.

"I do not know yet," Lydia said. "I will dye it as well as I can. But what is made from it will no doubt depend on who ends up buying it."

"You will sell the dyed silk, then?"

Lydia laughed. "Most likely. As much as I would love to wear the fabric myself, I do not have need of a gown so costly."

"You never know what sort of occasion might come up," Damon said. "You could wait and see."

"I do not think so."

"You do not think you will marry again?" Damon asked. She could not read the look on his face.

"I do not imagine I will." Lydia knew it was expected of her, but she did not see the need to bind herself to a man. She had money enough, and the security that came with it. There had been none who tempted her to consider it, to this point.

"I am sure that news will break the hearts of many men in Philippi and beyond."

"You do not need to flatter me any longer. I have already bought the silk."

He laughed. "There you go again, Lydia. Too clever for your own good."

They walked in silence for a few moments, and then Damon said, "My only condition for letting that silk go at that price is that you do not use it to make a garment for Felix."

"Felix?" She was not sure she understood. "The magistrate?" She could not think how Damon would even know the man.

Damon nodded. "Our fathers are cousins. I have seen him parading around in his purple garments. There is only one workshop that could make such fine clothing."

"You do not like him." Lydia tried to hold back a smile.

"What is there to like about a man who abuses his power and exacts as much as he can from those who have little?"

Lydia looked down. She could not speak out openly against one of her best customers. She may not like him, but she could not afford to lose his business.

"He has mentioned you more than once. He insists you deliver the fabric personally." There was something in his voice Lydia could not interpret.

"His orders are very costly." She tried to read the set of his jaw, the way he kept his eyes focused on the road ahead. "It is right that I see them to their destination."

"He has always had a fondness for beautiful things."

Lydia did not know how to respond. It almost sounded like he meant...but surely he must be referring only to the fabric. She cleared her throat.

"I did not know you were related to Felix. You are very different."

"Yes." Damon chuckled. "We are. My father made a point of teaching us to work hard, to use our talents, and to do good in the world. Felix's father...well, he, like his son, spent much time chasing the illusion of success."

"You do not think Felix is successful?"

Damon let out a long breath. "I suppose that depends on how you define success."

"How do you define it?"

Damon did not answer for a moment. A turtledove called from a grove of cypress along the road.

"I suppose it is when you live a life that does more good than harm. When you have enough and do not need more. When you have people you care about, and who care about you."

"You do not think your cousin has these things?"

Damon chuckled again. "I do not."

Lydia glanced at him again. "And what about you? Do you have success?"

"I have just brought the most beautiful piece of silk to the most beautiful woman in Macedonia," Damon said. "Most would say that I have success beyond my wildest imagination."

"But what do you say?"

Again, he did not answer. As the quiet stretched on, Lydia began to worry that she had been too forward, that she had mistaken their friendly business dealings for something more. But then he spoke.

"My wife used to love the story of Icarus," he said quietly. Lydia knew that his wife had died many years back. Some disease of the stomach, Andreas had said, but she did not know more than that. "You know it?"

"I do." Lydia nodded. "I did not always worship Adonai. I know the legends of the gods."

Damon turned his head. "I did not know that."

Lydia shrugged. "I suppose there are many things you do not know about me."

"Which god did you most often pray to?"

"Athena." Lydia felt ashamed to admit it now that she knew that there was only one true God.

"The goddess of war." Damon smiled.

Lydia nodded. "Also the arts, crafts, and skill."

"Ah. I see."

"My father owned a dye works back in Thyatira. His workshop made the most beautiful rugs you have ever seen, as well as wool and linen. I loved to be there with him, and I prayed that Athena would make me the best at dying and weaving."

"Your prayers worked."

"No." Lydia shook her head. "I do not believe they did, because I do not believe any of the gods hold power but Adonai, and His Son, Jesus Christ."

Damon's eyes widened and he pressed his lips together, and he did not say anything for a moment.

"I am sorry. I do not mean to offend you," Lydia said. "I know you pray to the gods."

"You do not offend me," Damon said. "You have given me much to think about."

Lydia did not know what he meant.

"I had heard that the Christians were staying with you," Damon said.

"The news seems to have traveled quite quickly."

"I wondered if it was true."

"It is. They are."

"And you…"

"I am one of them now. I believe that Jesus Christ is the Redeemer."

Again, Damon did not answer for a moment. When he finally spoke, his voice was low. "There are many who do not like what these men are doing."

"I was one of them until a few days ago. But God changed my heart."

"Right. But I mean—" He seemed to search for the words to say. "Please be careful. There are some with authority who find what the Christians are doing to be a threat. There are some who believe Caesar is the only one who should be worshipped. And as the Christians gain more followers, it is a threat to Rome."

Lydia remembered her conversation with Felix in his room. "Our numbers are quite small. We could not possibly be a threat to the Roman Empire."

"Your numbers are growing day by day," Damon said. "And yes, though it is small yet, there is fear the Christians will give their money to support this new religion rather than Rome."

Money. It always came down to money.

"We will continue to pay our taxes. Worshipping Jesus will not change that."

"Just be careful," he said. "Please." There was a look on his face she could not read.

They walked in quiet for a few minutes. Lydia pondered his warning from every angle. He was not the first to warn her of the danger of following Jesus. Paul had done so himself. But still, she did not see how a small group of followers of a peaceful man could pose any threat to the great Roman Empire.

Finally, when she could not take the quiet any longer, she said, "He flew too close to the sun."

Damon turned, and then, as her words registered, his face broke into a smile.

"You asked me about Icarus," Lydia continued. "He was the son of Daedalus, creator of the labyrinth beneath the palace of King Minos. Once the labyrinth was finished, Minos imprisoned Daedalus and Icarus in it, but they devised a plan to get out by building wings of wax and feathers. They flew out of the maze."

"I always liked to imagine how it must have felt once they got to the sky, to look down and see the earth from above." Damon smiled. "It must have been unbelievable." And after a moment, he added, "But then, I suppose that was Eunike's point."

Lydia supposed Eunike was Damon's wife. "What do you mean?"

"You know how the story ends."

"Daedalus warned Icarus not to fly too close to the sun, or the wax would melt," Lydia said. "But Icarus, intoxicated by the feeling of flight, ventured too far up." As they turned the bend in the road, the high stone walls that protected the city came into view, torches burning in the guard stands at regular intervals. His steps quickened, and she hurried her pace to match. "Just as his father predicted, the wings melted and he crashed to the ground."

"He got greedy," Damon said.

"He was flying. What person would not enjoy that feeling?"

"I don't know." Damon shrugged. "Eunike's point was that I tended to dream of things far beyond the scope of the possible. I dreamed of having ten sons to work with me. I imagined setting up the largest trading route in Asia, of carrying silk and spices and precious oils all the way from Serica to the far side of the earth."

That would be quite an endeavor indeed. The Silk Road was one of the most dangerous trade routes in the world.

"Your wife did not want these things?"

"She had a different definition of success. To her, it looked like a safe home, enough food to eat, health for our children. She believed there was no need to fly when you could walk and get there eventually anyway."

"It sounds as if you're saying she limited your ability to prosper."

"I do not mean that," Damon said. "Not exactly. She was right, in so many ways. It is because of her that our children turned out well and made good matches. It is because of her good sense that we had a comfortable life."

Lydia had supplied the scarlet linen his daughter Elena had worn for her wedding feast. She had married the son of a magistrate in the city of Corinth, and Andreas had told her the celebration went on for many days.

"But…?"

Damon laughed. "I suppose it is that she always warned against wanting more than was prudent."

"I see. She was always trying to keep you from flying too close to the sun?"

"Exactly. She wanted me to be content with what we had here on earth."

Lydia let out a breath when she saw that the city gates were still open. It was not safe to spend the night outside the gates. She inclined her head toward Damon.

"And are you?"

"Am I what?"

"Content to keep your feet planted firmly on earth?"

Damon was quiet a long moment, and then he looked at her. Although it was night, the moon cast plenty of light, and it looked as if he was gazing past her eyes and into her soul.

"No," he said softly. "I am not. I too want more than I can have."

CHAPTER SEVEN

At the next church meeting, there were more than forty worshippers. Lydia recognized many of the same faces that had shown up the week before, but she also met many new people—Syntyche, the wife of a wealthy business owner, and Epaphroditus, a guard at the temple of Poseidon, and Hypatia, who collected scraps to resell in the market. After they had worshipped, they ate together, Iduma turning out a beautiful roast lamb as well as bread with many dips to share among the believers. Lydia spent some time talking with Claes, the player at the theater.

"I prefer the tragedies," Claes said, but he said it in such a funny voice that Lydia had to laugh. He was outgoing and engaging and sometimes broke out into song for no reason at all. He was so different from Lydia, but she enjoyed his company. Lydia felt contentment in her soul as she broke bread with the disciples and fellow believers.

The next day, Lydia visited the temple of Caesar to retrieve the money she owed Damon. It was positioned in a prime location just off the agora, and as she passed by the gambling tables and market stalls, she saw Paul preaching once again and a commotion around the fortune-teller girl. Lydia wondered about the story the men had shared with her, that the girl had recognized them as representatives of the one true God, but Lydia did not go closer to investigate. She hurried to the Imperial temple, which had an imposing facade adorned with heavy columns and a striking pediment engraved with the name Caesar Augustus that proclaimed its power. A marble statue of the emperor stood on the steps, and another took up much of the inside. Lydia climbed the steps hesitantly, eyeing the half dozen Roman guards in their full armor plate. The tufts of red feathers on their helmets stood out brightly against the white stone of the building. She had not entered a temple to a false idol in many years, not since she had believed that Adonai was the one true God. But this was different. Caesar was not worshipped in the same way that the gods were. Not exactly. Still, she entered the building with trepidation. She did not stop to admire the statue of the comely emperor but went straight to the room down the stairs where money was kept and retrieved. More guards lined the corridor.

"I'd like to take out two hundred and fifty denarii, please," Lydia said to the man at the table when it was her turn. She told him her name and he unlocked a series of doors. He returned a few minutes later with her coins in a bag.

"Thank you." She turned, nodded at the guards, who did not acknowledge her, and she returned up the stairs and headed out of the temple. She would go straight to the home of Damon, and she would not feel comfortable until she no longer carried more than most men would make in many months on her person. She had never been to Damon's home before, and when she found the one he had described, she was surprised to see that it was quite large and very fine. His house was not far from the home of his cousin Felix the magistrate, but Damon's was higher up the hill and larger, with many windows.

Lydia had thought Damon was simply a trader in wool, but it would take a great amount of wool to pay for a home like this.

Lydia's curiosity was heightened when her knock was answered by a guard in armor plate. He did not wear the face-distorting helmet of the Roman guards but did wear a breast-plate and shin guards.

Lydia told the guard who she was and why she was there, and he took the bag of coins and promised to deliver it to Damon. Lydia thanked him and turned away, wondering how much she did not know about Damon. What man kept guards at his own home? Why would he do such a thing? Lydia did not know, but she hoped to find out.

The next day, Lydia went to the dye works and returned as the sun was setting. She found the lights in the upstairs windows blazing and smiled to think of the Christian men up there, praying and planning.

"Good evening," Elodie said after she'd unlocked the door and let Lydia into the house.

"Hello," Lydia said, handing the girl her cloak. "The others are here?"

"They are upstairs. They have eaten." Elodie folded the cloak over her arms. She would beat the dust off and air it out before Lydia wore it again. "Your supper is ready for you."

"Thank you." Lydia now heard excited voices upstairs, and what sounded like raucous laughter. The men were having a good time tonight. Well, good for them. They deserved to enjoy themselves after the hard work they were doing in the name of Jesus Christ.

After she had washed, Lydia sat down to eat, a lovely meal of roast lamb and spicy lentils, with apricots drizzled with honey afterward. While she ate, she went over the household accounts. Iduma was not wrong when she had said she needed more. The sum spent on food had gone up further than she had realized, and they were using far more oil than previously. The store of wine was also depleting more quickly. Iduma's notes indicated that Elodie was having to make many more trips to the nearby well to draw enough water, and her time was therefore limited. Well, all of that was to be expected, Lydia thought. It was not as if she did not have enough. She would simply need to pay attention to their expenses, and maybe ask Iduma to cut back on the amount of meat she bought.

After her meal, Lydia went upstairs and continued on to the floor where the men were staying. Merry laughter greeted her before she approached the door to the room where they had gathered. She knocked on the door, and heard Paul exclaim, "Come in!"

Timothy and Luke were lounging on cushions on the floor, while Silas and Paul sat in chairs at the table. Silas once again had a small knife in his hand and was carving into a piece of acacia wood.

"Lydia!" Paul exclaimed when she stepped into the room. "It is good to see you. We have had an extraordinary day!"

"What happened?" Had they been drinking too much wine? She had never seen them this excited. There was a hum of energy in the room, a sense of uncontained joyous celebration. She stepped into the room and closed the door behind her—she did not want Iduma to realize the state these men were in—but she hovered in the doorway.

"Do you remember that girl we told you about before? The one who tells fortunes?" Paul asked. His voice was loud, his eyes wide.

"The slave girl." Lydia nodded. "The one who recognized that you were servants of the Most High God."

"That is right," Paul said. "It happened again yesterday and then again today as we entered the square. As soon as we came near, she shouted the truth of who we are and who we serve. Her handlers rushed to settle her down and quiet her, but she kept calling out about it."

No, they had not had too much wine, she realized. This was not the sloppy, silly elation of drunkenness. This was something else altogether.

"You had mentioned she had a python spirit," Paul said. "We knew this meant she was possessed of a demon." Luke nodded at the man. Silas did not look up but kept his eyes fastened on the wood in his hands. The edge of his sleeve pulled up as he moved, and Lydia could just make out the lower edge of the tattoo he bore.

"That is how she could know the future, because she was consulting with a spirit from the other world," Paul said.

"A demon?" Lydia knew of *shedim*, the bad spirits in Jewish understanding, and the *daimones* of Greek culture. They were both associated with the gods and goddesses the pagans worshipped. That was how the girl supposedly told the future—she was said to channel the words from the god Apollo. But could these men really believe this girl was tapping into power from another realm?

"I see you doubt. Believe me, demons are very real," Paul said. "They are spirits sent by our enemy to fight against God's purposes. Jesus Himself encountered them, and they feared Him. He cast them out of many people while He was alive."

"He did?" Lydia had much to learn about the Christ and had not heard this yet.

"There was a man in a synagogue," Luke said, nodding. "And the men whose demons were cast into a herd of pigs. There were many others as well."

If Jesus had done it, it must be real. But Lydia still did not understand.

"But if this demon serves the deceiver, why would it call out that you are servants of the Most High God? Why wouldn't the spirit try to deceive those around it? Why would it not have the girl call out that you are fakes and that you are spreading lies?"

"Because even demons are subject to the power of God," Paul said. "There are many in this town who do not believe in the one true God, but make no mistake, the demons themselves do. The evil spirits may serve Satan, and they masquerade as power from Hera or Apollo or Saturn, but they are still subservient to the Most High God. They fear His power, but they recognize it and bow to it nonetheless."

Lydia tried to make sense of this. "You are saying that the demon inside the girl could not help but fear the power of God in you, and he caused her to cry out?"

"That is right," Paul said. He poured a little more wine from the decanter on the table into an earthenware cup.

"The first few days she called out to us, we had hoped that her message would help the others in the square to understand the truth of what she said," Luke said. It was an incredible thing to say—they had hoped that a girl possessed by a demon would help the people in the agora to understand the truth of Jesus Christ—but coming from even-tempered, logical Luke, it did not sound crazy. It almost made a certain amount of sense. If this girl who claimed to channel the god Apollo saw the truth, how could others fail to see it?

"But Paul was in a state this morning," Timothy said, grinning. "Perhaps he stayed up too late or had a bit too much wine last night."

"I did not intend for it to happen." Paul took a sip of the wine and set the cup down. "But I could not handle the commotion this morning. All of her screaming and then her handlers yanking her back, throwing curses at us, spitting at us. All the people scurrying to avoid the scuffle. It was too much."

"Paul could not contain himself," Silas said, a guilty smile on his face.

"What did you do?" Lydia's instinct was to fear the worst, but the way these men were grinning made her uncertain.

"I turned to her, and I yelled, 'In the name of Jesus Christ I command you to come out of her.' And in that moment, she shrieked the most horrible sound you've ever heard. Like someone was tearing off her arm, only the sound was deep, like a man's voice."

Lydia put her hand to her mouth. How could this be?

"Then suddenly, it just stopped," Paul continued. "And she fell to the ground and wept."

"It was crazy." Timothy still seemed shocked, recounting it now. "I have never seen it before. I wasn't sure it was even real, but…well, it's real, that's all I can say."

"You could tell instantly something was different," Paul said. "Everyone around could see something had changed."

"We tried to get close to her, to help her up, but the men responsible for her started to chase us, screaming for us to go away."

"The demon left her." Lydia wanted to make sure she understood. "Because of the name of Jesus."

"Even demons know the power of that name and are subject to it," Silas said quietly. What was this strange world she had stepped into?

"Have you done this before? Cast out demons?" Lydia asked.

Paul nodded, as did Silas. Both Luke and Timothy sat still. "Jesus gave His disciples the authority to do so," Paul said. "You too now have the power of His Spirit inside you."

Did she? Lydia didn't feel like she did. How would one do something like that, cast out demons? She could not imagine it.

"So what happened?" Lydia asked. "To the girl, I mean?"

"I do not know," Paul said. "We did not stay to find out, not with several large men chasing us."

"We did not preach in the square today," Luke said. "Instead, we went to the steps near the government building on the east side of the city, and we found that many who had witnessed the scene in the agora had followed us."

"So many wanted to understand the power that had rendered the girl changed," Silas said. "Paul preached, and dozens heard and were saved."

"Praise God," Lydia said, her eyes welling up. "That is wonderful."

"This city is hungry for Jesus," Paul said. "The message is touching so many."

"No wonder you are so merry tonight," Lydia said. "That is wonderful news."

"God is doing powerful things," Paul said. "And I'll tell you something, Lydia. He is using you as well."

"I don't—"

"You may not know it yet, but you will see. God is going to use you in powerful ways too."

CHAPTER EIGHT

Lydia was sitting with the men, listening to Paul teach about the life of Christ the next night, when they heard someone pounding on the door several stories below. *Thump thump thump.* All of them sat up a little straighter, listening as the pounding continued. Lydia pressed herself up, but Silas waved her down and started toward the door. Timothy was only a few steps behind him. The sky was dark, the evening meal finished. There could be no good reason for someone to be pounding on the door like that at this time, and suddenly Lydia was very glad to have several strong men among her household.

Lydia followed behind the younger men as they rushed down the stairs, Paul and Luke behind her, but she heard the yelling before she got to the main floor. A sense of dread filled her as she recognized the voice. Silas and Timothy were ahead of her, hurrying toward the entry, but Lydia yelled, "Stop!"

Both men froze but did not move away from the entryway. Anna came around the corner, yelling. Her face was red and streaked with tears, but this was not sadness. Lydia saw that at once. She was livid.

"Anna," Lydia said, stopping in her tracks. She heard Paul breathing heavily behind her. "What has happened?"

Elodie stood in the entry, a few feet behind Anna. Her eyes were wide, unsure of what to do.

"*What has happened?*" Anna's voice was shrill, and she jabbed her finger toward Silas and Timothy. "These men, these liars you have invited into your home. Do you know what they have done?"

"What?" Lydia's stomach turned sour. Had they done something terrible? She had believed them, trusted them. Had she been fooled after all? "What happened?"

"They have ruined Daniel's fortune-teller!" Now she waved her arm, indicating all of them. "One of them shouted at her about this Jesus you now claim to follow, and now she cannot hear the voice of the Oracle. She is ruined, and now so are we. What use is a fortune-teller who cannot tell fortunes?"

Lydia was so stunned by her words that it took her a few moments to understand. "The girl in the market?"

"Of course the girl in the market."

"She is owned by Daniel?"

"Yes!" Anna shouted. "Did you not know that?"

Lydia had not known that. How would she have known? Lydia shook her head. But with a sickening sense of dread, she saw that it must be true.

Owning slaves was not uncommon. Lydia thought it more fair to pay her workers, but slaves were a fact of life in many households and businesses throughout Macedonia. Still, the scriptures had strict rules about how to treat slaves, and exploiting an evil spirit hardly seemed like humane treatment. And how could a faithful Jew like Daniel profit from a girl who had channeled a false god?

"Daniel has many investments. Adria is among them. And she was a very profitable one, until these men ruined her."

Lydia felt silly for not recognizing it before. Surely the building trade could not have afforded Daniel the means to live as they did. She had never thought—

"How could you do this, Imma?" Anna was shouting through tears now. "It is one thing to throw away your own life, choosing to follow these liars and their false messiah. But it is completely another to ruin mine and destroy the fortune of my husband's family."

A thousand thoughts ran together in Lydia's mind, and she could not make sense of any of them. She had not known—but even if she had, what Daniel did was wrong—and she could not renounce the name of Jesus, not now that she knew its true power. Did Anna not see that this was proof? That these men were telling the truth?

Silence stretched out. Anna's outburst had silenced even Paul. Anna pressed her lips together, her nostrils flared. Lydia tried to think of what she could say. She could not apologize. She was not at all sorry for what these men had done. But she had not known and had never intended to hurt—

"This is too far, Imma." Anna's voice, which had been nearly hysterical just a few moments before, was now strangely calm. "Daniel is going to make sure these men are properly punished." She took in a breath and then continued. "And if you don't renounce this nonsense, you will not see me or your grandchildren again."

Lydia blinked. She had not heard her right. "Grand*children*?"

"Yes, Imma. Grandchildren." Anna moved her hand to her belly. "There is a baby due this summer. But if you do not renounce this heresy and send these men on their way, you will never meet him."

And with that, Anna turned and moved to the door.

"Anna. Wait." Lydia stepped toward her, reached out to grab her, but Anna was gone. The heavy door slammed behind her.

Lydia stood still for a moment. Her mind was filled with so many competing thoughts she could not make sense of them. She wanted to run after Anna, but somewhere in her she knew this was not the time to try to speak sense into her. Elodie, her eyes wide, was still watching her, and the men around her were avoiding looking at her. Surely they must be trembling with fear, Lydia thought, over Anna's threat to have them punished.

But when Paul spoke, all he said was, "Can we pray for you?"

Because Lydia did not know what else to do, she nodded, tears running down her cheeks.

After much intense prayer, the men had retreated to the rooms at the top of the house while Lydia went to her own room and lay down in her bed. She could not stop the tears that streamed down her face. Anna had never spoken to her that way before. She had never seen such hatred in her daughter's face or known such hurt. The things Anna had said—

Lydia felt another sob rise up. She had not known. She had no way to realize that the girl in the marketplace had been owned by Daniel.

But even if she had, would it have changed anything?

Could Daniel really have been exploiting the girl who was cursed with a demon? Had Anna truly been living off the profits of the false gods? The girl had been telling fortunes in the marketplace for many years. Surely Andreas had not known about this when he had arranged Anna's betrothal. But how could he have not?

Her mind kept returning to the news that Anna was having another child. The news, which should have brought her nothing but joy, was now tinged with sadness. Would she ever get to meet this grandchild? Lydia had no intention of renouncing her new faith. She could not expect Anna to understand, but she hoped that she might one day come to accept it. She would not really withhold her children from their grandmother, Lydia tried to convince herself. She would come around. *Please, Adonai, let it be so*, Lydia prayed.

There was a soft knock at the door.

"Come in." Lydia did not lift her head from the pillow, but she could tell it was Danae by the soft tread of her slippers as she stepped inside.

"I have brought you some cool water," Danae said. Lydia heard her set a tray down on the table next to the bed.

"Thank you." Lydia turned and saw that she had brought not only a pitcher of water to drink but also some in a bowl with a soft cloth. "You are good to me."

Danae ducked her head. "You are good to us," she said.

Lydia pushed herself up while Danae poured some of the water from the pitcher into a copper cup that glinted in the flickering light of the lamp. She held it out to Lydia, and she took it. But Danae did not move away. She was hesitating, as if there was something she wanted to say.

"What is it?" Lydia looked up at her servant.

Danae shifted on her feet. And then, after a moment, she said, "It is none of my business, of course. But—she was upset. She said things she did not mean."

Lydia felt a rush of emotion for Danae. This was not the first time she had comforted Lydia in her distress. It was she who cleaned up the mess when Lydia lost the babies, one after another, and had held Lydia close while she sobbed. Danae had been there for the worst moments of Lydia's life.

"I know," Lydia said. But knowing it was true did not make it better.

"She will come around." Danae picked up the cloth and dipped it into the bowl of water, and then she wrung it out. Gently, she placed it against Lydia's forehead. It was cool and refreshing, and the kind gesture helped to slow the tears.

"I hope you are right," Lydia said.

Danae dipped the cloth back in the water and held it to Lydia's cheek. "It may take a while. She was quite upset. But you are her mother, and she loves you. She will come around."

Lydia nodded. She was not sure, but Danae's words gave her peace. Danae wiped her face gently, and after a few minutes of quiet, Lydia felt strong enough to ask, "What about the others?"

"They are upstairs, ma'am. When I brought up more wine and sweets for them, they were gathered together praying."

"They were praying for Anna?"

"Yes." Danae hesitated again. "And for wisdom to know how to respond to the threat against them."

"Of course." Guilt swallowed her up as she realized that in her own private grief, she had momentarily forgotten the threat Anna had made. Daniel wanted the men punished for what they had done. Lydia did not know what he would do, but Paul and Silas and others had openly been spreading the Good News. It was a crime for which they could be arrested, or worse, and Felix had already made it clear that if Lydia did not accept his advances, he would take action against the believers. Lydia leaned forward, readying to stand. "I must go to them."

"You need to care for yourself first," Danae said, gently pressing her back. She smoothed the cool cloth across Lydia's forehead again.

"You are too good to me," Lydia said. "But I am afraid I must go to them. I should be praying with them."

This time Danae did not stop her, but she did help Lydia straighten her robes, and she held the cloth to Lydia's eyes to reduce the effects of her tears. Then Lydia walked quietly up the steps to the top floor. She pushed opened the door and found all four men in a circle on their knees. She crept into the room as Luke was asking God for wisdom and protection for all. None of the men looked up as she entered, but Timothy did move aside to make space for her in their circle. Lydia got down on her knees and joined with them in prayer. They asked for guidance and strength. They asked for courage and for clarity of speech. Luke asked that they be as wise as serpents and as harmless as doves. And Lydia asked that they fear no one but God and continue to spread the Gospel throughout Philippi and throughout the world.

The air in the room was heavy and still.

When they finally said amen, the streets outside were very quiet. Lydia's legs groaned as she rose to her feet, but none of the others stood. Instead, Paul swung his legs around so he sat on a cushion and said, "We should sleep. We must be back on the steps of the city building early tomorrow. There will no doubt be many souls who come to hear more about what has happened to the fortune-teller."

"You are—" Lydia's voice broke off. "You will go back?"

"Of course." Paul nodded. "There is still much work to be done."

"But Daniel does not make idle threats. He will very likely try to have you punished."

Paul shrugged. "We cannot live our lives in fear. We have a message the world needs to hear."

"He may try to have you arrested." Surely they did not understand what kind of man her daughter's husband was.

"I have been in prison before. I am sure I will see the inside of a jail again." Paul truly did not sound concerned. How could this be?

"I am not afraid to be in prison either," Silas added.

Timothy looked a little pale.

"But if you are arrested, how will the message of Jesus Christ continue to spread?" Lydia asked. Could these men not see that their being thrown in prison would be the worst thing that could happen? "Perhaps you should stay inside for a few days until Daniel's anger blows over."

"How will the message spread if we are too afraid to show up in the agora and preach?" Paul asked.

"Don't forget, the Gospel does not depend on us," Silas said. "God will make a way, whether or not it is through us."

Paul nodded. "Do you not see, Lydia? We will not be here with you always."

Lydia had known, of course, that they would not stay in Philippi forever. Paul had made it clear his goal was to carry the news of Jesus Christ throughout the world. She had not thought about... Well, she had not thought about what would happen when they left. But that was exactly why they must not be taken by Daniel's plans.

"Whether or not we are here," Silas continued, "whether we are in prison or have moved on to the next city or whether we are right here with you, we need you to make sure the Good News continues to spread. We need you to see that the church continues to grow."

"Silas is right," Paul said. "When we are gone, or..." Paul waved his hand. "We will need you to continue hosting the church here in Philippi."

"When we are gone," Silas said, "it will be up to you."

CHAPTER NINE

The knock on the door came early the next morning, no less loud than the night before. Elodie moved to answer it, but Lydia indicated that she should stop, and she went to answer the door herself. Lydia looked out the small window in the door, and then she opened the heavy wooden door, keeping the iron gate closed.

"Good morning." Lydia put a smile on her face and tried to act as though she was not unnerved, even as she found the three large men who had guarded the fortune-teller standing outside her door. She pretended everything was normal, as if this were just another day, though she was sure they did not believe her. She did not usually answer the door herself. Nothing about this was normal. "What can I do for you?"

"We are here for the men staying with you," the largest one declared. His hair hung in greasy hanks, and he was missing most of his teeth. Despite that, Lydia could see that he must have been handsome once, with his high cheekbones and strong jaw.

"Here we are." Paul appeared beside Lydia. Silas moved into the open doorway as well.

"Where are the others?" The leader was craning his neck, trying to see inside the house, but Silas blocked his view.

"We are ready to go now," Paul said.

Lydia saw then what Paul and Silas were doing. They were offering themselves up, trying to protect Luke and Timothy. And, she realized, herself. She did not know how to respond. Paul and Silas could not—

But then, Timothy was so young, and she suspected he would not fare well in prison. And Luke's skills were needed.

"There were four of you," a second man declared. He had bronze skin and a nose that had suffered more than one blow. "We are here to collect all four."

Paul opened the iron gate and stepped outside as though he hadn't heard, forcing the third man to step back to allow space. "Which way?"

Silas followed and immediately pulled the gate closed behind him. From her vantage point, Lydia could see the three men look at one another, uncertain how to react. The larger one said something to the leader in a language Lydia did not understand.

"The magistrate's offices are this way, are they not?" Silas said, pointing up the street. He began walking, and Paul went with him.

The men hesitated, and then the leader shrugged and said, "Let's go," and the men moved off. Perhaps they had decided taking two without a fight was better than risking violence to get four. Perhaps they were paid the same, no matter how many they got, or maybe they were content to get Paul. Or maybe, Lydia reasoned, the Lord was simply with them.

Lydia closed the door. Timothy and Luke were safe. Lydia pressed her hands against the closed door, and she started to turn back toward the room where they waited, but then she stopped. She knew what would happen now. Paul and Silas would be taken in front of the magistrates, and Daniel would try to convince the authorities to have them arrested and charged for disobedience to the emperor. She understood that her task now was to keep Timothy and Luke safe until they knew whether Paul and Silas would be released or thrown into prison and then to help them move along if needed.

"We should have gone too," Timothy said quietly.

"It is better this way," Luke said, though Lydia could hear in his voice that he was uncertain as well.

"Perhaps we should go now," Timothy said. "We could catch up with them."

"What good would that do?" Lydia shook her head. "It is better to have you two free. We do not know what will happen to them, but you need to continue to spread the message of Jesus."

They both nodded. Lydia sat back down and tried to eat, but she had a hard time forcing the yogurt down. With every moment, she was thinking about what was happening now—had they reached the magistrates yet? Had they been brought before the officials?

Neither Luke nor Timothy was eating.

Lydia should get ready to go to the workshop. But she could not imagine going to the dye works, not while Paul and Silas were in danger, and she could not sit here all day, wondering what was going on, hoping that the magistrates would have mercy on the men.

She would not, she decided. She could not.

Money was at the root of this. Daniel's complaint had been about lost income. And Felix's concern had been that the followers of the Way would not pay their taxes to Rome. Well, if money was the main issue, she could make that problem go away.

This was her home. It was her family and her city. She knew about how things were done in Philippi. And she knew the new praetor. She realized that she might know how to stop whatever was going to happen next.

Lydia stood quickly and walked to the cupboard where Elodie always hung her cloak, and she took it from the hook. She slipped it on, checked to make sure she had the small bag that contained her coins, and stepped out the door and into the street.

Lydia knew Daniel's men would take Paul and Silas to the municipal building to bring them before the magistrates to accuse them of treachery to Rome. That would be the excuse, though of course the real reason they were being dragged before the authorities is that in freeing the girl from her demon, they had taken away the income from a wealthy man used to having his own way.

Lydia's feet flew over the wet stones as she threaded past women balancing heavy jugs of water and workmen on their way to jobs. The market was already crowded, and the smells of roasting meat and spices and animal excrement turned her stomach as she made her way through. Up ahead, she saw the great marble building rise before her, its even columns and angled pediment creating an imposing facade, but she did not head toward it. She saw that the men had not been brought before the magistrates in the temple of justice after all but were being tried right here in the agora. A large crowd had gathered around the stage where Paul had preached, and he and Silas were held by the larger men, their hands tied behind their backs. They stood before a man in a deep purple robe. Lydia recognized the robe before she saw his face.

"What is the charge?" Felix called out. He turned so the crowd could hear his voice better.

Both relief and fear washed over her together. She had somehow known Felix would be involved in this. He had not been officially installed as praetor yet, but he was soon to be in charge of all justice and order in the city. It was natural that he would be the one to deal with this issue.

"These men are Jews, and they are throwing our city into an uproar by advocating customs unlawful for us Romans to accept or practice," the largest man said. Lydia scanned the crowd. Daniel was nowhere to be seen. "They are breaking our laws and agitating against our emperor."

These men seemed to know what to say to get the crowd riled up. Several jeered, and one man shouted for them to be crucified, just like the criminal they followed.

"What customs are these?" Felix asked, his voice booming out over the crowd. He seemed to stand up taller with every word.

Lydia pushed her way through the crowd, trying to get closer to the stage.

"They are followers of the zealot Jesus, and they have spent many days preaching from this very stage that there is only one god, and Jesus is his son," the man with the broken nose called out.

Many in the crowd shouted at this. Lydia continued to push her way through the crowd, working her way closer to the stage. Several pushed back or cursed at her, but she ignored them and continued on.

"They are saying that we have to be born again," the first added. "They say that it is sacrilege to offer sacrifices to our gods and that we owe our allegiance to their god even over Caesar."

Felix turned to Paul and Silas. Both looked directly at the Roman official, heads held high. Paul looked especially small beside the enormous guards.

"Is this true?" Felix asked. "Do you practice the rites of this forbidden cult? And have you declared allegiance to your god before Caesar?"

Felix stood taller as the crowd jeered. He was obviously relishing the attention and enjoying the act of punishing these men, just as he had threatened.

"There is no God but Adonai," Paul said, his voice loud and clear. "And Jesus Christ, our Lord, is His only Son."

Taunts arose from the crowd again, louder this time. More in the crowd were shouting that they should be crucified.

"They have disrupted our market," a man toward the front yelled.

"And driven many away from our businesses!" another added.

"Their curses have ruined the fortune-teller," someone yelled.

"Do you understand that what you have done is against the laws of Rome?" Felix asked.

Both men answered, "Yes."

"Crucify them!" came the roar from the crowd.

"Stop!" Lydia cried, still pushing her way through the crowd. "Felix, do not do this!"

Felix turned, and when he saw her pressing toward the stage, his lips curved into a smile.

"Please, Felix, stop this." Lydia was now close enough to the stage that she was able to see Paul's eyes widen when he noticed her. "You know these men pose no threat. I will deal with them. I will have them sent away."

"You say they pose no threat," Felix said. "But there are many in the crowd who say they have ruined the fortune-teller. They mock our gods."

He looked from Lydia back to Paul and Silas, tied up like prisoners, and then back at Lydia.

"I will take them away, and they will not bother anyone in this town again." Lydia was now directly in front of the stage, and Felix was looking down on her. "I will pay for their release," Lydia said. She would need Damon to take his silk back and return her money. She did not know how much their release would cost, but she was sure it would be dear. Still, the choice was clear. "I will pay the fortune-teller's owners for their loss. Just let these men go."

Felix let his gaze linger on Lydia for a moment, and a look crossed his face that Lydia could not read. For a moment, she thought it might be compassion. Would his heart be softened? Would he let these men go? Would he accept coins for their release? He turned back to the men who had Paul and Silas tied up.

"What do you say to this? This woman has agreed to pay for their release and to repay your master for the loss of his slave. Will you accept?"

Before they could answer, the crowd erupted.

"They have broken our laws!"

"They mock our gods!"

"They shame our emperor!"

"Crucify them!"

"Felix," Lydia said. "Please. I'll do whatever you ask of me."

Felix looked down at her, cocked an eyebrow. *"Anything?"*

Lydia willed herself not to imagine what that might be. "Anything you ask. Please, just let them go," she begged.

Felix held her gaze for a moment longer. There was something dark in his eyes, some deep ugliness that made Lydia tremble, though she tried not to show it. Then, with a shake of his head, Felix looked away. "It is too late, Lydia. You had your chance. You will not make a mockery of me again."

Then he turned back to the guards and shouted, "Have these men stripped and beaten."

Only seconds passed before the guards had pulled the robes off of Paul and Silas. As the crowd pressed forward, someone handed the guards whips, and they began beating the men. Lydia pushed forward, trying to get close enough to pull them to safety, but the crowd surged.

"Get her too!" a man next to her cried, and she felt several pairs of hands grasp at her. She shoved them off and tried to push closer to the dais. Lydia's breath came in shallow gulps as she heard the crack of the whip, again and again. Her skin felt too hot, and the bodies around her were too close, pressing too hard. As spots began to appear in her vision, she felt as if she was losing control of her limbs. And still, the whip sounded, a high-pitched whistle moments before it cracked, pounding against flesh. One of the men—she did know which—let out an anguished cry. "Crucify her too!"

A hand grabbed her arm. She tried to yank it away, but the grip was too tight. She pulled again, trying to move forward, but there was nowhere to go. The crowds were packed in too tight, too many bodies moving and writhing and shouting. She felt far from her body. The dark spots in her vision grew, blocking out more of her sight, and she was reminded again of the time she had fallen into the river when she was a child and had quickly been pulled under. She had felt this same distance, this same loosening from reality, in the moments before her father had pulled her out. The hand on her now pulled once again, but she barely felt it.

"Lydia."

Somewhere in her mind, she recognized the voice. She forced herself, with great effort, to turn toward it. Relief washed over her when she realized it was Damon.

"This way." He pulled on her arm again, and this time she let him. He tugged her closer as he guided her through the crowd. Several men shouted or spit at her as she passed, recognizing her as associated with the men, but Damon did not stop until they had reached the edge of the crowd.

"Are you all right? Did they hurt you?" His strong arm was still wrapped around her.

"I am not hurt." But Lydia did not move away from his grasp. She was not sure she would be able to stand without his support. The whips were still cracking against flesh. "They are killing them."

"Can you stand?"

She shook her head. She felt like she was still underwater.

"We must keep moving." Damon still held her body close to his and pulled her along, down the street where the tailor and butcher shops were. The crowds finally thinned, and he stopped. "You should not be here. Let's get you home."

"Have they killed them?"

"No." Damon shook his head. "Just as we were leaving the agora, Felix ordered the guards to stop."

Lydia did not know whether to believe him or not.

"They will be sent to prison, I am sure," Damon said. "But they are alive."

Was he trying to make her feel better? Lydia did not care. She let her body sag against his, and he held her, his arms around her, while her heartbeat slowed and her vision gradually returned. She pressed her face into his chest. He smelled like sage and woodsmoke. She knew it was immodest, even dangerous for a woman to be held by a man like this, but she did not care. What more could they do to her?

"All right?" Damon asked, slowly pulling back.

Lydia nodded.

"Okay then," Damon said. "We must walk."

He released her body but held on to her hand as he pulled her through the streets. The farther they got from the agora, the more her heartbeat slowed and the more she felt her head return to normal. And as it did, questions began to form.

"How did you get there?" Lydia let him lead her around a stagnant puddle. "How did you appear like that?" Damon did not hang around the market most days.

"I heard that the Christians were being brought to the market to be arrested," Damon said. "I was worried that you were in danger, so I came."

Lydia let those words sink in, and even in her muddled state, they brought a sense of security.

"Thank you," Lydia said. And then, thinking back to the awful moments when the whips first flew through the air, she said, "But I was not the one in danger."

"You are wrong about that," Damon said. "If I had not pulled you from that crowd, you could have ended up in that jail cell with those men. What were you thinking?"

"I had hoped I could convince Felix to let them go," Lydia said. "I thought he might do it for me."

"Then you misunderstand my cousin, if you think he does anything for anyone but himself."

His voice was chiding, but there was a tenderness in it too. His hand in hers was warm and strong as he led her through the crowded street. He probably did not need to keep hold of her now, but she did not pull away.

"And you are still very much in danger," Damon continued. "Especially now that Felix knows you will stand up for the Christians and be loyal to them. You are more at risk than ever before."

Lydia recognized the truth in his words. She had hoped she could convince Felix to let the men go, but there had been nothing but hatred in his eyes. Whatever opportunity Lydia might have had once was past. She understood that now.

"Where are the others?" Damon asked.

"At my home."

"They are not safe there. And you are not safe there as long as they are with you."

Lydia had no answer. Nor did she know what to do.

"I will help," Damon said. She should argue with him, convince him to keep himself safe and avoid getting mixed up with them, but she could not bear to say the words. Instead, she held tight to his hand the rest of the way to her home.

Elodie opened the door quickly when she knocked, and while Danae went to fetch tea, Damon stepped inside. Luke and Timothy came running to the door.

"Where did you go?" Luke demanded.

"I thought I could change the magistrate's mind." As the words left her mouth, Lydia realized how feeble they sounded.

"You could have been hurt," Luke said. "Or worse."

"She is returned, safe and sound," Damon said, and they both looked up, as if noticing him for the first time.

"Who is this?" Luke took a step closer.

"This is Damon. My friend." Lydia did not know what else to say. "He helped me."

Luke eyed Damon again for a moment and then nodded. "Luke. Nice to meet you. This is Timothy." Timothy nodded in response. "What happened?" Luke continued.

"Let us sit." Damon gestured toward the table. "We will tell you all."

Lydia was surprised. She had thought Damon would leave her at the door, as he had last time he'd walked her home, but Damon followed Luke into the room with the table and sat down. Lydia saw that Luke had been writing on parchment, no doubt recording the arrest. Danae set out sweet fig cakes and tea with bread while Damon explained what had happened in the market.

"I still do not understand why you went out," Timothy said. "It was dangerous."

"I thought I could influence the magistrate to change his mind."

"What would make you think that?" Luke asked.

Lydia knew that Luke did not mean to sound so harsh with her. He was scared. They all were.

"I—" Her voice faltered. She did not want to tell these men—any of them—what had happened at Felix's home. But they could not understand otherwise. "I have known Felix for some time." She glanced at Damon, who nodded.

"My cousin has taken a liking to Lydia," Damon said. The men took this in, no doubt trying to understand what exactly he meant by this.

"He offered me marriage," Lydia said. "And when I refused, he threatened all of us."

"He did *what?*" Damon's hand slammed against the table. "Did he hurt you?"

"It is all right," Lydia said. "I was not hurt. But I…" She did not know a good way to say this. "I went today to offer myself in return for the safety of Paul and Silas."

All three men started shouting, telling her how foolish she had been, how much danger she had placed herself in, chiding her. She knew they were right. She had been foolish. But instead of shame, she felt only fear.

"It did not work," Lydia said. "He told me it was too late, that he had been humiliated and would not be so again." She took a sip from the tea that Danae had placed in front of her. "That was when he ordered Paul and Silas to be beaten."

"They were beaten?" Timothy asked. "How can this be? They are both Roman citizens."

Damon's eyes widened. It was illegal to beat a Roman citizen, as they all knew. "Felix must not have known," he said. He looked at Lydia, then away. "Though I believe it would not have mattered if he had known. He was trying to prove a point today."

"They are in prison, then?" Timothy's face had paled.

Damon nodded. Lydia hoped he was right.

"How long until they are brought to trial?" Luke asked.

"There is no way to say. It could be days. It could be weeks."

"And they will be kept in jail until the trial?" Timothy asked.

"Yes. No doubt very securely locked up," Damon said. He lifted his cup and took a sip of his tea and then set the cup down again. "You two are not safe here. They know there are more of you."

"Surely they will not come for them now, after all—"

"I have no doubt my cousin will be even more anxious to get the others after he saw how much the crowd loved what he did today," Damon said. "It will be safest if you leave the city altogether. Do you have anywhere to go?"

Lydia tried to breathe normally. She was not ready for them to go. The church was so new. How would it survive if they all left?

"Paul instructed us to go on to Thessalonika," Luke said. "Last night, just before bed."

"That is where he planned for us all to travel next," Timothy added. "He reminded us that if something went wrong, we were all to meet up there."

"He planned to sacrifice himself, then?" Lydia understood now that he hadn't offered himself on a whim this morning. He and Silas had planned it out, knowing the threat was there.

Luke nodded.

"We must move quickly," Damon said. "Gather your things."

"Surely we can wait a few days, to see if they get out soon," Timothy said, but Damon shook his head.

"They know you are here, and they will be coming for you. You are in danger, and Lydia is in danger while you are here."

"I do not think—" Lydia began, but Luke interrupted.

"We will go now," Luke said, and started to push himself up.

"Get your things together," Damon said. And then, "I have an idea for how to get you out of the city safely."

As he told them his plan, Lydia was amazed that this man was putting himself in harm's way to help her friends. She trusted him, and his plan was good. She only hoped that it would work.

CHAPTER TEN

Damon sent Elodie running to his home and told her to ask for his servant Niko once she got there. She was to instruct Niko to bring the cart they used to transport large loads of pelts and to fill it with whatever old skins and fleeces were left in his workshop. Then Niko was to drive the cart straight to Lydia's home and take Luke and Timothy safely away.

Once Elodie had run off, Damon asked the men to dress in old garments. Lydia knew she did not imagine the hesitance in Luke's countenance as he traded his fine linen gown for a rough, worn one of plain wool. Damon then asked Leon to burn a candle against a plate and to collect the soot that gathered. This he mixed with a small amount of oil, and he used the paste that resulted to ink numbers into the men's forearms. If they were caught on the way out, Damon insisted, Niko would say that the men were Damon's slaves and knew nothing about the men who had been spreading the story about Jesus Christ.

When Niko arrived with the cart, he led the two men out, one tied to the other as if they truly were slaves, and loaded them into the cart. He then piled skins and hides on top of them, hiding them underneath, and pulled away from Lydia's house. He promised to get Luke and Timothy safely out of the city.

Damon also sent for two large men from his own household to stand guard at Lydia's home, stationing them inside the door. He introduced them as Galen and Grigory. Lydia argued that she did not need them, but Damon insisted, in case Felix or his men came to arrest her or to punish her in any way for what had happened today.

"I do not know how to thank you for your help," Lydia said just before Damon climbed into the cart that Galen and Grigory had arrived in.

"Please be safe. That is what I care about." Damon pressed his lips together, and he looked like he was about to say more, but the sound of hoofbeats against the stone down the road caused him to turn. "Send one of the men if there is anything you need."

He looked back at her just before he moved the cart forward. She closed the door and leaned back against it. What was she to do now? Was she supposed to just stay here alone, wondering what was happening? Were Paul and Silas safe? Were they alive? Would Timothy and Luke make it out of the city safely? Would they escape without being detained? Beneath all the worry and all the fear, she felt a strong surge of gratitude for Damon, for all he had done to protect her today.

"Come sit down, miss," Danae said, appearing from nowhere to usher her away from the door. The two guards stood at attention just a few steps away. "I will bring you some wine and some food. You need to eat."

Lydia nodded, even though she could not imagine eating with her stomach in such knots. But before she had gotten more than a few feet from the door, she heard voices. The gruff, deeper voice of one of the guards, and a softer one. Feminine. The guards were speaking through the hole in the door, telling her to move along, that no one would be admitted. For a second, Lydia hoped—could it be Anna, come to apologize? But when she pulled open the door, she found Syntyche. The woman from the church service.

"I am sorry," Syntyche said, ducking her head. "I did not know if I should come, but I heard what happened to Paul and Silas, and I thought—"

"No one is to enter the house," Galen said.

"I thought to come to the church and pray," Syntyche finished.

"Of course." Why had she not thought of this before? She did not have to do this alone. "Please, come in. We will pray."

"We have orders not to let anyone inside," Grigory began. But Lydia cut him off.

"Syntyche is a friend." Lydia waved her inside, but Syntyche hesitated.

"There may be others," Syntyche said. "Claes was going around to let us all know what happened, and to ask us to pray. Others, like me, may think to gather here to pray."

"Let us hope so," Lydia said. "May this house become a house of prayer."

She turned back to the guard. "If anyone comes here to pray, they are to be admitted."

"My orders are to admit no one," Galen said.

Lydia knew Damon had meant well, but she would not be a prisoner in her own home. "Any who come to pray are to be admitted."

He shifted his feet. Lydia heard the sword at his waist scrape against the ground. "How am I to know who is here to pray?"

Lydia was losing patience. "They will tell you they are here to pray. Let them in." Was this not her own home? Could she not admit whom she willed?

"The fish," Syntyche said quickly. "Anyone who is one of us will know the sign of the fish."

Lydia realized she was right and felt foolish. "Of course. They will know the fish."

The guard's eyebrow was cocked. "The fish?"

"If anyone says he is here to pray, ask him to tell you the symbol. Anyone who knows that it is the fish is to be admitted."

The guard let out a chuckle. "The symbol of your new religion is a fish?"

Lydia did not bother to explain. "Just let them come inside."

She ushered Syntyche inside and closed the door. Lydia turned to Danae, who was still standing nearby. "Please gather the others. We will pray."

Danae nodded and moved off to find Iduma, Elodie, and Leon. Lydia led Syntyche to the dining room and together they pushed the table against the wall to clear space on the floor, and then they sank down on their knees to pray. But

Syntyche had barely begun to speak to God when Lydia heard the guard outside speaking to someone else. She pushed herself up. A man this time, Lydia thought, as she walked toward the door. The guards moved aside and let Lydia look through the small window in the door, and she saw a man who had been at the church. Dimitri, she believed his name was.

Lydia opened the door. "He is welcome."

The two guards did not argue.

"Claes told me what happened to Paul and Silas," Dimitri said when he came inside. "He said to gather here and pray."

"I am glad you did. Please, come in."

Hypatia arrived, as well as Euodia and Eneas and many others. As the hour grew long, they were joined by Charis, Daphne, and Epaphroditus, still in his uniform of the temple guard. Claes came, telling her of his journey to alert the others. He was loud and warm and somehow made even his desperate errand seem funny, and Lydia was so grateful he was among their number. It did not take long for the room to become so full that Lydia had to ask the guards to help her move the table into the courtyard to make more room. Danae, Elodie, and Leon knelt with bankers, merchants, and beggars. The poor and the wealthy prayed together, beseeching God to intervene for His servants, to create a way for Paul and Silas to be freed, and for Luke and Timothy to escape the city unharmed. They prayed that the message of Jesus would be spread throughout the world and that the city of Philippi would see their witness and know that Christ was the King.

At some point, Lydia noticed that Iduma had not joined the group. Lydia found her in the kitchen, laying out trays of meats and cheeses.

"Iduma. Why are you not praying with us?"

The servant did not meet her eye. "The people have been here for many hours. They will be hungry. You do not want them to go hungry, do you?"

It was a fair point. Iduma had been thoughtful to get started. But that was not the issue.

"I asked you to come with us and pray."

"There are so many praying. I figured you would not miss one when there was work to be done."

"I did miss you. We need every heart praying for a miracle right now."

"As soon as I finish setting these out, I will come."

Lydia watched her for a moment and then decided not to cause a fight here and now.

"Please come soon."

Iduma nodded, and Lydia returned to the dining room and knelt down once again. Lydia became so absorbed in her prayers that at first she did not notice when another knock sounded on the door. So many had come now, and she expected many more would join in as well. The day was waning, and still they prayed.

It was only when she heard raised voices outside the door that she began to wonder if something was wrong. She stood and she saw that Galen and Grigory had their swords drawn, at the ready.

"What is it?" she called.

"There is a group outside who demands to be let inside," Grigory said. "But they do not know the fish."

Lydia walked closer and looked out the small window and saw Felix, surrounded by armed men. "Let me in, in the name of Rome!" he shouted. His men had their swords drawn also.

How had her home become a place where weapons were required? Suddenly, she found herself grateful for Damon's forethought and generosity. If these guards were not here, she would not know what to do.

"Lydia," Felix said. "Open this gate. We know there were two more Christians with the prisoners, and they are under arrest as well." He grasped the iron and shook it.

"No one is to enter this house," Galen said.

"I am not asking you." Felix ignored the guard. "I am telling you. These men are under arrest."

"Open the door, but keep the gate closed," Lydia instructed. When the door was open, she stepped forward. "You must want to punish them very badly to come here yourself," Lydia said. "Isn't this normally something you would send others to do, Praetor?"

"Many know there were others." Felix's face was twisted with anger. "They must be punished as well."

"For what crime?" Lydia asked. "For worshipping the one true God?"

"Do not keep speaking that way." Felix's voice suddenly lost its bluster, and he sounded tired. "I do not want to have to arrest you as well. Please, just hand over the men who were with the prisoners."

"They are not here. They have gone."

"Where have they gone?"

"I cannot say."

"You must. Tell me or I will arrest you as well."

Lydia felt her skin grow hot and her head grow light, but she steeled herself. There was an iron gate between these men and herself, as well as two large guards with swords. Felix could not arrest her unless she opened this gate. And if she did open the gate, she would be exposing all of the people praying inside. There was no telling what Felix might do when he found her home full of followers of the Way.

"I cannot tell you, because I do not know. They have left Philippi. They are long gone by now." Lydia prayed it was true.

"They cannot be. We have had guards stationed at every city gate. No men matching their descriptions have gone out of the city."

"Nonetheless, they have left."

"Do not toy with me, Lydia." Felix stepped forward and wrapped his hands around the scrolled ironwork of the gate. Andreas had spent a small fortune on it. Lydia prayed it was as strong as he had believed it to be. "Let me in."

"I will not. The men you seek are not here."

"Open the gate." He shook his hands, rattling the gate against its iron framework. "I am praetor. You cannot ignore me."

Lydia's mind swirled as one thought after another rushed into her mind. Ignoring him would be against the law. But then, so was worshipping Jesus, and there were dozens of people inside her home doing so right now. She remembered the last time she had been alone with Felix, and she suspected he would not be thwarted this time. Her mouth went dry, and her heartbeat quickened.

"Open the gate, or I will have the men in prison killed. They will be publicly executed at first light. I have the full authority of Rome behind me, Lydia. You cannot thwart Caesar and the might of his Empire."

"For what cause will they be executed?" Lydia asked. "What have these men done to deserve death?"

"For leading a revolution."

"A revolution?" Despite the fear that oppressed her, Lydia could not help but laugh.

"They have infected the city with their lies, and they make people lose all reason. Look at you. You were a successful businesswoman just weeks ago. And now, you have chosen their cult over the laws of Rome. You were not like this before you started associating with these revolutionaries, Lydia."

Lydia heard the poison in his words, and she realized that it was true. She had trusted in her own abilities and believed she could handle as much as any man. Now she realized that she could not handle anything without Christ's strength. It was a wonderful change.

"If you do not open this gate and come with me, you will be sending those men to their deaths."

Lydia did not doubt that Felix meant what he said. He acted under the authority of the emperor. He would do as he said. Lydia could not be responsible for the deaths of Paul and Silas. She must open the gate. But then—if she did, all of the people on their knees in the next room would be in danger. She would be in danger. What was right? Could she go out the gate without exposing everyone else inside? If she sacrificed herself, would it be enough?

She could not say.

Lydia closed her eyes, trying to block out his words and his face. *Lord, show me what to do,* she prayed.

And then, though she could not explain it, a sense of peace filled her. Her fears dissipated. Her mind settled and her body was filled with a strength that she did not herself possess. She remembered a story that Paul had told them about a night when Jesus took His twelve disciples out in a boat with Him. While Jesus slept, a storm raged, and the boat was tossed on the waves. The men with Him were terrified that the boat would be lost and they would all perish. The men woke Jesus, asking Him, "Don't you care if we drown?" Jesus had gotten up, unconcerned, and rebuked the waves and the storm, ordering them to be still, and the storm quieted. As Paul told it, the sea had become as smooth as silk, the sky clear as a summer evening. And then Jesus had asked His disciples, "Why are you so afraid? Do you still have no faith?"

Lydia let the words of her Savior settle into her heart. She saw no way out of the situation they were in. If she opened the gate, she and all the followers of the Way inside her home would be arrested. If she did not, Paul and Silas would be killed, and with them, the great hope of spreading the Gospel throughout the world. There was no good answer. No possible way out. She was afraid, the storm raging around her, the waves and wind threatening to swamp them all.

But, she realized, she was not alone in this boat. Jesus Himself was here with her, with all of them. Felix had the emperor on his side, but Lydia had the One whom even the waves and the wind obeyed. Jesus would calm this storm. She saw no way out, but God did. She simply had to trust.

"I am afraid I cannot open this gate," Lydia said. "I wish you a good day."

She stepped back and closed the door with a firm hand, and then she locked it. She heard Felix yelling on the other side of the door, and she heard the iron gate rattling. Lydia stood inside the door, listening, and it was not long before he stormed off, the armor of his guards rattling as they retreated down the street.

Lydia pressed her forehead against the door. The guards on either side of her stood still and tall, their swords at the ready. Slowly Lydia let out a breath, and then she turned back toward the believers still praying ceaselessly. There was only one thing she could do now. She must pray and trust that God would make a way, even when it seemed impossible.

CHAPTER ELEVEN

L ydia prayed long after the sun went down. One by one, the others left, needing to return to homes and jobs and families, and each was escorted home by one of the armed guards. Lydia was grateful again for Damon's thoughtful provision. When she finally readied herself for bed, the house felt empty and far too quiet. The believers had not been here more than a few weeks, but in that time, she had grown used to not only talking and praying with them but also enjoying their raucous laughter. Now the silence stretched out, even while Danae helped her prepare for sleep.

"Please, miss, try not to worry." Danae pulled back the covering stuffed with down and smoothed the linen sheet beneath. "The God who parted the Red Sea to allow His people to escape slavery is watching over Paul and Silas even now. He will make a way."

Lydia wanted to believe she was right. She nodded and sat down on the bed. Her thin nightclothes brushed against her legs as she slid under the covers. Truthfully, she did not really need help getting ready for bed, but Danae took pride in the task, and Lydia did not mind the company, especially tonight.

"You will see." Danae walked to the window and adjusted the covering, though it was fine.

"Thank you, Danae."

Danae blew out the lamp and trimmed the wick before she went out of the room, closing the door softly behind her.

Lydia had worried she would lie awake worrying, but she was so exhausted by the day's events that she did not have trouble falling quickly asleep.

Lydia dreamed of her childhood home. She dreamed she was playing with her sisters at the small creek that ran behind their home, as she had so many days as a child. She smelled the spicy scent of the meat that their cook had roasted on a spit for hours and the scent of the cypress trees after a storm. She dreamed that she was curled up in her mother's lap, hearing her sing softly, and then that she was in the bed she shared with her two older sisters, each girl squished up against the other. She dreamed that she was safe and warm and happy in her childhood home.

And then in her dream, the home began to shake. Lamps rattled against tables and the floor swayed beneath them. Slowly, Lydia was pulled awake with the frightening realization that the shaking was not just in her dream. Her bed was shaking, and the oil lamp had crashed to the floor. What was happening?

Lydia tried to sit up, but the room shook violently, and she struggled. Everything was the deepest black, with only the smallest glimpse of light from the window. From somewhere in the house, there was a scream and a horrible crash as something heavy smashed to the ground. The very earth was moving beneath them.

"God, help us!" she cried, but the earth did not stop its violent quaking. Lydia had felt many earthquakes, but this was like nothing she knew. It felt as if someone had picked up the house and was shaking it, and it seemed to have no end.

She watched in horror as a fissure opened in the wall that held the window and spread to the floor. Was the house going to fall apart around them? Would she die here, as the house crashed down around her?

And then it stopped, though it took her a moment to realize it. The bed still shook, and the curtains still swayed, but finally, everything settled.

Lydia threw back the covers. The lamp had rolled across the room, and she had no way to light it, so she went to the door without it and flew into the hall and down the stairs.

"Are you all right, miss?" Galen asked. He and Grigory still stood by the door, which was still intact. At least there was that. She was glad to see they had not abandoned their post.

"I am not hurt. How are you?"

"We are not hurt," Grigory said. "There is some damage, though, on the other side of the house. We heard a creak and then a crash."

"I will go look."

"Take this." Galen took a lighted lamp from the stand near the door and handed it to her.

"Thank you." Lydia hated to leave them in the dark, but she was grateful for the light. The servants slept in a series of rooms across the courtyard, and she found Danae running across the open space, coming toward her. Pieces of the roof had been shaken loose and littered the ground, and a portion of the wall had collapsed. Moonlight lit the courtyard, and Lydia was grateful for a clear night.

"Are you all right, miss?" Danae's eyes darted from one place to another.

"I am not hurt. How are you?"

"I am not hurt either. But one of the walls fell in. Maybe more than one."

Lydia followed her and found Iduma and Leon unhurt as well, though frightened. But Elodie's small room had been closed off by the fallen wall.

"Are you hurt?" Lydia called. They heard a soft sobbing in response. "Elodie?"

Leon was already using his hands to remove chunks of rock and plaster.

"Galen! Grigory! Please come help!" Lydia was once again grateful for Damon's thoughtful help of two strong men, though he could not have known how much she would need them this night. They ran toward the fallen wall, and they all worked together, scraping and heaving heavy chunks of brick, until they had cleared an opening. Lydia called to Elodie, and they heard soft moans, but the girl did not use words to respond.

"Elodie!" Lydia could not see into the dark space.

Grigory had taken the lamp that Lydia had set nearby and was already leaning into the small cleared space.

"She is awake," he called. "But her arm is pinned under a heavy rock. We must keep working."

As the guards and Leon worked to clear the opening, Lydia turned to Danae and Iduma. Danae had tears running down her cheeks, and Iduma was still, her eyes cast to the ground.

"Let us rest," Lydia said, and indicated that they should take a seat on the small bench at the edge of the yard. Danae nodded and walked to the bench, but Iduma stayed still.

"Are you able to walk?" Lydia had heard that people could be so frightened they were frozen in place, though she had never seen it.

Iduma nodded, slowly. "I can walk."

Lydia still moved closer to her and slipped her arm around her, guiding her to the bench.

"I was thinking about my niece and her family," Iduma said. "The home where they serve is not as well built as this."

Lydia wished she could offer words to put her at ease. She feared for Anna and little Eli as well, and also so many others. Was Damon safe? What had happened to Paul and Silas, trapped in a cell in the jail? "I am sure it must have shaken harder here than other places." She hoped the words were true, though she did not see how they could be. Lydia had never felt an earthquake as strong or as long-lasting as what had happened tonight. Still, the words seemed to bring Iduma comfort. Lydia helped her sit down on the bench, and she thanked her quietly.

Lydia turned to the pile of rubble and used all her strength to pull the fallen stones away. She prayed as **she work**ed, and she did not know how long it took, but finally there was a cry, and Galen pulled Elodie from the rubble. Her eyes were closed, and Lydia could not rouse her, but she was breathing. She looked so small in Galen's hands, and her left arm was crushed and flopped at her side.

"Bring her upstairs," Lydia said, and Galen carried her carefully inside and up the stairs of the home. If only Luke were still here. She had need of a doctor, and quickly. Lydia carried a lamp and led them to the top floor, where Paul and Silas and Luke and Timothy had slept—was it only the night before? Lydia could not believe how much had happened in the past day. She stepped into the room with the beds and gasped when she saw moonlight spilling into the room. A sliver of sky was visible through a hole in what had once been the roof, and a large section of the wall that faced the street had collapsed on the bed where Timothy had slept.

Thank You, Lord, for taking them away from here, she whispered before she turned and instructed that Elodie be brought to Lydia's own room. Perhaps God truly had protected them by forcing them away from her home. Still, she could not help but fear for all of them.

Once Elodie was resting in the bed, Lydia was able to see how badly injured she truly was. Her skin had grown pale and had a waxy sheen, and though she breathed, she could not be awakened. Her left arm had been broken in many places and was bent at a sickening angle. Danae had retrieved her kit of herbs and poultices, and she now placed a compress on Elodie's forehead. It smelled like camphor and eucalyptus, and Danae said it would cause her blood to fill out the limp arm and return it to its natural state. Lydia was not sure.

"We must fetch the doctor," Lydia said. She turned to the group crowded behind her.

"I will go," Leon said.

Lydia nodded and took him down to the room where the household accounts were kept to get ten denarii out of the locked box. "In case he needs to be convinced to hurry," she said.

Leon gaped at the amount but then told her he would return with the doctor as quickly as possible. After Leon slipped out the gate, Galen and Grigory returned to their post by the door, though Lydia assured them that it was not necessary, that no one would be coming to hurt them now. They did not disagree openly but moved toward the door and stood at attention once more.

Lydia went back up to her room, where Danae was tending to Elodie, but she quickly felt useless and unable to help. She considered going out herself, to check in on Anna, Sara, Andreas's mother, and Damon, but she knew that it would not be safe to do so until first light. So instead, she knelt down and prayed. She prayed that help would come quickly and that Anna was safe. She prayed that Paul and Silas had survived the earthquake and that the chaos that was no doubt reigning throughout Philippi would mean they would not be executed at dawn after all. She prayed that God would use the strange timing of this terrible earthquake to spare them, and she prayed that Timothy and Luke were safe, wherever they had slept this night.

A furious knocking on the door sounded. She opened her eyes and saw that it was light. Leon had returned, then. The doctor must have been tempted by the pieces of silver. Lydia pushed herself up and ran down the steps, but she did not find Leon and the doctor coming inside the house. Instead, she found Galen and Grigory shouting out the small hole in the door, "No one is allowed to enter."

"Who is it?" Lydia's heartbeat sped up. Had Felix sent some new round of guards, even in the midst of this terrible night?

"There are two men outside," Grigory said, turning toward her. "They say they are friends of yours. Do not worry. We will send them away."

"Who is it?" Lydia felt her throat close up. Had Timothy and Luke not been able to exit the city, as she had thought? Had they been sent back here? They would not be safe here. She moved closer to the door, trying to see out the window. The first glimmers of dawn had lightened the sky.

"Lydia!" More fists pounded on the door.

Lydia froze. No. It could not be. She recognized the voice. But it was impossible. Paul.

"Lydia, please let us in." That sounded like Silas.

"Let me see." Lydia pushed her way to the window. She gasped when she saw in the early morning light that it was true—Paul and Silas were outside her door!

"Open the door quickly!" She did not wait for Grigory to fumble with the lock, she undid it herself. She pulled the gate open and then the door, and she cried out as they rushed into the house. Paul quickly closed both the door and the gate behind them. Galen had his sword in his hand, but Lydia gestured for him to put it away.

"Is it true? Are my eyes playing tricks?" Lydia asked. Had the miracle they had prayed for really come to pass? "Were you not in prison?'

"We are here, in the flesh." Paul laughed, and Silas nodded. "You will not believe how God has been moving this night."

"Come in." Lydia ushered them inside the house. "No, wait." They were not safe here. This was a miracle, but they must not stay. "We must get you out of Philippi. Now that it is almost light, the city gates will soon open. You must go, now, before the authorities find you here."

"It is all right," Paul said. "We are safe."

"If Felix finds you here—"

"Just listen." Paul's voice carried an authority that made her stop. He did not sound fearful. She had already trusted him with so much. She knew she must trust him now as well.

Lydia nodded. "Let us sit. Tell me all." She gestured for them to follow her and then called to Iduma to bring them some wine and bread and to Danae to bring herbs to treat their wounds. Paul and Silas sat on the cushions gratefully. She had not noticed at first, in the darkness of the street, but now she saw that Paul's face was bruised and his nose broken. Silas walked with a limp. But their wounds had been treated, and both wore new clothes. How could this be?

"How are you here?" Lydia could not convince herself that this was real, that they were truly in her home. "What happened?"

"You saw that we were arrested," Paul said.

Iduma set a tray of bread and cheese in front of them, but though they must have been starving, neither man moved to take any.

"You were flogged and beaten first," Lydia said. "And then thrown into prison."

"We were placed in the inner cell," Silas said. "Chained, and our feet put into stocks."

"And yet we spent the day praying and singing songs of praise to God," Paul said.

Perhaps Lydia should not have been surprised, but she still found herself impressed by the news. "How could you praise God, even after you had been treated so terribly?"

"Our reverence for God does not depend on our circumstances," Paul said. "I have learned that we can survive any situation as long as we remember that God is in control. Even when I want to despair and to give up, I do not, because Christ gives me His strength. That is the secret to being content in any situation— the knowledge that through Christ, I can do anything."

Lydia nodded, taking in the words. She recognized their truth, but she still had so many questions. It was so like Paul to issue forth a message while she was desperate to know what had happened.

"But how did you get out?" Lydia asked. "How were you freed if you were in chains?"

"We continued praying and praising God into the night," Paul said. "The jailer did not like it. He smacked his sword against the walls, ordering us to be quiet, but we continued to praise God anyway."

"Even when he told us that there was an order that we would be executed at first light, we continued to pray," Silas said.

"That seemed to anger him further," Paul said.

"We later learned why that decision had been made," Silas said. "We were told that you had refused to give up Timothy and Luke, and we were so glad."

"I could not give them up. They were already gone," Lydia said. There was so much to tell them. "They had already been ushered out of the city. But many of the church members were here praying. I would not let Felix's guards in because I would not let them be hurt. I did not know what the right thing to do was, but I could not—"

Paul held up his hand. "You made the right decision. We are grateful that you and the others were safe."

"We did not know any of this at the time, of course," Silas said. "All we knew was that we must hold fast to the truth of Jesus Christ and keep praising God."

"And then, about midnight, there was a terrible earthquake," Paul said.

"It was very strong. Parts of the house have collapsed," Lydia said. "And Elodie is upstairs, waiting for the doctor. She was trapped under the rubble for quite a while. She is not conscious. I fear…"

She could not put the thought into words.

"I am sorry to hear that. Let us pray for Elodie."

And then, Paul bowed his head and asked God for mercies for Elodie. He asked for swift healing and that she would wake soon. And then he looked up and continued on with his strange tale.

"It must have been a very large earthquake." Paul poured some of the wine into a cup in front of him. "Your house is in better shape than many. There is damage all over the city. Some buildings are completely destroyed."

"I feared that," Lydia said. There would be much suffering in the coming days and weeks.

"It is terrible," Paul said. "But one of the buildings that was destroyed was the jail. As the building shook, walls were cracked and tumbled like blocks. The roof collapsed, and the stocks pulled away from the wall. Our chains fell off, and the prison doors flew open."

Lydia could not believe it. "And yet you were safe?"

"We were not hurt. We were not even touched. Once the shaking stopped, we stood, and there was nothing keeping us inside."

"So you escaped?"

"Yes," Silas said at the same time that Paul said, "No."

Lydia looked from one to the other, waiting for an explanation.

"We started to leave," Paul said. "We realized that God had provided the miracle we had been praying for. But then the jailer came and found that we were loosed."

"When he saw that we were free, he drew his sword," Silas said.

Lydia nodded. A guard who let a prisoner escape would be executed, by order of the law. It would not matter that a strong earthquake had caused their release. This guard had no doubt decided to spare his family the embarrassment of a public execution.

"But Paul shouted for him to stop," Silas continued. "I tried to silence him, but he would not be quiet."

"You gave away your chance to escape?" Now Lydia was confused. Had they not just been given the answer to prayer they had been asking God to send? "Why would you not simply keep running?"

"I could not believe that God would send our freedom at the expense of this man's life," Paul said. "I knew, without a doubt, that God had answered our prayer, and yet I could not imagine that He intended this guard to die as a result of our freedom. I do not believe that God would see this man's life as less valuable than our own."

Were their lives not more important? Weren't they the key to spreading the Good News? Lydia considered it. She did not know whether she would have had the strength and fortitude to make the same choice.

"Paul called out, 'Do not harm yourself, we are all here!'" Silas said. "And the jailer called for lights, and several men rushed in with torches, and they found us all there, waiting."

"And then the jailer fell down on his knees, trembling, and asked what he must do to be saved." Paul took a sip of the wine.

Lydia felt her mouth fall open.

"Paul told him to believe in the Lord Jesus," Silas said. "And he did, then and there."

"Praise God." Lydia could not believe it. The events of this night got more and more miraculous.

"Our new brother in Christ, Clement, helped us walk out of the prison," Paul said. "He took us to his home, where he cleaned our wounds and fed us, and he gave us new clothes. And we told them about Jesus Christ, him and his whole family, and they were all baptized. What started as a night of fear and terror became a morning of rejoicing and praising God."

"That is wonderful." Lydia still could scarcely believe it. She closed her eyes, thanking God for His mighty provision. But she still had so many questions. "But why are you not afraid? Felix will be even more angry now. You should be on your way out of the city before they come for you."

"They will not come for us," Paul said. "This is the point in the story where another miracle occurs."

The earthquake that had freed them and the baptism of the jailer's entire family were not miracle enough? Lydia did not know what could possibly come next.

"Officers were sent by the magistrates to Clement's house," Paul said.

"We believed they were there to fetch us back to prison," Silas said. "Or to execute us. We came forward with our arms up."

"But they were not there to kill us," Paul said. He was swirling the wine in his cup, a smile on his face. "They told us that the magistrates had decided that we were free to go in peace."

"They..." Lydia could find no words. "They did what?"

"We could hardly believe it either," Paul said. "But we asked what had happened, and we learned that the praetor went to the temple of Poseidon after the earthquake to offer sacrifices."

Poseidon was said to be the god of the earthquakes, as well as the sea. She was not surprised to hear that Felix had brought him an offering after the terrible shaking of the night.

"While he was praying to the false god, he was approached by a guard," Paul said, a smile on his face. "One we know well."

Lydia thought for a moment. "Epaphroditus?" He worked as a guard in the temple of Poseidon. "He was here praying for you two just yesterday."

"God must have answered his prayers, because he was there to help us when we needed it," Paul said.

"Epaphroditus told Felix that *we* were responsible for the earthquake," Silas said. "He told him that there would be further earthquakes and that they would be much larger, unless we were freed. And so, we were released."

"Praise God," Lydia said. "It is truly a miracle."

"It is, except that then this one would not keep his mouth shut." Silas jerked his thumb toward Paul.

"What did you do?" Lydia hoped he had not said something that had put them all at risk again.

"I reminded the officers that they had beaten us publicly and thrown us in prison without a trial and that we were Roman citizens," Paul said. "And I demanded that the magistrates themselves escort us so that all would know of our innocence."

"You did what?" Lydia was astonished. Why would he have said such a thing instead of accepting God's providence?

"I was thinking of you, Lydia," Paul said. "And of the other believers here in Philippi. If we had slunk off into the night, taking our freedom without making it clear that we were innocent, you and all the church would have been seen as suspect. This way, all will know that we are innocent and we were beaten and imprisoned unfairly. I wanted all in the city to know that they cannot treat servants of Jesus Christ in this way."

Lydia considered this. Could it be true? "And what did they do?" she asked.

"They were afraid," Paul said. "The magistrates had not known that we were Roman citizens when they had us beaten. They came themselves to escort us from the guard's home to here, making it clear that we are innocent."

Lydia shook her head. The story got more and more incredible.

"So that is it? You are free to continue preaching with the blessing of the magistrates?"

"Oh, no." Paul laughed. "No, they asked the two of us to leave the city. We are no longer welcome here. But you are safe. All will know that we were beaten unfairly and wrongly imprisoned, and they will not believe that you and the other believers here are at fault."

Lydia was not so sure. She asked them to repeat parts of the story, trying to imagine this all playing out while she and the others here were tending to Elodie.

Just then, there was another knock at the door, and Leon entered, the doctor following along behind.

"I am sorry it took so long," the doctor said, bowing before Lydia. If he recognized Paul and Silas, he did not show it. "There are many injured in the city this morning. Your man Leon was faithful and worked hard to track me down."

"I am grateful," Lydia said. "She is upstairs."

Danae showed the doctor upstairs to the room where Elodie slept. Lydia would join him soon, but for now, she focused on Paul and Silas. "Did they tell you when you must go?"

Paul looked at Silas, who shrugged. "I am pretty sure they meant immediately," Silas said.

"But we could not leave the city without coming to see you," Paul said.

"Thank you." Lydia sat back. "I am grateful."

But inside, her mind was reeling. What would they do now? The church was just starting to grow. How would they go on without their leaders?

"Will you come back and teach?" Lydia asked.

"No." Paul shook his head. "No, I am not sure we will be allowed back in this city. That is why we needed to see you, Lydia. We needed to make sure you will agree to lead the church going forward."

"I will *lead* it?" Lydia stared at him. "I cannot teach about Jesus Christ."

"Well, yes, you and others." Paul waved his hand dismissively. "Perhaps you will not teach. But the church will meet at your home. You will bear the burden of keeping it going, and you will be responsible for overseeing its growth. Before we leave, I needed to make sure you are committed."

Lydia took in the words he was saying to her. She had fought so hard to be allowed to take over the dye works instead of handing it over to a male relative. Women did not do such things. And now, these men were placing her in charge of this fledgling congregation. They were not asking her—they were informing her that the continuance of the church at Philippi rested on her.

Jesus truly had turned everything on its head.

"I am willing," Lydia said.

"Good then." Paul rose from his cushion. "We must go. I will write when we are safely in Thessalonika."

"Wait." Lydia also rose and headed, for the second time this morning, to the small room where she kept the locked cabinet. She unlocked it and counted out thirty denarii. Then she locked the safe again, tucking away the key, and brought the coins to Paul.

"Take this," she said.

Paul hesitated a moment, his eyes downcast, and then he looked up at her. "Thank you, in the name of our Lord Jesus Christ."

"Be safe, and go with God."

As Paul and Silas walked out the door, she wondered if she would ever see them again.

CHAPTER TWELVE

T he doctor tried to set Elodie's arm, but it was crushed in too many places.

"I do not know if she will be able to use it again," he told Lydia quietly. "For now, all I can do is give her medicine to dull the pain. Let her lie still, and fetch me again if she develops a fever or the skin begins to change color."

Lydia promised she would, and then, at Danae's urging, she sat down to a meal. Lydia had not realized how hungry she was, and she ate heartily of the lentils and cheese and bread. Then Danae encouraged her to lie down and rest, but though she was tired, deep down in her bones Lydia knew she would not be able to rest.

Her first thought was for the church. The members who had prayed so fervently for Paul and Silas's release the day before needed to know of God's miraculous provision. She sent Danae out with a message to deliver to Claes—all who could should gather at Lydia's home at sundown to hear about the miraculous answer to their prayers. She drank a cup of strong tea, and then she took her cloak and ventured out into the streets herself.

Paul had told her there was great damage to the city, but it was still shocking to see houses flattened and some with roofs missing. The smell of smoke hung in the air, and she saw several dark plumes rise in the cool air. Many homes on Lydia's street had cracks in the plaster or gaps where stones had been, but they were still well off compared to some of the devastation that had visited other parts of the city. Many smaller homes, built of less sturdy materials, had collapsed completely. *Lord, have mercy*, she prayed.

Lydia made her way first to Anna's home. It had only been two days since Anna had screamed at Lydia, but Lydia hoped that the events of the past few days and especially the frightening night had softened Anna's resolve. Still, she felt her heartbeat quicken before she turned onto the street where Anna lived.

The street appeared to have largely been spared. The homes here were set on deposits of granite, and they stood tall and proud and were largely safe from the devastation of the poorer areas. Lydia knocked, and Emira came to the door, but she kept the outer gate closed.

"Good afternoon, miss." Emira bobbed her head.

"Hello, Emira. Is Anna available?"

"I am afraid she cannot be disturbed just now," Emira said.

From somewhere deep inside the house, Lydia heard Eli shrieking. "Is she safe?"

"Yes, miss. It is just that she cannot see you now."

Lydia's heart sank. "In that case, can you tell me if she is well? Was anyone hurt in the quake?"

"No, miss. We are grateful. This house was largely spared and none were hurt."

Lydia wanted to push her way inside, to see with her own eyes that Anna and little Eli were safe, but she knew she could not.

"I am glad to hear it."

Well, if her daughter would not speak to her, Lydia would turn to the second reason for her visit. "I am in need of a builder to repair the damage to my house. I would like to hire Daniel's family to do the work."

"I will let the master know," Emira said, nodding.

"May I speak to him about it?"

Emira pressed her lips together, and she seemed almost to be in pain as she shook her head. "He is very busy today. There are many who require his services."

Lydia had no doubt that was true. However, not all of them were his wife's mother.

"In that case, will you please tell him I would like to hire him as quickly as possible? I will pay him well." That might motivate him, if the other reasons did not.

"I will let him know." Emira nodded again.

"Thank you." Lydia hesitated, and before she turned to go, she said, "Please give Anna my love."

"I will, miss." Emira closed the door, and Lydia turned away, her heart heavy. Anna was upset, Lydia knew. But she could not stay angry forever—at least, Lydia hoped she could not.

Lydia received the same reaction at the home of Sara and also of Andreas's mother. None of her former community would see her. Lydia mourned inside, and she tried to understand their feelings, but she could not. Was she not still the same person? Was she not still their family? But apparently they did not see it so.

Many were out in the streets, some cleaning up fallen stone, some wandering, seemingly dazed. Many were begging on the streets, much more than normal, and Lydia dropped coins in front of each. She also saw the sobering sight of bodies wrapped in sheets.

Lydia then went to see Damon. She had sent the guards home that morning, after Paul and Silas left. They were no longer needed once Paul and Silas had gone free. But Lydia hoped to make sure he was well and also to find out what had happened to Timothy and Luke.

"He is not here," the girl at the door of Damon's house said. "He is helping to clear the rubble from a house nearby."

The girl gave Lydia directions to the site where she would find Damon, and she easily found him among a group of men helping to clear stones from the front of a home. The roof and most of the ceiling over the second floor of the home had collapsed. Lydia prayed there had been no one inside those rooms when the earthquake struck.

"Lydia." Damon straightened up and smiled. "It is good to see you. I am glad to see you are well." Around him, men were shouting, hefting large stones, and moving in all directions, but Damon stood still, and she felt as if he was looking into her very inward parts.

"You as well." Tears sprang to her eyes, and she fought them back. "I also wanted to thank you."

Damon brushed his hands on his robe and stepped away from the rubble. "I hear it was quite an exciting day you had." He moved closer to her. The way he was looking at her made her feel as though there was no one else in the world.

"I am very grateful for the guards you sent to help us. I do not know how we would have made it through the day without Grigory and Galen standing guard."

"I am glad to hear it." He stopped when he was a short distance from her. "Though Grigory tells me you fought off our new praetor on your own."

Lydia laughed. "I would not say that. The presence of an iron gate and two strong men were important factors."

"I enjoyed imagining you standing up to him." He gave her a look that she couldn't read and then gestured down the street. "Come. Let us walk. There is something you need to see."

Lydia nodded, wondering what it could be, but she walked alongside him toward the bath house. She had always enjoyed his company and even felt a strange excitement around him recently, but now she felt something different. She felt...safe.

"What of Luke and Timothy?" Lydia asked.

"Luke and Timothy made it out of the city just fine," Damon said. "My man was able to take the cart out with no one taking a second glance."

"I am so glad." Lydia had not realized how worried she had been until she heard the news, and felt a knot in her belly loosen.

"He drove them as far as Amphipolis. There, they were delivered to a friend of mine, with the message that she was to give them shelter and keep them safe."

"Please thank your friend for me. I am most grateful."

Damon nodded. "She can be trusted to keep quiet."

Lydia wondered how he knew this friend and what sort of relationship he had with her.

"She does not need to keep them in hiding. They are not in danger any longer."

His eyebrows raised, and she told him the story as they walked. She explained how the believers had gathered to pray and how God had sent the miraculous earthquake to free Paul and Silas and the wonderful conversion and baptism of the jailer. She told him about the message from the temple guard and that Paul and Silas had been released, the magistrates quaking in fear that they had beaten and imprisoned Roman citizens.

The Via Egnatia was crowded, but she saw that the bath still stood. And though some of the facade of the library had fallen, the temple to Apollo, which stood next to it, was almost totally destroyed, its columns fallen like sticks, its roof collapsed onto the very ground. Lydia could not help but see the hand of God in that.

Lydia told Damon how the officials had ordered Paul and Silas to leave and never return to Philippi.

"That is quite a story," Damon said once she had finished.

"It is amazing, is it not?" Lydia still could hardly fathom it.

Damon didn't answer for a few minutes, but he was turning it over in his mind, she could see. They approached the East Gate, and the crowds thinned, but there were more buildings with damage from the quake.

"Isn't it possible," Damon began, "that the quake was a natural occurrence, not a miracle brought about by your god to free those men?"

Lydia had not been expecting the question. "Are you saying that it could be a coincidence?" Surely she could not have heard him right. "How could it be?"

"Earthquakes are not uncommon in this region," Damon said, his voice calm.

"Yes, but this was the largest I have ever felt. Have you ever heard of one strong enough to break the walls of the jail and set prisoners free?"

"I have heard of earthquakes large enough to send entire cities falling into the sea," Damon said.

"That cannot be true," Lydia said.

Damon shrugged. "And yet you believed that this huge quake, with all its devastation, was sent just to free two men from prison. I do not see how this is any less strange."

The words stung, though she tried not to let them.

"You have told me that your god created all and loves all," Damon said. "Isn't that right?"

"Adonai is love." Lydia nodded. "And Jesus loved us all enough to redeem the world from sin at the cost of His own life." The very words sounded beautiful as she said them.

"Right." Damon nodded.

"You are used to capricious gods," Lydia said. "False idols who must be mollified with sacrifices and bribed with good behavior. Adonai is not like that."

"Is he not?" Damon shook his head. "Don't the Jewish people offer sacrifices to Adonai to atone for sins? And did you not just tell me that Jesus sacrificed himself to appease your god's hatred for sin?"

She hated how much his words hurt. He misunderstood her words and her faith.

"It is not like that," Lydia said. Words crowded her mind, arguments for why he was wrong, but she was overwhelmed by the feeling of loss. She had known Damon did not believe in Jesus, and yet she had hoped… After the ways he had helped and all that had happened…could he really not see?

"Adonai is not like the other gods," she said again.

"You do not need to convince me of this. I do not place much trust in the gods worshipped by many around us," Damon said. "They seem to me petty and fickle. But I do pay attention to the great teachers. I take much from the writings of Plato and Aristotle. They have a very logical way of understanding the world. And I am inclined to believe that there is much that happens in our world that is not orchestrated by any deity. That, sometimes, things just…happen."

Lydia's own father had enjoyed the writings of these thinkers. She was familiar with their arguments.

"I do not claim to understand the mind of Adonai," Lydia said. "And I do not know if things 'just happen' or if He causes them. But I do believe that we prayed for a miracle that would set Paul and Silas free, and a few hours later, they were freed. It is hard not to see the hand of God in that." How could he not see this?

Damon stretched his hand out and touched her arm. She did not shake him away, though she knew she should. They had passed the city gates and followed the Via Egnatia, stepping around the sections where the stones had buckled.

"I am not saying it is not true," he said slowly. "Maybe your god did orchestrate this whole earthquake to free Paul and Silas. But if He did, what of the suffering caused this night? What of the homes destroyed and the families who mourn those crushed by the rubble? Does He not care about them too?" Damon continued. "I guess what I am saying is, what kind of god would cause so much suffering in order to free His servants? Does that not show that He loves some more than others? That His love is not any less fickle than the favor of the gods you call false?"

Lydia did not know what to say. He did not understand. And yet... She thought back to Elodie, lying still in her own bed. All around Lydia was suffering. She had seen it herself on her walk through town. She trusted that Adonai was in control. But was there an element of what Damon was saying that held some truth?

"But they are spreading His Gospel," Lydia said.

"So your god does care more about the people who believe in him than everyone else?"

"No." He was twisting her words around, confusing things. "He loves all. But He did use the quake for the spreading of His Gospel. He does protect His people."

"And what of the rest of us?"

More than anything, Lydia felt a sense of sorrow. She had hoped...but she'd been silly, of course. Damon was a kind man, a good man. He had helped her, and she'd allowed herself to believe that he felt something more than friendship for her. She had allowed herself to imagine that he might feel for her what she was beginning to recognize as feelings for him. But even if he did—even if there was more between them than she'd begun to hope—it could not go anywhere, she realized. There could be no future with a man who didn't believe in Jesus. She had never let herself think it before, but she realized now that it was true. No matter how safe she felt with Damon, no matter that she felt alive with him, that she felt parts of herself she had never felt before when she was with him—none of it mattered. She knew the healing power of Jesus, and she would never stop talking about it. She could not see living with a man who belittled her faith.

She was responsible for the church in Philippi, Paul had told her just before he left. She was responsible to see it grow. She could not be with a man who did not share her goal.

"You think our God is silly, and yet you helped Timothy and Luke escape," she said. Lydia knew she sounded like a petulant child, but she could not keep the hurt from her voice. "They are ministers of the Gospel, and you helped them escape to spread what you see as lies."

"I may not believe what they preach," Damon said. "But I would do anything to help you. I saved them because of you." At this he moved his hand from her arm and took her own hand in his. Lydia did not resist, but she did not feel the same giddy excitement she might have just a little while ago. She felt...hollowed out. Damon did care about her—she had not imagined that. But she realized now that tender feelings were not enough. How could they have a future together when they did not share the most essential beliefs? Was it possible? Lydia did not see how.

Lydia had not loved Andreas when they were married. She'd had no expectation of tender feelings. Her father had arranged the match with a suitable man from a good family, and that was enough. As a condition of her betrothal, she'd had to abandon worship of the false gods and agree to worship only Adonai, and at the time she had not understood why this was necessary. Now all these years later, she recognized the wisdom in it. A house divided against itself, as Jesus had said, could not stand.

"Perhaps if you came to our church and heard the message, you might feel differently," Lydia tried.

Damon shook his head. "I would follow you just about any-where, Lydia, but not there."

"Perhaps you will be persuaded." She tried to the keep the warble out of her voice.

"I very much doubt it." He rubbed his thumb against the back of her hand as they walked. "I have never seen any need to believe in gods and powers we cannot see. If your god wants to change my mind, he will need to make me believe other-wise. He will need to make me believe in the miracles you so readily see."

"We prayed for a miracle to free Paul and Silas, and look what happened. Would you not call that a miracle?"

"I would call that very lucky timing." He shook his head. "Surely your god, if He is truly great, could have created a miracle that did not cause destruction to so many."

Lydia had no answer. After a few beats, she said, "I cannot explain it, but I know, with all my being, that Jesus is the Son of God."

"Then I suppose we are at an impasse," Damon said.

They walked in silence for a moment, Lydia turning the words over and over in her mind, and then Damon turned onto the road that led to the dye works. "I want to warn you that it is not good," Damon said, and it took her a moment to realize what he was talking about.

Goodness. The dye works. In all the activity of the past day, she had barely thought about the dye works. But with a sickening sense of dread, she realized why Damon was bringing her this way. Hyperion's shop, the first along this road, had lost its whole front wall. Hektor's was not much better.

"You came out this way earlier today?" Lydia did not understand.

"I came this morning. I wanted to see... Well, I had hoped to bring you good news."

But he could not. He did not say it, but she understood. While parts of the city were built on strong rock, this area was less desirable for building, which was why the smelly dye works had been relegated here. At Joran's workshop, the roof had fallen in completely.

Lydia felt weariness overcome her. She had barely slept, but she had not realized how tired she was until this moment, when she felt her strength abandon her. Suddenly the warmth of Damon's hand in hers felt like a lifeline.

Finally they approached Lydia's workshop. It had fared better than the others, which she saw immediately. Thank goodness for Andreas and his insistence on using heavy sandstone. But portions of the side wall had collapsed, and stones had spilled out onto the ground around it. The roof above it was tipped at an awkward angle, like it was not sure whether to stay in place or fall.

"Thank goodness this happened in the night," Lydia said. "What is it like inside?"

"I did not enter the building," Damon said.

Lydia pulled the key out of her pocket and felt silly as she inserted it into the slot in the door. Anyone who wanted could enter the building through the open side wall. But when she stepped into the front room, there was not much damage. The locked box was still there, though dented by a few bricks that had fallen, and a chair had been knocked over. But when she entered the storage room, she gasped. Most of the earthenware jugs that had kept powdered pigments had fallen to the ground and smashed, spreading plumes of color all over the floor.

"I am sorry," Damon said. He knew as well as she did that this represented many years of work and hundreds if not thousands of denarii.

Lydia took a deep breath to steady herself, and then she walked farther, into the loom room. She could not stop the cry that erupted when she saw the looms crushed under fallen stones. Damon took her hand again, and it steadied her. She moved on to the spinning room. The wheels had been tossed every which way, and some also had been flattened like the looms. But Lydia did not have time to process this, because she had seen a purple stain spreading across the floor, no doubt from the dye room beyond. Lydia's head grew light as she realized what this meant. The vat of dye was gone—there could be no other explanation. That also was thousands of denarii lost.

But also—

"Giorgio?"

She ran into the back portion of the building, looking for the dye master. The east wall had fallen in completely, and the roof had fallen with it. Where the vat had been was now only a pile of rubble. "Giorgio!"

"Was he here?" Damon scanned the wreckage. His voice had taken on a sense of urgency. He had not seen Giorgio earlier, then.

"He was staying here at night, monitoring the batch of dye." How had she not thought of Giorgio until now? She had been so caught up in the safety of her family and household that she had not thought to check on her most faithful worker. She felt an overwhelming sense of guilt, but it was quickly tinged with fear. The dye had spilled, so the vat must be buried under the rubble somewhere. Was Giorgio there too?

Damon was already pulling heavy chunks of brick off of the pile and tossing them to the side. Lydia joined him and used all of her strength to heft stones off the pile and onto the ground.

"Perhaps he went home for the night," Damon said. "Perhaps he is safe."

"No." Lydia knew the answer with a sick sense of certainty. "He would not have left his post."

"Then we will find him." Damon's voice was calm, but there was a strength to it that Lydia wanted to wrap herself in. He hoisted large stones, and Lydia found strength unknown and pulled off as many stones as she could.

"The vat is here," Damon said as he uncovered a sliver of dusty iron beneath the rocks.

That was when Lydia felt sure that Giorgio was buried under the rocks somewhere. She began attacking the rocks with a fierce energy. They worked together, moving stones until they had uncovered most of the vat, and they kept digging. The sun moved toward the horizon, the daylight slipping away, and still they dug.

It was Damon who found him. Crushed beneath the fallen stones, faithful at his post. When she saw, Lydia looked away and collapsed on the rocks beneath her. Damon pulled Giorgio's body free and laid him on the ground, and then he came toward Lydia and wrapped his arms around her and held her as she cried.

CHAPTER THIRTEEN

That Lord's Day there were more than a hundred gathered in Lydia's home to worship Jesus. Among the new faces was Clement, the jailer who had been converted by Paul and Silas the night of the quake. His entire family was there, praising God and His only Son. Other new visitors were there because they had seen a change in their loved ones and were curious to meet the God who had caused it. Some had been drawn to the church by the witness of Paul and Silas in the face of mistreatment. Some were searching for answers and hope in the face of the devastation their city had faced in the past few days.

Hundreds were dead, including two that Lydia knew of in their own fledgling congregation. Daphne, the woman who begged by the city gates, was among them. Lydia found herself remembering Damon's question about why God would cause the quake to save the lives of two of His servants while taking the lives of two others. She could not understand it. Thousands of buildings were damaged or destroyed. There was so much weeping and wailing, so much suffering.

In the days that followed the quake, the city had been rocked by smaller quakes, and each one sent another wave of panic through all of them. Thankfully, none of the aftershocks had been as strong as the first quake, but they all lived in fear that another would strike.

Lydia had buried Giorgio in the cemetery in the city, next to Andreas and the babies that had not lived. She had not asked Andreas's family for permission, and she did not care that they were upset. They could not hurt her any more than they had.

Elodie's crushed arm had begun to fester, the skin turning hot and red and puffy and eventually black in spots. The doctor had taken it the day before, and the girl still rested in Lydia's own bedroom, asleep and hopefully oblivious to the pain.

Also on the day before, Lydia had received a letter from Paul, and she read it to the congregation this morning. It was some comfort to hear that he and Silas had made it to Thessalonika. He told them that they had met up with Timothy but that Luke had been called home. His wife was sick, and Paul asked them all to pray. He inquired about the church members and hoped that they were safe after the quakes, and he thanked the church for their prayers for him and for the spread of the Gospel. He also reminded them their present troubles were achieving in them an eternal glory, and he ended with the exhortation that Christ was coming back soon and to not lose hope.

Lydia tried to not lose hope, but in the midst of so much suffering, it was difficult. She had not heard from Anna, though she had sent many messages and brought loaves of fresh bread. When Lydia had been with child, bread was all she could stomach, and she hoped it would help Anna now. But though Emira accepted the bread, Lydia was not allowed to see Anna.

Damon had helped her secure workers to rebuild her home and workshop, since Daniel would not do the work, and he had made himself available for any help she needed. Damon himself was very busy, and Lydia learned from her servant girl that Damon's family owned many of the buildings in the city, and he was seeing to their repairs. This helped her understand how he afforded personal guards and also made her even more grateful he had sent some of the workers at his disposal to help her. He had showed once again that he cared for her, but she grieved to know that they could not have a future together, not unless he believed in Jesus Christ.

Lydia and her household dragged their way through the days. Danae cared tenderly for Elodie, while Lydia spent much of her time overseeing the workers who had been hired to clean up and repair the workshop. Lydia tried not to show it, but she was growing worried about money on top of everything else. The collection of coins at the temple was growing ever smaller as she hired workers to repair her home and her workshop and paid the doctor. She would not sell any cloth anytime soon. In fact, it would be many weeks before she was able to use the space again at all, and then she would need to start all over again, bringing in the equipment and pigments and murex shells needed to create just one batch of the dye. She would need new looms and all new fibers. It was overwhelming. Lydia had put money aside, thinking she would be ready for any tragedy, and yet she worried it would now not be enough.

Which is why it was so shocking when an officer arrived at the workshop one afternoon the following week, wearing the armored breastplate and helmet that marked him as an officer of Rome. He asked for Lydia and then handed her a papyrus.

Lydia read the words, and then she looked up at him. "What is this?"

"Do you need me to read it to you?" The man's voice was mocking.

"No, I do not. It says a new tax has been levied against my business. A very steep one. And I am trying to understand why."

"The city suffered much damage from the recent earthquake. Our leaders need to raise funds to repair the municipal buildings and to keep the city running."

"So I am being taxed forty percent of my last month's profits?"

"There is much work that needs to be done."

"I have already used most of that money to pay my workers and my suppliers. What is left must be spent to repair my own building."

"Forty percent of it must be sent to the government first."

Lydia leveled her gaze at him. The helmet masked part of his face, but she saw he was younger than she had first realized and still had acne along his chin.

"This tax is being levied against other business owners as well?"

"Others are being taxed at the appropriate rate."

Lydia took that to mean that certain businesses were receiving higher taxes than others. Those owned by Roman citizens were certainly not taxed at the higher level, but she wanted to understand where she fit.

"Why am I being taxed at such a high rate, then?"

"It is not for me to say. I am just the messenger."

Even if she had the money to pay this tax, which she did not, it would erase any margin of profit going forward.

"Who do I speak with to appeal?"

"This message comes straight from the praetor himself."

Ah. Lydia understood now. She was being punished for Felix's bruised pride. He had been quietly installed in the position, though the public ceremony had been pushed back due to the earthquake.

"And if I don't pay?"

"Those who do not pay their taxes end up in prison, as I'm sure you know." With this, the officer turned and walked away, the metal on his armor clanging with each step.

Lydia looked down at the page before her. This would mean another trip to the temple. This would mean even more of her reserve vanishing. *Lord, help me,* Lydia prayed. She had barely enough there to pay the workers.

She would need to trim the household expenses again. Iduma would not be pleased. And she could cut back on the food at the meal she served to the church after the service— but no. That meal was the fellowship of believers. She would not cut there, not while she could still provide it.

She would need to find other places to trim her budget.

A new letter arrived from Paul a few weeks later, and Lydia was pleased to read it to the church, which had grown larger still. They had moved from the cleared dining room to the courtyard, and still they had trouble fitting everyone inside. The workmen had mostly repaired the wall that had collapsed on Elodie, and though there was still much work to be done on the rest of the house, Lydia did not feel unsafe any longer.

Lydia read aloud that Paul had learned that the earthquake that had freed him and Silas had been felt in Thessalonika as well, though the damage was not as severe there. He told the church about how he had approached the synagogue in Thessalonika and begun to reason with those inside, quoting from the scriptures, teaching that Jesus Christ had suffered on the cross and died. Many believed, including some of the Jews, as well as many God-fearing Greeks and several prominent women. "I am beginning to see that strong women will be the backbone of the church," Paul wrote. "They are faithful servants, both in prayer and hospitality as well as in financial provision, who will help carry the church to the four corners of the earth."

Paul continued to tell of how some of the Jews in the town were jealous of their success and had rounded up some bad characters from the marketplace, formed a mob, and started a riot in the city. The rioters went to the home of Jason, with whom Paul and Silas and Timothy were staying, to drag them before the crowd.

"I am growing weary of such antics," Paul wrote. "I pray that this does not continue in every city we are to visit."

But when the crowd did not find Paul and Silas at the home of Jason, they took Jason and some other brothers and dragged them before the officials and accused them of welcoming the men who had already caused trouble all over the world into their homes. The crowd accused them of defying Caesar's decrees, saying that there is another King, called Jesus. The crowd and the city rulers had gone mad at this but allowed Jason to post bail and guarantee that the men would be leaving the city at first light. Jason had been released. The next morning, Paul and Silas and Timothy went on to Berea.

"Praise God!" Epaphroditus called, and his voice was echoed by a chorus of others. Epaphroditus had quickly become something of a leader within the congregation, and he offered prayers during the service, while Claes, who had a strong, clear singing voice, led them in a simple song he had composed about Christ's sacrifice. They broke bread after the service, and one man, a widower named Keoin, sought Lydia out and sat by her. Though he was clever and witty and what some would call handsome, she did not feel the same draw toward him that he seemed to feel toward her. Instead, she could not help wishing that Damon was among their number.

That afternoon, after the church members had left and the furniture was put back into its place, Lydia met with Iduma to go over the household expenses.

"We will need to cut back on what we spend once again," Lydia said. "I am sorry to say that we must have less meat and less fish as well."

"We already have meat or fish rarely," Iduma said, scowling. "I cannot make meals out of what I do not have."

"We will survive," Lydia said. Then she looked down at her list again. "We will need to cut back on lamp oil as well. Also, fuel for the stove. We must try to find another source, one that is cheaper."

"Cheaper fuel does not burn as clean." Iduma crossed her arms over her chest.

"That is something we will be forced to live with," Lydia said.

Iduma did not answer right away. Her lips were pressed together, and she was shaking her head, just slightly. Then, she pulled in a deep breath, and she spoke. "There are other ways we could cut back."

Lydia had heard her grumbling about preparing a meal for so many after the church gathering this morning.

"I will not stop feeding the church. Breaking bread together is one of the most important things we do."

"It costs more and more each week."

"We serve the simplest food." Today, they'd had braised lentils in oil, bread, and yogurt and herbs. They had diluted the wine.

"Some no doubt come only for the free meal." Iduma sniffed.

"I do not mind. If they come for the meal and hear the Gospel, that is just fine with me."

"The neighbors are starting to complain about the noise and the traffic of so many coming and going each week."

Lydia did not ask how Iduma had heard this news. She knew that Iduma spoke with many of the servants in the other houses nearby and that servants spread gossip faster than fire.

"So be it. I will not stop hosting the church."

Iduma pressed her lips together once more.

"There are other ways to cut costs," she said after a moment.

"What do you propose?"

"You are still paying Elodie, are you not?" Iduma arched an eyebrow.

"Yes." Where was she going with this?

"She will not be much help with one arm." She gave Lydia a knowing look.

It took Lydia a moment to understand what Iduma was suggesting.

"You want me to fire her?" Lydia could not believe the words that were coming out of her mouth. "And do what? Put her out on the street?"

"No." Iduma, perhaps responding to the anger in Lydia's voice, began to backtrack. "Not put her out in the street. But she will not be able to work as hard as the rest of us, that is all. Perhaps another situation might be found for her."

"She will not be able to work as hard because a wall of my house fell in on her," Lydia said. "It is no fault of her own. I will care for her as long as I am able."

"She could be sent back to her family."

"No." Lydia would not betray Elodie's confidence. Iduma did not need to know that Elodie's family did not want her. "That is not an option." Lydia was quickly tiring of this conversation. "We will find other ways to cut back."

Iduma held her chin up high, and Lydia held her gaze until Iduma finally lowered hers.

"And while we are speaking, please know that if you plan to continue serving in this house, you will serve the Living God. I cannot make you believe the Gospel in your heart, but I can insist that you pray when I ask you to, and you must stop worshipping idols."

Iduma blanched.

"You have a choice," Lydia said. "You may serve Jesus, or you may find another position."

Iduma did not look at her as she turned and walked back to the kitchen.

Repairs were continuing at the dye works. The stones were removed, the crushed vat hauled away and melted down, and the rear wall rebuilt. The looms were repaired, and the broken jugs cleaned up, the costly dyes washed out of the rock floor. Damon's men worked fast and well and did not take long breaks like many of the workers in the city. In a matter of weeks, the dye room was ready. Soon, they would bring a new dye vat in, and Filip, who had worked with Giorgio, would oversee the dye room. Lydia did not know how she could stand to see someone else in Giorgio's place. Things would never be the same here, but they must move forward. She would not be able to afford to pay her workers if she did not make and sell some fabric soon.

Damon stopped by the dye works on various pretexts over the next few weeks. He said he wanted to check on the workmen he'd hired, or he stopped by after trying to receive payment from Hektor. One time he came with a cart full of the softest fleece wool, though he knew she was still many weeks from being able to use it. Lydia could not help the way her heart jumped each time he entered the room. As the weather warmed and his skin grew darker, he seemed to become more handsome, his hair more glossy and full. He would joke with her, trying to make her laugh, and he would tell her she was beautiful. Lydia felt like a young girl giggling in the marketplace, and every bit of her seemed to come alive when his hand brushed hers and when he let his fingers trail against hers while showing her a fleece. This longing from deep down in her was like nothing she had ever felt before. Every part of her wanted to draw closer to him.

And yet, with each visit, her despair also grew. She had stumbled into something she did not understand, and she felt that she was playing a dangerous game, allowing herself to care about someone she could not marry. Though everything in her wanted to pull him toward her, she knew she would be wise to push him away. Her heart ached with loss after every visit, and it became so difficult that Lydia almost wished he would not come.

When the door of the workshop opened a week after his last visit, Lydia looked up, expecting to see Damon again, but it was a woman in a simple robe with a large hood. When she pulled the hood back, Lydia saw that it was her sister-in-law, Sara.

"Sara!" Lydia brightened. Lydia came around from behind the worktable and moved to embrace her friend. Sara had not responded to any of Lydia's messages. "How are you? Are you well? I hope you did not have damage from the quake." She had not spoken to Sara in many weeks, not since Sara's last disastrous visit to the dye works. She had not heard from Daniel's family at all, or from Anna. She felt her heart lighten to see her friend, but a look at Sara's face made it clear this was not a simple friendly visit. She had her eyes lowered, and she was biting the inside of her cheek. Lydia stopped short. "What is wrong?"

"I am sorry to have to come here and ask you this," Sara said. "But there is no one else, and I thought, well, I hoped maybe you would help."

"What is wrong?"

Sara pressed her lips together "It is Dorit. She is very ill."

Lydia felt a jolt. Andreas's mother was very ill? "What is wrong with her?"

"There is a large mass growing inside her belly. She says it has been there for some time, but only recently has it grown so large, and it has made her very weak and sick."

"That is terrible. I did not know."

Sara nodded. "You have not been around."

Lydia bit back the frustrated answer that threatened to come out. She had not been around because none of the family would see her.

"What do the doctors say?"

"The doctor says she needs a special medicine. It comes from Egypt and it is called quicksilver. It will cure her, the doctor has promised."

"Then she must have it." There was not a question. Andreas would have done anything for his mother, and she would do the same.

"I am glad you agree." Sara took in a breath. "There is only one problem."

Lydia waited for her to go on, but she realized the answer before Sara spoke.

"It is very costly," Sara said sheepishly.

"How much?"

"Enough to cure her will be nearly one hundred and fifty denarii."

Lydia took a step back. It was a staggering amount. An inconceivable expense.

"Can Tobias pay it?"

Sara shook her head. Tears welled up in her eyes.

"But he is a tax collector." The tax collectors were known to pocket a portion of every payment they brought in. He had to have thousands of denarii hidden away by now.

"He is…" Sara touched the hem of her robe to her eyes as tears spilled over. "It seems that he had been playing with dice more than we realized."

"How often?" The Romans were very fond of gambling. Everyone from common workers to the highest paid governors sometimes tried their hand. Andreas had not cared for the games and Lydia saw no point in throwing away money, but she had heard stories of some who had gotten too deeply into the games and had lost much more than they could afford to lose.

"Every day, or nearly. There is"—her voice cracked—"there is almost nothing left."

"Oh, Sara." Lydia wanted to step forward and embrace her sister-in-law, but her erect carriage made Lydia hesitate. "I am so sorry."

"He hid it well. We all thought things were fine. It was only when men started coming to our home to demand payment that we realized."

The officers, then. No doubt similar to the ones who had come to her workshop. "Was he able to pay them?"

"Not at first." Tears were spilling down her cheeks now. "They took him to prison. I sold my dresses and my jewelry."

Lydia noticed then that Sara did not wear the ruby ring nor any of her bracelets or necklaces.

"I am sorry, Sara."

"It is all right." She lifted her chin, trying to be brave. "After I got Tobias released, I had some money left, but our home was damaged in the quake, and the rest of it went to pay for its repair. You know Tobias would have given anything to help his mother, but we have nothing left. And we know you have joined the Christians now, but we wondered if family loyalty might allow you to help us."

The words stung more than Lydia wanted to admit. She wanted to argue that she had not pushed them out—she had been told she was no longer welcome. The fact that she had found faith in Christ did not mean she did not care about her family.

But she did not say any of that. She could not afford the doctor's fee. She could not come anywhere close to that. But she could not say no. She could not refuse Andreas's family. Maybe this would be a way to buy her way back into the family's good graces, she thought.

Instead, what she said was, "Of course I'll help."

CHAPTER FOURTEEN

That evening, Lydia had not been home for long when a knock sounded on the door. Lydia had come to hate that sound the past few weeks, as it rarely brought good news. But a few moments after Danae opened the door, she came into the room where Lydia was preparing to eat.

"You have a visitor," Danae said, bowing her head. "He is waiting at the door for you."

"Who is it?" The way Danae was smiling, it must not be terrible news.

"You will see."

It was an odd answer. Danae was not usually this coy.

"You must invite him in, whoever it is."

"I did, but he insisted he wanted you to come with him."

"What is this?" Lydia did not like to be kept in the dark.

"Just go see," Danae insisted.

"All right." She pushed back from the table and stood, smoothing her robe. She followed Danae to the door and found Damon waiting on the far side of the gate. She could not help the way her heart leaped. He was wearing a deep blue robe made of fine linen, and his hair and beard had been neatly trimmed.

"What is happening?" Had something gone wrong?

"I was hoping you could come for a walk." Damon smiled, and her insides twisted. He was so handsome.

"I am not sure I—"

"We will hold supper." Danae practically shoved her out the door.

"Well, all right." Lydia wished now that she'd had a few moments to prepare. She would have liked to have put on a clean robe and smooth her hair. But as she stepped out into the street next to Damon, she still felt a lightness she had not felt before.

"I hope you are well." Damon was smiling at her.

"I am. Hungry, but well."

Damon laughed. "I am sorry to interrupt your dinner."

"It is all right. I am glad to see you."

"I'm glad to hear you say that." There was a hint of a smile in his voice.

"Although the last time you took me for a walk, it did not end happily."

"No." He let out a sigh. "I do hope this walk will be different."

"Are you going to tell me where we are going?"

He turned his head, seeming to consider for a moment, and then he nodded. "I don't see why not. We are going to the theater."

"To the theater? Will there be a show?"

The theater was built into the hillside, with rows upon rows of seating leading down toward the stage. Andreas had declared the place a marvel of engineering for the way a sound muttered on the stage could be heard in the top row of seats. But she was not aware of any shows playing now.

"No, not tonight." He laughed as he took her hand and pulled her down the street, across the Via Egnatia and toward the hill. The sun hung low in the sky, bathing the stones of the city in a golden light, and the air was warm and fresh.

"Then why are we going?"

"Lydia?" Damon stopped short, and as Lydia also stopped, he took a step toward her. He stood just a little ways in front of her, and for a minute, she thought he was going to lean in and kiss her. She held her breath and felt her body arc toward him. But instead, he said, "Trust me."

Before she could think of a response, he starting moving again, pulling her along by his hand, which was threaded through hers. She did trust him, she realized. She knew that what he said was true and that his word was his oath. She knew that if she let herself depend on him, he would not let her down. But she also realized that she could not allow herself to do so.

Soon they arrived at the entrance to the theatre, its mammoth columns tall and proud behind the stage. The seats sloped up the hill in a half circle. It had survived the quake largely unscathed. It was enormous. And it was empty.

"Are we allowed to be here?" Lydia asked. Surely they did not simply let people walk in here at all hours. Then again, there was nothing to keep them out.

"It is all right." Damon led her in through the gap in the stone that served as an entrance and then led her past the stage and toward the steps.

"We are going up?"

Damon nodded. "All the way to the top."

"Oh my." Andreas had always liked to be close to the stage so he could see the actors better. She had never thought to go up.

"You can do it." He started up the steps, the hard leather soles of his sandals smacking against each step. "You are not afraid of heights, are you?"

"No. Just strange men leading me to out-of-the-way places at odd hours."

"Are you calling me strange?" He cocked his head but kept walking. She followed him. She was breathing heavily by the time they got to the top, and her legs were aching, but Damon reached out his arms and pulled her to him and then turned her around.

"Oh. Goodness." From up here, the city was sprawled out before them, the buildings tumbling one after another down the hill. Lydia had never seen the city from this angle, and in the orange light of the setting sun, the stones seemed almost alive.

"People do not realize that the cheaper seats present the best view. This is where I always choose to sit."

Her body was warm where it pressed against him, and he held her so firmly but so gently.

"It is lovely." It was all so perfect—the beautiful evening, the warm light, the man she had come to care about more than she had realized.

No, Lydia realized. *No. This is not right.* As much as she wanted to stay, she knew she needed to go.

"I must get back."

"We just got here."

"It has been a lovely walk. But I must get back."

"I was hoping to talk with you." Now he dropped his arms from her and took her hands, so he was facing her, and he pulled her close. "I wanted to ask you something."

"You can ask as we walk back," Lydia said.

"Lydia." He pressed his lips together, tilted his head. "I think about you night and day. My every thought is about you. You are the most beautiful, the most talented, the most precious woman I have ever met."

They were the words she had longed to hear, and yet she could not enjoy them.

"You feel it too."

"I feel the night air is starting to set in."

"Even now, you joke? Lydia, I have just emptied my soul. For once, please, let down your guard."

Lydia felt so many emotions swirling through her that she could not begin to process them.

"Am I wrong? Do you not care about me in the same way that I care about you?"

"I—" Lydia was at a loss for what to say. She could not deny it.

"Let us get married. That's why we're here. I wanted to ask you—will you marry me?"

Lydia's heart soared. She had never known how lovely it felt to be desired. Her marriage to Andreas had been arranged, a financial transaction of sorts. But this—this was totally different. She was old enough now and independent, and she could do as she pleased without asking for permission from anyone. Damon wanted her for who she was. He had chosen her. He cared about her. It was special in a way she had never before experienced.

She wanted to tell him that she loved his laugh, his smile, the way he had protected her. She wanted to say that she felt safe with him and that her body came alive in ways she'd never imagined before, when he was near.

But Lydia said none of this. She did not know how to answer. She was torn in half—part of her wanted to say that of course she felt the way he did, of course she wanted nothing more than to be his wife. The other part of her knew it was impossible.

"Lydia?"

She could not draw this out any longer. She needed to tell him the truth.

"It is just…" She took in a breath, trying to steady herself. "The church."

"Is that all?" Damon's face registered relief. "That does not bother me. It is not a problem that you are a Christian."

It didn't bother him? It was not a problem? This was the faith that was at the very core of who she was. Something inside her fell.

"Naturally, the church could not continue meeting in your home. Or my home, or whichever we chose. But we could find a suitable space, and I would not mind if you continued to attend."

Lydia took this in. "They could not meet in our home?"

Damon's brow furrowed. "Lydia. The church is illegal. Surely you must see why I can't have it meet in my home." He meant because of his position and because of his wealth. He must have seen how the words wounded her, because he quickly added, "But I do not mind at all that you remain a part of it. You may worship whatever god you choose. I will love you, just the same, until I die."

Lydia had known that Damon did not believe in Adonai, let alone Jesus Christ. But she had hoped...well, she had hoped for all kinds of things that now seemed completely silly. Damon would let her continue to worship Jesus Christ, he'd said. But the saving grace of Jesus was so much a part of her that she could not imagine it simply being tolerated. He had said that she could continue to be part of the church. But she had promised Paul that she would lead it and help it to grow.

"I cannot stop hosting the church," Lydia finally said.

"Lydia." He rubbed the back of her hand with his thumb. "You have shown such care for the church. No one could have done a better job. But it will be fine hosted in another home. And you will be free to worship your god."

The sun had slipped below the horizon, and shadows were beginning to creep across the city below them.

Lydia chose her next words carefully. "He is not *my* God. He is the God who created the world and all that is in it. He is the Alpha and Omega and all that is in between. He is the God of the heavens and the Author of all life. And He has redeemed His people."

"Okay," Damon said. "That is fine. I still want to marry you. Please, Lydia. Say you will."

With everything in her Lydia wanted to say yes. She longed to wake up with this man and go to bed with him. She was never as alive as she was when she was with him. She loved him. She had not admitted it to herself until this moment, but it was true. She loved him. And yet she knew she could not marry him.

She pulled her hands free and felt tears sting her eyes. "I am sorry."

Damon looked more surprised than wounded.

"I do want to marry you. More than anything, I do. Please believe that. I love you." She used the back of her hand to wipe away a tear. "But my heart belongs to Jesus first. And I cannot marry a man who does not feel the same way."

"What are you saying?" Damon appeared stricken.

"I have made a promise to host and lead the church," Lydia said. "And as much as it pains me, I cannot do anything that will come before that."

"You can still attend," Damon said. "You would refuse me because of the church?" Damon now looked genuinely confused. "You would give up your happiness—and mine—for this?"

"I am sorry." Tears were now streaming down her face, and she did not bother to wipe them away. "Many have given up far more. Paul has spent time in chains, being chased out of town after town. Stephen was stoned. I suppose this must be my sacrifice for the sake of the Gospel." She squeezed his hands. "I wish it were not so, Damon. I do love you. I do want to marry you. But I cannot."

They stood just a little ways apart from each other, but suddenly completely distant. She felt as though the strength had gone out of her body.

The light was fading fast from the sky, and with it, all of her hope. For the first time, she began to wonder if the Gospel was truly worth sacrificing so much.

Lydia barely slept that night, replaying the scene with Damon endlessly, crying out to God and sobbing. She had just thrown away the very thing she wanted most, and she asked God again and again whether He really needed her to make such a sacrifice. The answer that came to her was the image of the sinless Jesus Christ, nailed to the cross for the sin of the whole world. Was her sacrifice really all that great? She knew, in her heart, that it was not. But that did not make it hurt any less.

The next day, Lydia dressed carefully and painted her eyes with kohl, hoping to disguise the dark circles under her eyes. Then, after the midday meal, she and Leia took the silk from the locked cabinet and loaded the bundle into the cart. They set off toward town. The cart was pulled by a donkey, while Lydia and Leia walked beside it, Lydia steering the donkey's reins. Lydia would not approach Felix alone again. She had learned that lesson.

"It is a shame to sell this beautiful silk," Leia said as they walked the streets of the town. "I keep dreaming of all the beautiful things that could be made with it."

"I wish I did not have to," Lydia said. Lydia did not need to be reminded of the loss of this fabric, which was even greater than Leia realized. She had promised Damon that she would not use the fabric to make something for Felix.

"It is stunning. I have never seen so much silk all together," Leia continued.

"Yes," Lydia said. Leia did not need to remind her what she was giving up.

"It would make such a stunning gown, dyed deep purple. It would be fit for a queen."

"I know."

Leia did not seem to get the hint. Suddenly Lydia wished Asuman was with her, but she had not yet been called back to the workshop. Leia had been working every day to restore the looms.

Technically, Lydia was honoring her promise. She would not be making something for Felix from this fabric but simply hoped to sell him the raw material. But what did it matter anymore anyway? Damon had been so crushed last night, so surprised and heartbroken, that Lydia was certain there was nothing that could be done to make him hate her even more. And she needed the money. With her business still not able to operate and her collection of coins at the temple nearly gone, she had no other way to get the funds needed to buy the medicine Dorit needed.

Leia chattered about the embroidering she imagined on the gown she would make and dreamed of the fine jewelry that would set it off as they led the donkey through the city gates.

Lydia nodded at the guards, enjoying the cool air beneath the arch for the few moments before they emerged into the bustling city streets. Many of the buildings were under repair. There had been a high demand for builders after the quake, and Lydia had no doubt that Daniel had replaced a large amount of the income lost from the fortune-teller with the increase in the need for builders in the past few weeks. She did not know for certain, because Anna still would not respond to the notes Lydia sent, but she prayed that Anna and her family were doing well enough.

When they approached the municipal building, Lydia tied up the donkey and together, she and Leia hoisted the heavy silk and carried it up the marble steps, past the statue of Caesar, and through the colonnaded edifice. Lydia told the guards by the door that she was here to visit the praetor.

"The praetor does not have time for visitors."

"Please tell him Lydia is here to see him and that I have something he will want to see."

"He cannot be disturbed."

"He will want to be disturbed for this."

The guard looked her over uncertainly, perhaps trying to ascertain what kind of woman she was. Lydia kept her chin up and tried not to let this guard intimidate her, though inside she was trembling. The last time she had seen Felix, he had threatened to arrest her. Would he want to see her after all? What would he do if she did get in front of him? Would he have her arrested now? Lydia hoped that the silk would be too much of a temptation for him and that he would forget all else.

"We will let him know." The guard indicated a far corner of the floor where they could wait. There were no chairs or benches. Lydia and Leia set the bundle down and stood. They waited as a guard was sent with the message and returned, and while the guards conferred. Many people came and went from the building, and shadows lengthened. Lydia did not know how much time had passed while they stood here, but her feet and back ached and her stomach grumbled. Leia, mercifully, was silent beside her.

Finally, while many workers streamed from the building to return home for the evening, one of the guards approached them.

"The praetor will see you now." He showed them up the marble stairs and into a large room with an oiled wood desk and a thick carpet in a pattern that reminded Lydia of designs from the east. She prayed for the right words to say and for favor in the eyes of Felix.

"Lydia." Felix did not look up from the parchment in front of him. In the flickering light from the oil lamp, Lydia saw a jeweled ring on his finger, crusted with rubies and emeralds, as well as a fine gold chain around his neck. "What is it now?"

"The ceremony that will publicly install you as praetor is coming up, is it not? You will need that new robe, as we discussed before."

"I have found a new supplier, Lydia. I have no more need of your services."

Lydia tried not to show the fear this news caused her. Felix was loathsome, but if she could not count on his orders, her struggling business was in even deeper trouble than she had known. She should have seen this coming, she recognized that now. But still, it was a shock.

Lydia steeled herself. She must focus on why she was here.

"Nonetheless. I have come with the hope that you will be interested in the most stunning fabric I have ever seen. I am certain you will want to see it." Lydia gestured for Leia to open the bag, which they had set on the floor, and she hoisted the bulk of the fabric and handed it to Lydia. She unfurled a section and spread it across Felix's desk.

"This is silk, all the way from Serica."

Felix looked up, and his eyes widened.

"Go on. Feel it. It is as smooth as the petal of a rose."

He reached out his fingers and stroked it gently. "Where did you get this?"

Lydia could not think about Damon. She would not let herself remember that magical evening when he had brought her this beautiful material. "I have my ways."

Felix glanced up and gave her a long, penetrating look before returning his gaze to the fabric.

"There is enough here for a very fine robe."

"It is plain."

"I will have it dyed. It will be the most regal robe anyone has ever seen."

He was rubbing the silk between his fingers, testing its feel.

"Your shop is able to dye?" He cocked his head. "You have not paid taxes on any new sales."

Lydia pressed her lips together. He had been paying attention to what she had and had not paid.

"We will be ready to begin dyeing again very shortly." This was not strictly the truth. It would be a few weeks before they were scheduled to receive the first shipment of the murex shells, and it would take some time after that before the dye was ready. But perhaps she could hurry the process. She would do whatever needed to be done. She needed to sell this silk.

"How much?"

"I have never seen this much silk together in my life. It is very rare to find such an excellent piece."

"How much?"

"It came all the way from the far side of the earth."

"Lydia. Do not toy with me. Tell me the cost."

"I have many customers who are interested," Lydia said. She did not know if anyone but Felix would pay this much for the silk. "But because of the importance of the occasion and the good business it will bring me when the public admires you in the most stunning robe they have ever seen, I will give you a special price of two hundred denarii."

"You are trying to rob me."

"When the public admires your good taste as well as your leadership, it will be worth every penny." The words were sour in her mouth, but she forced herself to smile as she said them.

"This is not worth one coin over fifty denarii."

"It is worth far more than that. But because you have been so gracious, I will sell it for one hundred seventy-five."

He wanted the material. She could see that in the way his eyes lingered on the soft sheen of the fabric. He was no doubt imagining himself draped in it, standing before the city.

"Seventy-five."

Lydia shook her head. "I am afraid I cannot let it go at that price. I will take it to another customer, one who will give me a fair price for it." She started to pull the fabric back, but he pressed his fist down on it.

"Seventy-five denarii, and for that, I will not have you sent to prison."

"Sent to prison?"

"The Christians continue to meet in your home, Lydia. Do not think we are oblivious to the illegal actions for which you are responsible."

Lydia straightened her shoulders. "I have done nothing wrong."

"You are practicing a cult that is forbidden by the emperor. Your members continue to spread its poison, and it is infecting the city like a disease."

Lydia felt the first cold fingers of fear grip her. He could not really mean this, could he? "We share the saving grace of our Lord."

"You teach that there is but one god and that even Caesar should bow to him."

Lydia did not argue. Even Caesar himself needed Jesus.

"I have overlooked it because of you, Lydia. But people in this city, especially those at high levels, want the Christians to be wiped away from this town."

Lydia tried not to let her face reflect her fear. "What have we done, then, to cause so much harm?"

"We are getting many complaints from your neighbors about the crowds that gather at your home."

"We will try to be more quiet."

Lydia heard Leia shift behind her.

"Many are upset that fewer offerings are being made to the gods. They worry that the gods will retaliate with another earthquake, or worse."

"They need not worry about that. Those false gods hold no power."

Felix leveled his eyes at her. She did not look away.

"If I do not take action to stop this uprising, they will think I am weak."

"It is not my business what others think of you." Lydia could not believe the boldness of the words that were coming out of her mouth.

Felix did not move.

"They say you are revolutionaries, plotting to overthrow Rome."

"Nothing could be further from the truth."

"Our revenues have gone down as more and more citizens are giving their money to the church first and paying their taxes afterward."

That was it, then. That was the heart of the matter. If there was less money to send to Rome, that reflected poorly on the praetor and his management skills.

"If there is a problem with the sums you collect from the city, it is not the fault of the followers of the Way. We all pay our taxes. Our Lord instructed us to render unto Caesar what is Caesar's. Though the taxes on many have increased, we pay them without complaint. I am afraid your shortfall must come from another source." She looked at the ring on his finger and then at the gold chain around his neck. He pounded his fist on the table.

"That is it. Action must be taken. Whatever has happened with these Christians, it has changed you, Lydia."

He meant it once again as an insult, but Lydia could not see it that way. She was changed, heart and mind, and she could not be more grateful.

"I have overlooked too much, I see that now. I did not want to hurt you, Lydia, because of the respect I have for you as a businesswoman."

Lydia thought back to their last encounter in his home and could not trust his words.

"But the time has come when I cannot ignore it any longer. You must declare your loyalty to Caesar."

"Of course I am loyal to Caesar."

"To Caesar over this god that has caused so much trouble and created so much upheaval in Philippi."

Lydia's breath went short, and her mouth suddenly felt dry.

"You have just told me that you give to Caesar what is his. So go on. Tell me that your loyalty is first to Caesar, and you will not be punished."

Lydia's skin tingled, and every sense sharpened. He could not mean this, could he?

"I can see that I was mistaken. I will find another buyer for the silk." She started to lift the package off the desk.

"Tell me that you are loyal to Caesar, Lydia, or I will know that you are indeed a revolutionary and must be punished as one."

How had this meeting turned so quickly? She had come here only searching to sell the silk, and now she was being threatened with—what? She was not sure. She could not believe it.

Felix's voice had gravel in it. "Declare where your loyalties lie, Lydia. With Caesar or with Jesus that they call the Christ?"

Lydia tried to think of something to say, but her normally quick mind had gone blank. The answer was clear. But the consequences of declaring that truth could be disastrous. She could not think how to get out of this.

Help me, Lord.

She took a deep breath in and let it out, and slowly, a steely, centered calm settled over her. She knew, without a doubt, how to give an answer. Only the truth would do. God would protect her, just as He had protected Paul and Silas and so many others. And if He did not—if her fate was like that of Stephen or the others who had faced terrible consequences for their loyalty to the faith—then so be it. She could not deny what she knew to be true.

"I believe in Jesus Christ, the Son of God, Creator of all that is. I will worship Him above all else for the rest of my days."

Behind her, Leia let out a gasp.

Felix did not move for a moment. He seemed to not know how to respond. Lydia was aware of the edges of her vision starting to blur and her breath going shallow in the silent moments that seemed to stretch on forever.

But then, he shoved his chair back, stood, and yelled, "Guards! Arrest this woman!"

The last thing Lydia felt before the world turned black was a pair of strong hands clapping chains onto her arms.

CHAPTER FIFTEEN

Prison was even worse than Lydia had imagined. She had known to expect the small cell and the chains. Because the prison at Philippi had been ruined by the earthquake, she was now held in a small room under the municipal building, along with three other women. The men were held in a separate cell, and she could hear them shouting and crying out not far away, but she did not know how many were there or what was causing them such pain. The guards walked the halls, the metal of their breastplates clanging at all hours. Their helmets covered their faces, as if they were dressed for battle—and judging by the sounds that came from the other cells, it seemed that perhaps they were.

When she had first arrived, Lydia had tried to talk to the other women in the cell, to tell them who she was and find out about them, but the one with the light hair acted as though she did not hear, while the one with only three teeth snarled at her. The last, an older woman with a raspy voice, introduced herself as Marit, but though she smiled kindly, she lay back down on the floor and turned to face the wall. The guards had given Lydia a thin blanket, but there was nothing but the cold slab of floor to lie on. An earthenware pot in the corner of the room, out in the open and shared by all, was the only place to relieve oneself. It was emptied once a day and stank like nothing she had ever known. Weak light filtered in through a small ventilation hole near the ceiling. The guards brought stale bread and water twice a day, and those meals quickly became the highlight of the day, as they were the only thing to break up the tedium of staring at the walls.

The first day, Lydia sang songs, just as Paul and Silas had, but the woman with few teeth told her, in coarse language, to be quiet. The woman with light hair threatened to throw the pot at her. After that, Lydia began to sing the songs only within her mind. She also spent hours in prayer, asking for God's mercy and for His blessing on the little church. She wondered whether the others had heard what had happened and if they would still meet. She wondered whether Anna knew she had been arrested and if she was well. She wondered if Anna would ever forgive her. The days and nights ran together, and Lydia also wondered how long it would take before she was brought to trial and whether she would lose her mind before that happened.

On the third day, Lydia received a letter. The guard banged against the door and then slipped it through the crack in the same stealthy way they delivered food. Lydia never saw more than a glimpse of an arm or a foot. Lydia was pleased to see that the letter was from Epaphroditus. He said he was shocked to hear what had happened and prayed she was well, and he promised the church would continue to meet on the Lord's Day. They were all praying for her, he said, and asked her to remain strong in the hope of their Savior. He also promised that those of the church with connections were doing all they could to help with her swift release. Lydia wondered what that could be, but mostly she treasured the note, knowing that people of the church cared for her. Thoughtfully, Epaphroditus had also sent along parchment and ink so that Lydia could write letters of her own.

She first wrote back to Epaphroditus, thanking him for his dedication and his thoughtfulness, and encouraging the church to keep meeting and praying together. She knew some in the congregation might be afraid after her arrest, but she urged them to gather anyway, because the Lord was more powerful than earthly rulers. She tried her best to believe it herself.

Lydia also wrote a note to Anna, telling her daughter what had happened and that she was well. She also told her how much she loved Anna and always would. Anna might not want to hear from her, but Lydia would send it anyway.

"What are you doing?" Marit asked, seeing Lydia crouched in the light of the small window to write her note.

"Writing a letter." Lydia moved the parchment so she could see.

Marit nodded and did not turn immediately back to the wall. Lydia sensed that she wanted something, but she did not know what.

"My friend sent me several parchments. Would you like one, to send a letter?"

Marit shook her head slowly, but she still did not turn away. Lydia had not seen her interested in anything but the wall since she had been here. Lydia went back to her writing, but

Marit continued to watch her, her brow knit. She followed each stroke of the quill with her eyes.

After a few moments, Lydia tried again.

"Is there someone you would want to send a letter to, if you could?"

Marit didn't answer at first. She bit her lip and cast her eyes down. And then, slowly, she nodded. Then Lydia understood.

"Would you like me to help you?"

Again, Marit didn't answer at first, but then she asked, quietly, "Would you?"

"Of course."

Lydia set aside the note she was writing and gestured for Marit to come closer. She scooted across the floor and sat next to Lydia. Aside from meal times and relieving herself, it was the only time she had seen Marit move from her spot by the wall since she had arrived.

"Who would you like to send a letter to?"

"My son," Marit answered. "Stefan."

"Tell me what you want to say, and I will write it for you."

Marit nodded and began to dictate.

Stefan, she said. *This is a note from your mother. A kind woman is writing this for me. I am fine. I miss you. I am sorry that I am not able to be there with you. I want you to know that I do not regret what I did. I would take a hundred loaves of bread if it meant little Deondre's belly would be full. I only wish I had been quicker and not been seen. I miss you and I hope to see you soon. Give Deondre my love. Mama*

Lydia fought to hold back her tears as she wrote the message. She had known there were many in the city who were hungry and that things had gotten worse since the quake. Lydia, too, worried about money, but she was not anywhere close to having to steal bread for a child to eat. How many more were there in the city like this? How had she not known any before this? And, she wondered, could the church help?

After that, Lydia felt more tenderly toward Marit, and though the two women hardly ever spoke, Lydia thought of her as a friend of sorts.

On the fifth day, the woman with the light hair was pulled from the cell by one of the guards, shrieking and kicking the whole way, and she never came back. Lydia did not know what had happened to her, and though Marit said she was no doubt sent home, Lydia did not believe her.

On the sixth day, Lydia received another letter. She hoped it was a response from Anna, but when she saw the seal, she recognized it as belonging to Damon. Her heart began to beat faster as the guard slipped it through the cracked door. Damon! He would rescue her. A man like Damon would know the right people to get her out of this prison.

It was a cloudy day and the afternoon was waning, and there was not much light in the cell, but Lydia still began to read.

Lydia,

I heard today what my cousin has done. It is unforgivable. I am sorry you are trapped.

I have also heard why you went to see our praetor. I know that you sold the silk to him after all. This, I think, hurts me more than anything else that has happened between us.

If you needed money so badly, why didn't you come to me?
I would have helped you. It is not a sign of weakness to ask for
help. On the contrary, I believe it portrays strength. Instead,
your foolish pride has ended in this.

I am trying to help speed your trial. I will do all I can.

I remain, as always, yours.

—Damon

Lydia read through the letter many times, trying to understand. He was angry, that was clear. And how could she blame him? He had asked her not to let Felix get the silk. She supposed that Felix had now gotten it for free, since he possessed it and had not paid her. But she had needed the money, and Felix was the only one who could help.

Felix was the only one who she'd *thought* could help. She wondered now if what Damon had said was true. Would he have helped her? She had not thought to ask, not after she had rejected him. What kind of man would help her after she had stomped on his heart?

A good one, Lydia thought. She clutched the letter to her breast. The kind of man any woman would want.

Lydia did not sleep much that night. Truthfully, she did not sleep much any night since she'd been in this cell, but tonight she was kept awake not only by the hard ground and sound of rats scurrying and men shouting. Her mind spun, remembering the way Damon had flirted with her, finding excuses to call on her. She thought of how excited he had been to bring her that silk, the most amazing bolt of fabric either one of them would see in their lifetimes. She thought about the time he pulled her from the market when the crowds had pressed in and how strong and sure his arms were. She thought, too, about how he had sent his men to protect her after Paul and Silas's arrest, and how he had held her when they had discovered Giorgio. And she thought of the silent walk back to her home after she had told him she could not give up the church for him.

As she lay there, trying to find a comfortable position on the hard floor, Lydia could not help thinking about all that she had given up since the followers of the Way came into her life. Andreas's family, who would no longer talk to her unless they wanted money. Her daughter, and the chance to see her grandson and welcome the new baby when born. Her business. It was not lost entirely yet, she admitted, but with the taxes levied on it she did not see how she could sustain it for much longer. Damon. And now, her freedom. Would she ever be released from this prison? Lydia had none of the protections that a Roman-born citizen would be afforded. There was nothing to say she had to be released anytime soon.

Had it all been worth it?

Lydia did not have to think long on that. The answer was yes. The saving grace of Jesus Christ was worth everything she had suffered and more. It was almost as if the Gospel had stripped away everything that mattered so she could see that none of it was as important as she had thought. All the things that had once defined her—her wealth, her standing as a businesswoman, her reputation as a dealer of purple cloth, her hope for a marriage born of love, even the love of her precious daughter—all of it was gone. And with it, all the things that kept her from seeking, first and only, the kingdom of Jesus Christ. Now that all the things she had thought would be what she was known for were gone, her legacy, if she ever got out of here, would be building up the church at Philippi to spread the Gospel throughout the world.

"Could you stop moving?" Marit called out.

Lydia muttered an apology and lay still.

Felix could try all he wanted to squash the church. He would not succeed. He could punish her for leading it and arrest those who followed in her wake, but he would not silence them. Epaphroditus had sent another letter saying that even more had come to worship this past Lord's Day. In only a few months, they had grown from just a handful of worshippers to nearly one hundred thirty this week. The church was growing so fast they could not keep up with each convert. Try as hard as they could, Lydia thought, the officials would not stop God's people from meeting. If they killed her, another leader would rise up. If they burned down her home, the faithful would find another place to meet.

No, Lydia decided. Even if the magistrates brought the full power of Rome to bear, it could not compare to the power of the Living God, who would not let His faithful be silenced. It was too late for that, and the faithful were too many in number.

The church at Philippi would survive.

Even if she never got out of here, she understood, the church would last.

CHAPTER SIXTEEN

A few days later, a bundle was delivered to the cell. Inside, Lydia found a feast with pieces of dried fish and lamb, walnuts, dates, raisins, and dried apricots. The note attached said, *Be well, Imma. Love, Anna.*

"Come see." Lydia spread the contents of the bag on the fabric and told Marit and the woman with few teeth, whom she had learned was named Elena, to eat. None had had a full belly since she had come here, and Marit for some time before that. They all three ate quickly and greedily, until there was none left. It tasted better than any food Lydia had had in her life.

"Thank you," Marit said before scurrying back into her corner.

It was not the food that pleased Lydia the most, however. It was the fact that Anna had not stopped caring. Perhaps there was hope for them yet.

The day after that was the Lord's Day again, and though Lydia could not join with the congregation in their worship, she joined them in spirit, praising God until the dirty looks from Elena silenced her.

That night, once the evening bread had been delivered and the dishes collected, the three women lay down to rest.

There was not much else to do once the sun went down and the room was cast into darkness.

After rocking from side to side, trying to find a spot that did not hurt her sore hips or shoulders, Lydia finally fell into a dreamless sleep. Sometime later—she did not know how long—she was startled awake by the clang of the door. She sat up, and by the light of a torch, she saw that Marit and Elena were also up, eyes wide. Marit held her blanket up, as if to protect herself. One of the guards held out the torch, looking from one face to the next, before he settled on Lydia. Beneath the helmet, she could only see his eyes, which were wild with—what? Lydia wasn't sure she wanted to know.

"That one." He pointed to her as another guard came in from behind him and crouched down.

"What is happening?" Lydia hated the tremor in her voice.

"You are coming with us." The first guard spoke.

"Now?"

"Now." The second one was stabbing at the lock on her chains, trying to unlatch it.

"But where?" At this time? The sky was black as ink outside. Lydia had never heard of anyone taken from a cell in the night.

"Don't ask questions," the first guard barked.

"Hurry," said the other.

The kneeling guard had to jiggle the key, but finally it caught, and the lock snapped open. Lydia was free of chains for the first time in nearly two weeks, but she did not have time to enjoy the sensation before the man grabbed her and hoisted her up over his shoulder.

"Set me down!" she shrieked. She pounded on his back with her fists.

"Let's go." The first guard—the one with the torch—moved out into the hallway and slammed the door shut behind him.

"Quiet," the other hissed.

"Set me down!" Lydia yelled again, and when the first guard shushed her, the one holding her set her down. Suddenly, Lydia stood between them, free of chains. What was going on?

"We must hurry," he said and gestured for them to follow him. "But please, be quiet."

"Where are you taking me? What is going on?" The guard behind her pushed her, gently, urging her to follow the first one down the hall. She reluctantly did.

"You will find out soon enough. For now, please, go quickly, and be quiet."

At the end of the hall, the guard used a key to unlock a door, and they went up a staircase, down another hall, and then out another door. And then, Lydia was standing under the open sky, its surface dotted with stars. Lydia felt as though she had never seen a sight so glorious in all her life.

"Let's go." The second guard pulled her into a chariot that was parked at the side of the building, while the first waited by the door. As soon as they were inside, the driver cracked the whip, and the horses began to move, pulling the carriage forward with Lydia and the guard inside.

"What is—"

But before she could get the words out, the guard took off his helmet, and in the moonlight Lydia saw who it was. She let out a shriek. "Is it really you?"

Claes laughed. "It is. Did I play a convincing guard?"

"Oh my." Lydia could not help it. All the terror she had felt just a moment before now bubbled up as laughter. "But how did you—"

"Clement," Claes said.

Lydia clapped her hand to her mouth. "That was Clement?" The guard who had accepted Christ the night of the quake had intervened to let her free tonight.

"He wanted to break you out the first night, but we convinced him to wait."

"Why did you wait?" Lydia laughed again, now that the terror was fading. "It was miserable in there."

"We needed to wait until we had a plan to keep you safe once you were free," Claes said. "Somewhere for you to go."

Somewhere for her to go. Lydia had not thought about it until this moment, but where would she go? She could not go back to her home. The magistrates would come looking for her there as soon as they realized she was gone.

"Where are we going?"

"You will see shortly."

This night had been full of surprises, but they all faded away as the chariot stopped and Lydia saw where they were.

"This is where I am to be kept safe?"

Claes shrugged. "For now." He jumped out of the chariot and helped her down.

Lydia took a deep breath. "Let us go, then. Before we are seen."

Damon rushed toward them as Grigory and Galen ushered Lydia and Claes inside.

"You are safe."

"Damon." Tears spilled down her cheeks before she could stop them. She was overwhelmed by gratitude, by fear, by exhaustion. By how happy she was to see him, even despite all that had happened. He was moving toward her, and before she understood, he had wrapped his arms around her. For a moment, she stiffened, unsure, but then she let herself relax into his arms, and she never wanted him to let go. "It is good to see you. Thank you."

Damon held her tightly for a moment longer, and then he pulled back. "Bring some wine and some hot food," he said to a servant who watched from the corner. The young man turned and scurried out of the room, and Damon took her hand and led her to the couch. He settled her and then sat next to her. Claes sat on the couch across from them.

"How did this happen?" Lydia asked. She still could not wrap her mind around all that had occurred this night.

"The people of your church were very concerned about you," Damon said. "As was I."

"Yes, but…" She looked from one face to the other. They did not know each other. Or they had not until now. "But how did that happen? How did you make this happen?"

"We can explain more later," Damon said. "For now, know that we have been working closely together. But there is not much time, and there is a lot to do."

"Your friend Damon has been most generous to us," Claes said. "He even attended our service last week."

"You did?" She turned to Damon.

"I needed to know whether they could be trusted," Damon said. "I was not convinced of their message, but I was convinced that they were trustworthy. So here we are."

Lydia still did not understand, but she nodded. The servant set down a jug of wine and a bowl of stew made from some kind of meat. Lydia's stomach groaned.

"Eat, please," Damon said. "Eat all you can, for there is a long journey ahead of you."

Lydia had picked up the bowl and the spoon, but she paused with the spoon halfway to her mouth. "A journey?"

"You cannot stay here, Lydia, as much as I wish it were possible. They would find you immediately."

Lydia realized that he was right. It would not take Felix long to guess where Lydia had been taken. She spooned some of the stew into her mouth. It was thick and spicy, the meat tender. She quickly spooned up another mouthful.

"We must get you out of the city before the jailers realize you are gone. Clement will keep them from discovering that you are missing as long as he can. But he will not be able to keep them from the knowledge forever."

Lydia was starting to realize how much thought and care had gone into this plan and she felt a surge of gratitude. But then she had another thought. Clement had been on the verge of running himself through with his sword when Paul and Silas were freed. The punishment for an escaped prisoner was death. "What will happen to Clement when I am discovered missing?"

Neither Claes nor Damon answered for a moment. Then, carefully, Claes spoke. "It was a risk he was willing to take."

"What?" The stew turned quickly sour in her belly. Lydia started to stand. "No. He has a wife, a family. He cannot be sacrificed that I may go free."

"Lydia, please sit." Damon sounded weary. "Much thought has been given to this."

"And many prayers as well," Claes added. "Also, your friend has been quite generous." He gestured at Damon.

Lydia looked at Damon, searching for the meaning of these words. "I do not understand."

"A generous offer has been made to the head guard to look the other way," Damon said. "If all goes as it should, Clement will not be punished."

Damon had bribed the head guard then. Lydia shook her head. Surely her life could not be worth all of this. But also, she knew this could not be the end of it.

"But he was not the only one who knew I was there. This came down from the praetor himself. What will happen to him when Felix discovers I am gone?"

Neither man answered at first. "It was a risk he was willing to take," Claes repeated quietly.

"And that is why we must move quickly," Damon said. "The sooner you are brought to safety, the sooner everyone else in your church will be safe."

"Where am I to go?" Were they sending her back to her family's home in Thyatira?

"There is a house that belongs to my uncle," Damon said. "It is remote, up in the hills near the border with Thrace. Only the caretakers reside there. You will be safe there."

Lydia started to protest, but Damon quickly added, "It is not the side of the family that includes Felix. He does not know this uncle and will not think to look for you there."

"You must leave the city at first light, as soon as the gates open," Claes said. "Before they realize you are gone."

Lydia nodded. "How?"

"We will do it the same way we got Luke and Timothy out," Damon said. "You will be in a cart, covered with wool and fabric. You will need to stay very still and quiet for a long time."

"That is all right."

"It will not be comfortable," Damon said. "I am sorry about that. But it is the safest way."

"I will not mind. Compared to where I have been, I am sure it will feel like paradise."

While Lydia ate a second helping of the stew, the two men went over the details of the plan with her. Galen would drive the cart. She was to lie still in the back of the cart for the length of the journey, which would take two days. They would provide her with some food and a wineskin of drink, and they must only stop for the barest of necessities. The couple who kept the house in the hills had been alerted to expect her and to keep her safe.

"Thank you," Lydia said. She could not understand how so much trouble had been made for her, but she was grateful.

"You are concerned," Damon said. Lydia nodded slowly. He could read her so well.

"What about Anna?"

"We will watch out for her," Claes said. "We will let her know you are safe, but we will not tell her where you are."

Lydia nodded, grateful. "But what of my home here?" Lydia asked. "And the dye works? There are many who depend on it for work. Who will run it while I am gone?"

The men looked at one another. Claes pressed his lips together.

"What?" There was something they were not telling her.

Finally, Damon said, "Felix has seized the dye works."

"He what?" Lydia did not understand. "He can't do that!"

"A tax was levied on it," Damon said.

"I know about the tax," Lydia said. "When I am able to start producing again, I will pay it."

"This was another tax," Claes said. "A new one. Due immediately upon receipt."

"But you were not there to pay it," Damon said. "So the dye works was seized. It now belongs to Rome." He put his hand on hers. "I am sorry, Lydia."

"But…" Lydia could not even think of what to say. "That cannot be. How can he do this?"

"I do not know that he can. I believe he has overstepped. We will fight to get it back," Damon promised. "But for now, getting you to safety is the most important thing."

"The sun will be coming up within the hour," the servant boy said from the corner.

"Right. We must get you ready."

Before she could think how to argue, Lydia was taken to refresh herself for the long journey and then escorted out to the cart.

"If I need to tell you something, I will rap three times, like this," Galen said, knocking quickly on the side of the wagon. "If you do not hear that sign, do not move or speak."

Lydia nodded to show that she understood, and Damon pulled her toward him one more time. He wrapped his arms around her and said, "Be safe, Lydia." Then he pulled back and planted a soft kiss on her cheek before indicating that she should climb into the cart.

"We will be praying for you," Claes said.

Lydia was wrapped in cloth and bundled into the bottom of the cart, surrounded by wool and soft fabric that pressed down on her. Sound became muffled, and the clop of the horse's hooves over the stones were but a soft thud as the wagon started to move.

Lord, protect them all, Lydia prayed. So many had risked so much. *Keep them all safe. And may Your glory and Your power be made clear.*

The wagon slowed and Lydia heard voices, but she did not know what they were saying. They must be at the city gate, she decided. But soon, the wagon moved again, and they were off, following the stones of the Via Egnatia. The ride was rough, and though she tried to relax, she could not, thinking on the news that Damon had just shared. Felix had seized the dye works for Rome.

The dye works was her business, but it was also her life's work. She was Lydia, dealer in purple cloth. Who was she without that? How would she pay her bills, her servants? The medicine she had promised to buy for Andreas's mother? For food? Her savings were gone. She had nothing left.

It was but one more thing her faith had cost her.

At some point, she slept, and she was woken by three taps on the side of the wagon. She sat up and saw that it was late afternoon, and they were parked under a grove of cypress trees not far from a dirt path at the base of the foothills that led to the east.

"Let us take a short break," Galen said. He helped her up and gave her privacy while she went farther into the grove to relieve herself, and then he did the same. After a quick meal of dried lamb and nuts, he bundled her back into the wagon and they continued on. Thus they continued for the rest of that day and night, taking only short breaks to rest the horse and refresh themselves. Lydia had plenty of time to think about all that she had lost and who she was without the dye works. And by the time the sun rose again on the second day, Lydia knew the answer. She was not Lydia, dealer in purple cloth, any longer. But she was, and would always be, Lydia, a child of the Living God.

Late the second day, the wagon stopped and Lydia heard three raps again. When she emerged, she saw that they had arrived. A beautiful house of golden stone was set on a hill surrounded by eucalyptus and cypress trees. All around them were hills, as far as she could see in every direction, and there were no other buildings in sight. Grapevines spilled down the hillsides in neat rows, and an orchard farther down sheltered olive and fruit trees.

"This is stunning."

Galen nodded beside her, and a man came out to tend to the horse. He introduced himself as Nestor and told them to head to the house. Before they arrived at the tall wooden door, it opened, and a stooped woman answered the door. She identified herself as Kali, and she led Lydia to a room with a stone tub that sat over a fire. Lydia sank into the hot bath gratefully. She used sweet-smelling soap to clean herself for the first time in weeks, and when she emerged, a soft, clean robe was waiting for her. Kali brought her a meal of fish and greens and fresh melon and then helped her climb into bed, where she fell into a deep sleep. It was the next afternoon before she awoke.

Lydia pushed back the soft blankets and took in the high ceilings, the large windows, the spacious room. Damon's uncle, whoever he was, had this beautiful home just sitting empty. She had so many questions, but knew she would not get many answers just yet. It was cooler up in the hills, and she pulled the robe around her and then walked to the window. All around her, grapevines glowed green in the sunshine, and beyond them, the golden hills spread out in all directions. The whole place seemed bathed in sunlight.

Lydia saw that new robes had been placed in her room while she slept, and she chose one of fine linen and dressed her hair as best she could. She wandered out and found Kali in the open-air kitchen, cooking lamb.

"How can I help?" Lydia asked.

"You are to rest and relax," Kali said. "Please, recover your strength. That is your only duty."

Lydia wanted to argue, but she felt suddenly so tired. After a meal of lamb and bread, she returned to her bed and slept again until evening.

At the evening meal, she and Galen ate alone at a long table. "When will you be returning to Philippi?" Lydia asked. She thought he must be planning to return as soon as he and the horse had rested.

"My orders are to stay here as long as you are here," Galen said.

Lydia hid her surprise and then realized she should not have been shocked after all. Damon had always looked out for her. Why would he not do so now?

The days passed. Lydia spent her time wandering in the olive and lemon groves and walking among the vines, enjoying the feel of the sun on her skin. Slowly, she recovered her strength. She tried to talk with Kali, but though she was polite, she was reserved. She and Nestor had lived here and cared for the house for more than thirty years, she told Lydia. Their children were long grown. The man who owned the house came only every few years. It was a peaceful life. She was happy enough.

Lydia wrote letters to Damon and to Anna and to Claes, asking for word on what was happening at home. Iduma knew where the coins were kept. She would make sure she and Danae and Elodie and Leon could eat for the next few months. After that, she did not know what would happen to them or how she could help.

Lydia also spent hours in prayer, asking God in His mercy to protect the others back in Philippi. She asked that Felix would change his mind and return the dye works. She felt bad sitting here in this luxurious house while the others were left to face the consequences of continuing to meet and pray together in defiance of the law. She prayed that Anna and Eli and the baby would be well, and that she would be reunited with them someday. More than anything, she prayed that God would make a way for her to thank Damon for all he had done for her. She asked for a way for them to be brought together.

As the weeks passed, Lydia came up with a plan. She knew she could not return to Philippi. Her life there as she knew it was over. But she had committed to growing the church. She could still do that, she realized. It would just look different than she had thought. She would send a letter to Paul. She would meet up with him and Silas. She would help spread this Gospel around the world alongside the leaders of the faith. She could handle sleeping on the hard ground and trusting God for her next meal. She was not afraid.

Lydia had been at the house for almost two months when the sound of approaching horses sounded on the drive. Lydia had long since grown used to the noise. Deliveries of supplies from the village, a great distance away, arrived nearly every day, and she had no reason to suspect this was anything different. She continued her walk under the olive trees, taking solace from the summer sun in their cool shade. It was only when she heard footsteps that she emerged from the rows of trees and she saw him.

Damon looked different, standing in that golden sunlight. His skin was darker, and his hair was bleached lighter by the sun. He was dressed in linen, and his beard and hair had grown longer.

Lydia could not help herself. She let out a small cry, ran toward him, and threw her arms around him. He laughed, and his strong arms wrapped around her and lifted her off the ground.

"Is it really you? Are you really here?"

"Lydia." He set her feet back on the ground and grasped her hands. "I have missed you."

Lydia studied him up close. She admired the familiar curve of his cheek, the strong jawline, the deep brown of his eyes. She loved the contours of his face. But still, she saw again that there was something different. There was something altered about his countenance. He seemed...lighter, somehow.

"I have missed you too." Lydia's voice came out husky, and she did not know why.

For a moment, they both stood still, looking at the other. The air felt heavy, sultry, and there was a kind of energy in the air, as just before a lightning strike.

And then, before she even realized what he was doing, Damon leaned forward and kissed her. His lips were soft but insistent, and as she felt herself melt into him, a spark of excitement ran through every part of her body. His beard scratched against her skin, and it made her feel more alive. She had never felt such drive, such desire. She wanted every part of him close to her. In that moment, she forgot about every reason they could not be together. But as she tried to pull him closer to her, Damon slowly, reluctantly, pulled away.

"You are even more beautiful." Damon's voice was hoarse as he rubbed his hand across his face. "I did not dare believe my memory."

Lydia wanted to pull him close again, to return the kiss and deepen it, but she stood in front of him, waiting. She breathed in deeply, smelling his scent. "You came."

"I came," Damon said. "And I bring news. Much has changed since you left Philippi."

"Yes?" As Lydia's heartbeat began to slow and her breathing returned to normal, she remembered all that she had wanted to ask him. "Please, tell me."

"Come," Damon said. "Let us return to the house, and I will tell you all."

Lydia did not want to return—she wanted to stay here in this beautiful, secluded orchard where they were alone. But for that reason, she nodded, realizing the wisdom in his words, and reluctantly followed him back toward the house. He held her hand, and as they walked, he told her that he had checked in on Anna weekly and that she was doing well, and her belly was growing day by day.

"Did you tell her who you are?" As far as she knew, Anna and Damon had never met.

"I told her I was a friend of her mother's," Damon said. "After what you had told me about her, I was worried she would slam the door in my face, but she allowed me in. She cares about you, Lydia. Truly, she does."

"She is not angry?"

"I think her anger has had time to cool," he said. "She seems to genuinely want to know that you are safe. I have a letter from her to pass on to you."

Lydia thanked the Lord for this small bit of good news. When they were back at the house, they sat at a small table on the patio, in the shade of the eucalyptus trees. Kali brought out a carafe of wine and bread and olive oil.

Damon told her that Felix had installed one of his own men to run the dye works and that they were now turning out cheaply made dyes that streaked the fabric with uneven, muddy color. Hyperion had hired Leia, and Asuman and Filip had found work with Hektor. It made Lydia glad to know that at least her workers were cared for, even if the dye works was no longer hers.

Damon told her that he had visited her home regularly and the servants were doing well, even little Elodie, who was gaining strength and confidence. They were well fed. They were taken care of. They would be all right, for a while, at least.

"And Clement?" Lydia could hardly bring herself to ask. "What happened when my absence was discovered?"

"Ah. Now that is an interesting story," Damon said, dipping a chunk of his bread in the golden olive oil.

Lydia took a sip of wine, waiting for him to go on.

"Felix, as you might have guessed, was not happy when it was noticed that you were gone."

"I would have been surprised to hear otherwise."

"He ordered the guard responsible to be executed."

"Oh no."

"But the head guard—"

"The one you paid?"

"Exactly. He did an admirable job. He might join your friend Claes at the theater if he decided to retire from being a guard."

"What do you mean?"

"He assured our praetor that the order would be carried out."

"Felix did not need to witness the execution himself?"

"My cousin is…" Damon trailed off. "He is squeamish. He once fainted at the sight of a pig being slaughtered when we were children. Still, the guard asked if the praetor would like to see the man's head as proof."

Lydia's stomach roiled. "What if he had said yes?"

"It is a good thing I know my cousin well. He did not need the proof, and Clement walks free to this day."

"I am so glad." Lydia let out a breath she hadn't realized she'd been holding. "And the rest of the church? Did Felix retaliate? He must have known that they were involved."

"They are fine. They still meet. As of yet, they have not been molested or disturbed."

"I am so glad." Lydia did not know how this was possible, but then, God was in control. Even the waves and the wind obeyed Him. As long as Jesus was in the boat, they did not need to fear.

For a long moment, neither spoke, and the call of a turtledove was the only sound on the patio. Jasmine filled the air with its perfume, and the afternoon light bathed the surrounding hills in golden light.

Lydia was so grateful for the news, and yet with it came the reality that she was completely cut off from her own life. She did not know how long she could stay here, but what would happen if she came back to Philippi?

"I have been thinking," Lydia said. "About what happens next."

"I have as well," Damon said. "I have thought of little else."

"I cannot return to Philippi," Lydia said.

"Not unless something drastic changes," Damon said. "If you return now, Felix will simply have you thrown into prison again."

"And yet I cannot stay here forever," Lydia said.

"You may stay as long as you wish," Damon said. "My uncle will not need the house."

"I am grateful to be here," Lydia said. "But I have an idea about what I will do."

"Good. I have also had an idea." Damon drained his cup of wine and set it down. As she was about to tell him about her plan to sail around the world with Paul and Silas, Damon said, "I can see only one way for you to return to Philippi."

Lydia started. She had not been expecting this. "What is that?"

"The only way you would be protected from Felix is if you were a Roman citizen," Damon said. "He could not arrest you without a speedy trial. He could not levy excessive taxes. He may still try to eliminate the church, but he could not hurt you as easily. It would be the only way."

Lydia knew what he was suggesting.

"You are saying I should marry you because you are a Roman citizen. As your wife, I would be protected."

"No. I am saying you should marry me because I love you, and because you love me."

She could not deny the truth of his statement. She did love him, deeply and without reservation. But love, in this case, was not enough.

"I cannot—"

"Wait. Before you tell me that you are going to throw away my happiness and yours because of your commitment to the church, I need to tell you something."

"No, I—"

"Lydia. Please stop arguing and listen to me."

She bit her lip and gestured for him to speak.

"I told you that the church was meeting and that Felix had not interfered with its gatherings. I did not mention why that is."

"Why?"

"He cannot interfere, not when it meets at the home of a Roman citizen."

"They do not meet at my home?" Lydia struggled to understand. "Where do they meet?"

"They have been meeting at my home since you left Philippi."

Lydia was so shocked by this news that she did not say anything at first. Then eventually, she asked, "What?" She had heard him wrong, surely.

"Believe me when I say I did not want them to. Not at first anyway. But I knew if it mattered to you—mattered enough to you that you were willing to go to prison rather than renounce your faith—I decided I could not keep pushing them away. Not if I wanted to convince you to be my wife. I told Claes to spread the word. They now meet at my home."

Lydia was still speechless. "You are serious?"

"I also knew that it would make Felix very angry. I would be lying if I did not say that played into my decision as well."

Lydia let out a laugh.

"You truly let the followers of the Way meet?"

"I do not understand why you don't believe me. Have I made a habit of lying to you?"

"No. But…" She had no other words.

"The funny thing is, after listening to them talk about Jesus for a few weeks, it did not seem as crazy as it did at first."

"Really?"

"I am not saying I believed it all. Don't get me wrong. It took quite a while for me to believe that anything they were saying was different from any other made-up god. But eventually, it did not seem as strange." He picked up the carafe and poured more wine into his glass.

"How so?"

"This Jesus character—He did not seem to match what I had heard about Him. I had been told He was a revolutionary and that He claimed to be more important than any man who had ever lived. But during the service, I heard about a man who laid down His life for His brothers. Instead of a zealot bound on overthrowing the empire, I was told about a man who asked His followers to care and sacrifice for others. Slowly, I realized that I did not think His followers had everything wrong."

Lydia sat still, trying to absorb all he had said.

"And of course, there was much to plan, and when Claes and Epaphroditus began to come over and talk to me about the service and how they would be run, our conversation often turned to talking about why they believe and what it means to follow Christ."

Lydia gasped.

"You are surprised."

"I am," she admitted. "Pleased, but surprised." She took in a breath. "What happened to everything having a rational explanation? To needing to see a miracle to believe that they are possible?"

"I did see a miracle."

Lydia leaned forward.

"The thing is, it looked nothing like I was expecting," Damon said. "I wanted a sign in the sky or a light coming down from the heavens to tell me Jesus was the truth. I did not see that. Instead, I saw a group of people who cared for one another, even when it cost them. Who shared food, with those who had more giving to those who had none. I saw them stand, fearless, firm in their faith, before a ruler who wanted them to renounce it. I saw brave souls who pledged loyalty to Jesus Christ instead of their own gain. And I realized, slowly, that the existence of believers like this was a miracle."

"So…" Lydia was not sure she understood. "What are you saying?"

"I am saying that, despite my determination not to, I believe. I cannot stop myself from thinking Jesus's message is the truth."

Lydia did not expect the tears that rose up from somewhere deep inside her, but they spilled over before she could stop them.

"It's not as bad as all that," Damon said, pulling a square of fabric from his pocket. He held it out to her. "I like to think the Christians could do a lot worse than me."

Despite herself, Lydia laughed.

"So…" Lydia did not know how to phrase this. "If I married you, you would not mind if I continued to host the church in our home?"

"I would insist on it."

Lydia sat back, absorbing all of this. It was too good to be true. And yet it was true. Her prayers had been answered but in a way she had never dreamed possible.

"Do you know what this means, Lydia?"

She pressed her lips together, shook her head.

"It means you no longer have an excuse not to marry me."

She leaned forward and kissed him, and this time, he did not stop her.

EPILOGUE

The sun streamed in through the window as Lydia dressed for the Lord's Day service.

"You should wear that one," Damon called from the bed, where he was still lounging lazily. He pointed to the deep reddish-indigo robe she had worn for their wedding. He had tried to get her to wear the robe each week to the service since, and she had always refused.

"I will choose something more suitable," Lydia said, selecting a plain linen robe.

"You are beautiful, even in a plain robe," Damon said. "But I will always associate that color with you. I love to see you in it."

"I am no longer a dealer in purple cloth," Lydia said.

"You will be again soon." Damon sat up in the bed. "As soon as those shells arrive, you can begin your first batch."

They had bought a small building that had fallen into disrepair just down the road from where her old dye works still stood. Together, they had restored it, and Lydia was starting her new workshop with a small amount of material. It would be nothing like the old workshop, but that was all right. She would start small, and she would build it up slowly. She would make purple cloth once again.

"What I mean is, that is not *all* I am. That is not how I am defined now."

"That's right." Damon held out an arm, gesturing for her to come closer. She walked toward him, and he hooked her with his arm. "You are my wife as well."

She leaned over and planted a kiss on his lips, and he tried to pull her down onto the bed, but she laughed and stood, though he held on to the string on her robe "Not now. There are already people beginning to gather downstairs."

"Let them wait." He pulled her toward himself. "They all understand what happens when you have a wife as beautiful as mine."

Lydia laughed and pulled back. "Later. For now, you must get up."

Damon sighed and climbed out of bed. Lydia could not help but watch him as he walked across the room. She still could not believe she was married to this incredible man.

They had wed in a quiet ceremony not long after they had returned from the mountains. Damon's daughter Kasandra had attended, but Anna did not. Anna had visited several times since the wedding, though, stealing away while Daniel thought she was visiting with friends. Those moments were precious to Lydia, and she hoped that someday Anna would feel that she was allowed to reconnect with her mother openly. Lydia prayed for it every day, and she tried to be patient. There would be time.

She had sold her home and used a portion of the money to buy the quicksilver Andreas's mother had needed, but she died soon after drinking the treatment. Still, the act of buying it had allowed Andreas's family to speak to her again. She prayed that their relationship would continue to improve over the coming years.

"Miss?" Elodie knocked on the door, balancing a tray of tea against the wall.

"Come in."

Elodie set the tray down on the table in the corner and poured the tea into two cups. It took Elodie longer than it took the others, but Lydia did not mind.

"They are starting to gather, miss," Elodie said.

"Thank you." She heard the chairs and tables being pushed out of the way and the sound of voices.

"Euodia and Syntyche have already begun to argue over the correct placement of the dais," Elodie said. "You may need to help settle the argument again."

Lydia sighed. All members of the church were important. But not all of them were easy to deal with. "We'll be down shortly."

As Lydia dressed, she considered how different her life looked than it had last winter, when she had met a group of ill-kempt vagabonds on a riverbank. The message they shared had turned her life upside down and changed her heart forever and, in the process, had changed everything. She had been financially ruined, imprisoned, forced to run for her life. She had lost everything she had thought made her who she was. Everything that she had believed was important in her life—her Jewish community, her family, her business, all of it— had been taken from her once she had embraced the message of God's grace.

But she had gained so much more.

She tightened the strings on her robe but had to leave it a little looser than the previous week. Soon, others would start to notice, but for now, she could still hide the small bump of her belly.

"Are you ready?" Damon came up behind her and placed his hands on her belly.

"Yes." Lydia turned and kissed him again. "Let us go down."

Damon held open the door and followed her down the stairs. They had agreed that if it was a girl, they would name her Eunike, after Damon's first wife, and if a boy, he would be Giorgio. Lydia had worried about choosing names so early, but already this child had lasted longer than any of the others save Anna. Besides, they both trusted that God was in control of this as well.

Together, they walked down the stairs to the church service that would soon begin. Together, Damon and Lydia were building a family. But also, with all the believers now gathered in their home, they were building the church. No matter what happened next, Lydia knew that this was really all that mattered.

Someday, they hoped followers of the Way would not need to hide. They dreamed of a world where Christians could practice their faith openly, where it was accepted—even endorsed— by the government. But that world was very far off. She had faith anyway.

Lydia knew the world would never know her name. People would never know that a dealer in purple cloth had encountered followers of Jesus on a muddy riverbank and believed with all her heart. The world would never know what her faith had cost her. It did not matter. Lydia and her new husband had agreed that even if it cost them everything, they would continue to spread the Good News throughout the world.

"Ready?"

She nodded, and together she and Damon walked into the church service and began to praise the Lord, along with all the saints.

Those who came after her might never know there had even been a church in Philippi at all, or what it had cost to see it flourish, even if it were remembered.

But even if it cost Lydia every last thing she had, she would make sure that the world would know the name of Jesus Christ.

That was the only thing that truly mattered.

AUTHOR'S NOTE

Dear Reader,

I have read the book of Acts many times, and I knew the story of Lydia. I mean, I thought I did. She was a dealer in purple cloth and converted, and then she let the disciples live in her house. That's pretty much it, right?

But as always happens with a closer look at the Bible, I quickly realized that the story is much more complicated and layered than that. Once I started digging into Lydia's story and writing about her life, I kept coming across moments that I hadn't really taken the time to understand before.

Take the story of Paul losing his patience with the fortune-teller and casting out a demon, for instance. That's from Acts 16:16–18. The more I dug, the stranger that story got. I had never taken the time to understand the connection to the Oracle of Delphi and the Greek god Apollo, or what it meant that the fortune-teller recognized what others in Philippi had not: that these men were truly representatives of the Most High God. I also saw how strange and plausible it was that rich men had been exploiting this girl and how angry they became when what they considered their property—what they saw as theirs by right—was taken away. That impulse hasn't changed with the centuries.

I had always heard the Sunday school story of Paul and Silas escaping from prison after an earthquake and never thought beyond what a great miracle it was. But as I was writing, I realized what an immense quake that must have been and how much damage it must have caused, not just to the prison but to the whole area. Sure, it was an incredible answer to prayer for Paul and Silas—but what about everyone else? It became more complicated the more I thought about it, and hopefully you'll see my wrestling with what this miraculous answer to prayer must have meant for others in Philippi in these pages.

I also enjoyed looking at the book of Philippians—the letter Paul wrote to the church at Philippi—to learn more about what the church there must have been like. Some of the characters mentioned in that letter appear here. My personal favorites are Syntyche and Euodia—what were they fighting about? I don't know, but I have spent enough time in churches that this felt surprisingly, hilariously familiar to me.

I was initially intrigued by Lydia's story because she was (from what we can tell based on what we're told in scripture, anyway) a single, independent woman of means, and I was interested in exploring how women were so often responsible for the spread of—and the financing of—the early church. It's a chapter in our church history that I wanted to learn more about, and I hope this gives a glimpse into what the life of one early woman of faith might have looked like. I sure did enjoy writing it.

Blessings,
Beth Adams

FACTS BEHIND
the Fiction

❖

WHEN PAUL MET LYDIA

Paul had no intention of going to Europe. He was touring what is now Turkey on his second mission trip, which started in about AD 49 or 50. But something happened that changed his mind.

He had planned to revisit cities where he and Barnabas planted small house churches in central Turkey. Then he wanted to head to the west coast, perhaps to the city of Ephesus, a major port of entry for anyone sailing in from Rome, "but the Holy Spirit would not let them preach in Asia" (Acts 16:6 CEV). So he headed northwest, then planned to double back eastward along Turkey's northern shoreline. There, in what is now northwestern Turkey, Paul, his new associate, Timothy, and possibly Luke sat and waited.

The mission team was in Troas, a port city on Turkey's northeastern corner, a short two-day voyage to Europe across the Aegean Sea. "During the night, Paul had a vision of someone from Macedonia who was standing there and begging him, 'Come over to Macedonia and help us!'" (Acts 16:9 CEV).

This is where scholars say Luke may have joined Paul's mission entourage. "We [note this doesn't say "They"] began looking for a way to go to Macedonia" (Acts 16:10 CEV). That's the first time the writer

A TYPICAL SAILING SHIP FROM PAUL'S DAY.

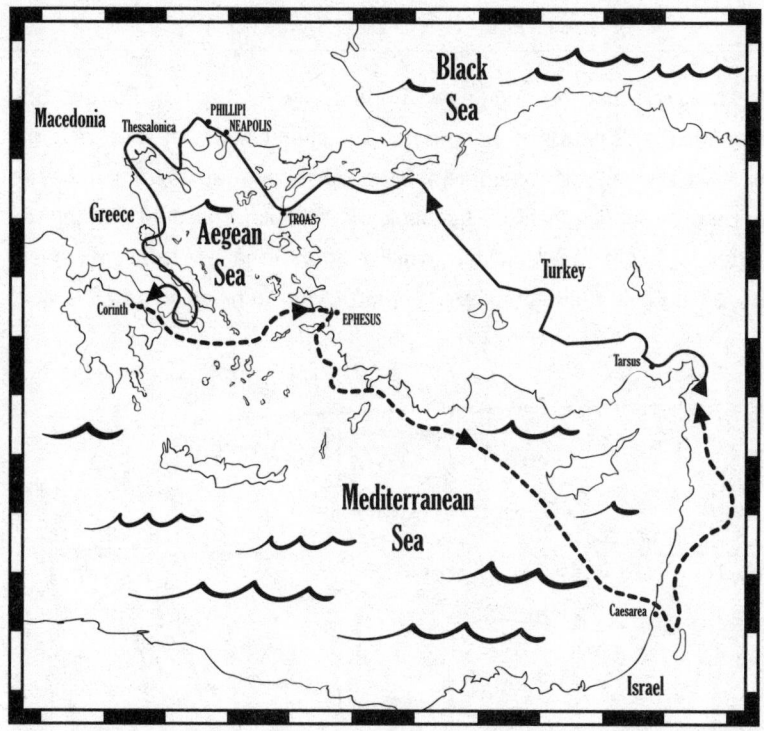

of Acts includes himself in Paul's missionary adventures. And they *were* adventures, sometimes dangerous.

Two ships and two days later, the group landed in the Macedonian port city of Neapolis, now Kavala. From there, they moved on to neighboring Philippi, roughly a three-hour walk inland, about eight miles (13 km). There, by a stream during a Sabbath prayer meeting, the men met Lydia— a complete stranger—who believed what they said about Jesus and invited them to stay at her house. Paul had felt led to go to the river: "Where we thought people would be meeting for prayer" (Acts 16:13 NLT).

Josephus, a Jewish historian from the first century, confirmed in the book *Antiquities of the Jews* that there was a community of Jews in Philippi. But perhaps not enough to start a synagogue. That would explain why locals met for prayer by the riverside. God had clearly orchestrated this otherwise seemingly coincidental string of events.

LYDIA, PAUL'S PATRON

Lydia wasn't just the first-known Christian in what is now Europe. She became Paul's patron, or benefactor. The church she hosted in her home became his only known source of financial support, aside from money he earned by making tents. The book of Philippians is Paul's thank-you letter for a gift they sent him while he was in jail. "I have all I need, because Epaphroditus brought your gift to me" (Philippians 4:18 NCV).

ST. PAUL PRISON IN PHILIPPI, WHERE PAUL IS SAID TO HAVE WRITTEN THE LETTER TO THE PHILIPPIANS.

It might have been unusual at the time for Paul to accept help from a woman, but he was in good company. Jesus had accepted help from "Mary Magdalene, from whom he had cast out seven demons; Joanna, the wife of Chuza, Herod's business manager; Susanna; and many others who were contributing from their own resources to support Jesus and his disciples" (Luke 8:3 NLT).

Lydia, like some of the women in Jesus's traveling entourage, seemed remarkably independent. She ran a business catering to the rich and famous. She was a "merchant of expensive purple cloth" (Acts 16:14 NLT). Purple cloth was a luxury item made from the dye of sea mollusks known as rock snails.

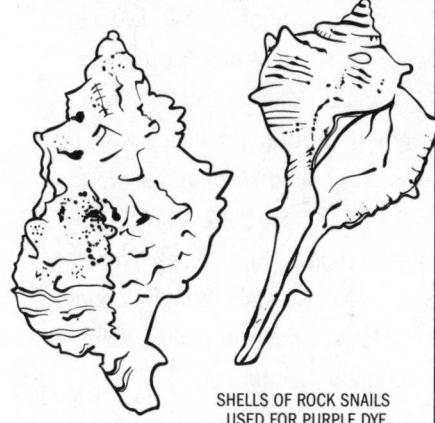

SHELLS OF ROCK SNAILS USED FOR PURPLE DYE.

It took many people to pick thousands of murex sea snails, carnivorous gastropod mollusks, from rocks along the shore and process them for dye. They could crush the dye out or boil it out in huge vats for days—producing a nose-twisting stench. It took even more time if the dye-maker decided to milk the mollusks as a renewable source of dye. The murex snail secretions aren't purple to begin with. They're clear. The heat and light work on the chemicals in the secretions to turn it purple.

QUESTIONS ABOUT LYDIA

Lydia came from Thyatira, an industrial center in western Turkey famous for producing purple cloth. But Paul met Lydia and converted her to Christianity in Philippi, in what is now Greece. What was she doing there, some 300 miles (480 km) north of home?

Some scholars say she was probably on a sales trip to see some of her wealthy clients. But she had a home in Philippi. She also had a household of people—servants, if not children, and possibly a husband, though Luke doesn't mention one and some scholars believe she was a widow. "Come and stay at my home," she told Paul after "she and her household were baptized" (Acts 16:15 NLT). All of this happened on day one—the first time she met Paul.

Some might think it would not have been acceptable for a Jewish woman to invite into her house a group of men she just met. Jewish

PHILIP II OF MACEDON, WHO NAMED
THE CITY OF PHILIPPI AFTER HIMSELF.

women in some communities weren't even supposed to speak to men. Jewish leaders were expected to distance themselves from women in public.

One explanation for Lydia's behavior is that since the time of Alexander the Great (356–323 BC), women in this province, which Romans called Macedonia, were well-known for their leadership roles in society. In that case, most people wouldn't have thought it odd for Lydia to show strangers some Macedonian hospitality.

LYDIA'S SAME-DAY BAPTISM

It might seem extraordinary that Paul—almost at first sight—converted Lydia to Christianity. She was a complete stranger. They had just met beside the river outside Philippi, and Paul immediately baptized her right there. That would seem strange to many today. But in Paul's day, it would have been inappropriate to leave the riverside without taking advantage of the opportunity to baptize a new believer.

In New Testament times, when Christianity was still just a movement in what looked like a new branch of Judaism, all Christians got baptized. There are no exceptions in the New Testament. Jesus Himself said, "Go and make disciples of all the nations, baptizing them in the name of the Father and the Son and the Holy Spirit" (Matthew 28:19 NLT).

Peter preached the Jerusalem sermon that saw the conversion of over 3,000 Jews in one day. He told the crowd, "Each of you must repent of your sins and turn to God, and be baptized in the name of Jesus Christ for the forgiveness of your sins (Acts 2:38 NLT).

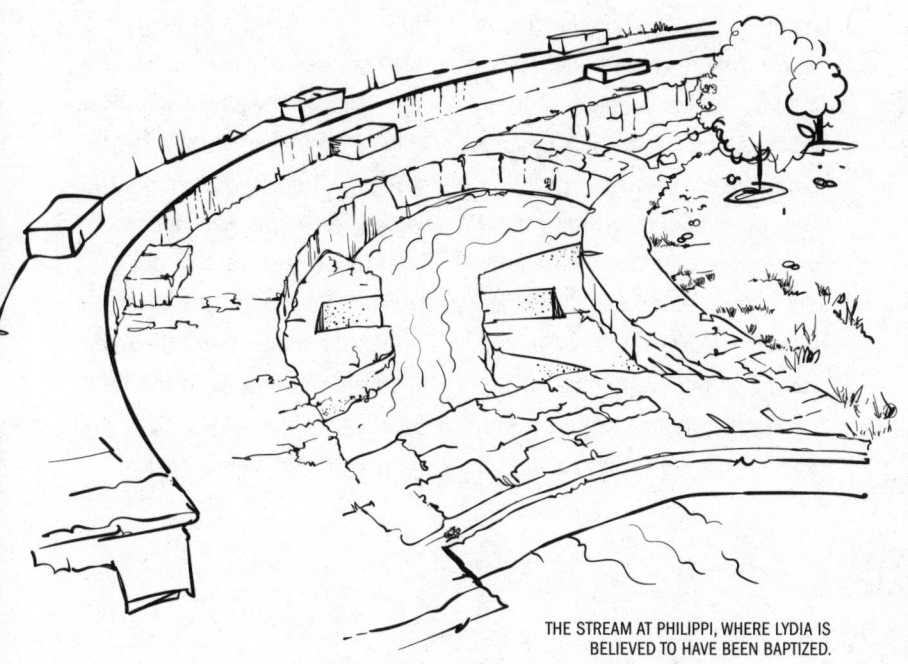

THE STREAM AT PHILIPPI, WHERE LYDIA IS BELIEVED TO HAVE BEEN BAPTIZED.

THYATIRA: LYDIA'S HOMETOWN IN TURKEY

There's not much left of Lydia's hometown of Thyatira, the ruins of which are buried under the modern city of Akhisar, near Turkey's west coast. But there are plenty of inscriptions supporting what the Bible says about it.

Luke reported that Lydia was "a merchant of expensive purple cloth" (Acts 16:14 NLT), or, as the King James Version poetically says, "a seller of purple." Inscriptions chiseled on stone to honor leading citizens reveal

Thyatira was a manufacturing center specializing in wool and in dyed fabric—especially expensive purple cloth.

Inscriptions uncovered so far commend workers and business owners who produced linen, wool clothing, leather products, robes, and dyed fabric. These inscriptions reveal there were more guilds of dyers in Thyatira than in any other city in the region Rome called Asia. This sprawling province covered about a fourth of Turkey, starting on the western coast.

Thyatira is one of the seven cities in western Turkey to receive a message from God in Revelation. Thyatira did not get a complimentary letter. The writer says Jesus is upset with Thyatira's idol worship and immorality. In that letter, Revelation's prophet depicts Jesus in terms the residents of Thyatira would have understood well: "This is the message from the Son of God, whose eyes are like flames of fire, whose feet are like polished bronze" (Revelation 2:18 NLT). He urged Christians there to reject this behavior and keep the faith: "hold tightly to what you have until I come" (Revelation 2:25 NLT).

RUINS OF ANCIENT PHILIPPI.

HOW ROMAN ROADS WERE BUILT. SOME, SUCH AS THE APPIAN WAY, ARE STILL IN USE TODAY.

BUILT TO LAST

Rome built an international network of stone-paved roads throughout the Mediterranean world—50,000 miles (80,000 km) of them. They did it for military reasons. They wanted their army to be able to rush to any hot spot of rebel activity and crush it quickly—without getting bogged down in muddy trails.

Romans built their roads in layers, though not always the same way. In some of the more important roads, the layers reached five feet deep and stretched 50 feet wide (1.5 by 15 m).

- Start with a deep trench of native ground rammed tight.
- Add a thick layer of stones, each one big enough to fill a hand.
- Layer on rock rubble, broken stones, and lime.
- Add a layer of Rome's discovery: limestone concrete made with crushed pottery.
- Top it off with large flat stones. Arch the middle of the road above the sides so it sheds water like a turtle's shell and it drains to each side.
- Add raised edge stones to mark both sides of the road.

Rome's paved roads provide one important reason that Christianity spread so quickly and explain why Paul was able to cover an estimated 10,000 miles (16,000 km) during his mission trips. Some of these roads still exist, including those preserved at Pompeii, buried under ash and lava of Mount Vesuvius's volcanic eruption in AD 79.

Fiction Author
ELIZABETH ADAMS

Elizabeth (Beth) Adams lives in Brooklyn, New York, with her husband and two young daughters. When she's not writing, she spends her time cleaning up after two devious cats and trying to find time to read.

Nonfiction Author
STEPHEN M. MILLER

Stephen M. Miller is an award-winning, bestselling Christian author of easy-reading books about the Bible and Christianity. His books have sold over 1.9 million copies and include *The Complete Guide to the Bible*, *Who's Who and Where's Where in the Bible*, and *How to Get Into the Bible*.

Miller lives in the suburbs of Kansas City with his wife, Linda, a registered nurse. They have two married children who live nearby.

Read on for a sneak peek of another exciting story in the Ordinary Women of the Bible series!

THE PROPHET'S SONGBIRD: ATARAH'S STORY

by Roseanna M. White

The prophet was coming, and the thrill of it made notes of joy burst in Atarah's mind and spill from her lips in a hum. She pulled the last round of bread from the side of the oven and offered it to her mother with a grin. Tonight, perhaps, Elisha himself would dine with them. Or tomorrow. Soon he would arrive, and the entire School of the Sons of the Prophets would feast together to welcome him.

"Thank you, Atarah." Imma took the bread and slid it onto the table, huffing a breath when the twins darted by, nearly knocking her from her feet. "Channah! Havah! Sit and eat."

Her little sisters jostled each other for their favorite spots, ignoring their mother's chiding. Atarah pressed her lips against another grin. Barely in their fifth year, those two could try the patience of anyone. Imma might be capable of making the hardest of hearts crack in grief when she lifted her voice in mourning, but inspiring the twins to behave themselves was another talent altogether—one only Abba seemed able to master.

Fortunate, then, that he strolled in now, silencing the twins with one well-aimed glare before sending a wink Atarah's way. "Something smells delicious." He settled against his usual cushion and smiled at them all. He would have been out already, helping the other prophets care for the animals, teaching his students how to listen for Yahweh in every stirring of the breeze, every bleat of a lamb, every buzz of a bee. "Our God is a living God," she'd heard him saying to Tavi last week, "so we seek Him through the tending of life. We see the sacred in the miracle of this world He has created."

Tavi—a student at the school only for the past three years but unquestionably Abba's favorite—had nodded in that solemn way of his.

Channah snuggled against Atarah's side the moment she folded her legs and sat. She turned her sweet little face up to her too. "What song are you going to sing when the prophet arrives, Atarah?"

Her stomach danced a bit at the question. It was Elisha himself who had first invited her to sing a psalm of praise before the school, when she was scarcely older than Channah and Havah were now. But it still made her anxious to do so when he was here—anxious and eager both. It was Yahweh she wanted to praise and please with her voice, ultimately, but...but one could not get much closer to Him than His prophet.

"The one hundred forty-fifth, I think." It was the first song she had ever sung in front of the school. *I will extol thee, my God, O king; and I will bless thy name for ever and ever.*

Havah grinned at her. "What about this morning? Will you sing the one about Him training my hands for war?" Havah pulled her arm back, as if she held a miniature bow.

Abba gusted out a sigh. "Havah. Leave the warring to your brothers."

Havah's brows drew together like a thundercloud. The storm was only cut off because two of those brothers chose that moment to hurry into the room, all elbows and knees as they jostled each other into place.

Atarah grinned at the boys—eight and ten now—and tried not to miss the eldest of them too much. Joshua had been away from home for two years as he studied to be a scribe, but she had yet to get used to his absence.

Imma turned to the table with the last of the breakfast dishes in her hands, sending a weary look toward the twins. "Perhaps Atarah should sing a plea for relief from persecutors today."

She chuckled and then let the conversation drop while Abba led them in a short prayer of thanksgiving. But while talk afterward turned to the weather and when Elisha might arrive, Atarah let the many songs she knew float through her mind. Which one today? Something joyful, because the prophet was coming. Something happy, because the Lord had blessed the school so richly. Something…something that had a hope of teasing a rare smile to Tavi's lips.

"What do you think, Atarah?"

"Hmm?" She looked up at her father. His plate was empty. Even more surprising, so was hers.

His smile was as soft and warm as the bread she could scarcely remember eating. "I was only saying it will be a joy to see Gahazi again. And that perhaps you could plan to sing his favorite song after the meal too."

"Of course." She reached for his empty plate, stacked it with hers, and then raised a questioning brow toward the twins, neither of whom had finished their yogurt yet. Channah stopped her giggling long enough to scoop some onto an apple slice and stuff it into her mouth.

Abba's hand landed on Atarah's shoulder. "Whenever they arrive—be it tonight or tomorrow—we will have another announcement too. Something I think you will be most pleased to celebrate."

The last time her father had worn that particular expression, it had been when he informed the family that arrangements had been made for Joshua to be educated as a scribe—a true honor, and one that had made her elder brother beam with joy. *She* had not been quite so happy to say farewell to him, though she was of course bursting with pride.

Was this news that he had completed his studies and would be coming home? Or perhaps that final arrangements had been made for his marriage? Atarah would certainly be thrilled when Joshua returned and wed Sahar—then she would finally get to claim her friend as her sister.

The younger children were bustling away from the table with their usual noise, so she asked for no clarification now. She simply smiled and nodded, noting that the light in Abba's eyes was the simple kind. Not the one that shone from them on those occasions when the Spirit of God came upon him and he spoke something divine. This was not Johash son of Ner, one of the prophets, who spoke—just Abba.

"Hurry, Atarah!" Channah shouted from the doorway. "I see Tavi and Abner coming!"

It was all the inspiration Atarah needed to rush the plates to the bench and fly back to the sleeping chamber the girls all shared for her head covering. They would scour the breakfast dishes later, after the school had joined together for prayers and song and then dismissed the students to their classes and tasks.

She joined her sisters outside just as the two young men reached their house. Abner smiled as he lifted a hand, revealing twin rows of straight white teeth. "Good morning! How are the loveliest ladies in Ramah today?"

He never missed an opportunity to smile at her or compliment her or Imma. He was without question the handsomest student at the school and the most charming, and he was of an age to choose a wife and start a household of his own. Every girl in the region had been vying for his attention, trying to convince her father to enter negotiations with his.

Atarah tucked a strand of hair under her headscarf as Imma, a step behind her, greeted him. She barely kept a frown from her brows. She had always found him handsome too, of course. It was a simple fact. And a few years ago, she had entertained dreams about becoming his wife someday. It had seemed likely. Their fathers were friends, both teachers at the school, their families equals.

Now, though, the thought made no notes of anticipation trill through her mind, no song spring to her lips. Abner was a friend. But she had no particular yearning to be his wife.

That was not the news Abba would have for her...was it?

Her gaze darted past him, to Tavi. Two inches shorter, not quite as handsome if one were judging a face by symmetry and whatever else made one person more beautiful than another. Never did he greet anyone with a carefree smile.

But his hands were already caught, one in each of the twins', and he was listening to their chatter with rapt attention, nodding along to whatever they were saying as they tugged him toward the central courtyard of the compound.

She could still see him as he had been when first the prophet brought him here, three years ago. Lanky and thin, yes, but worse than that. He had been hollow. A pottery shell surrounding a void. As if all his heart, all his spirit, had drained from him when he watched the Syrians slaughter his family in a raid.

Elisha had seen something in him though. He had brought him here and whispered a few words to her parents. Abba had taken the young man under his wing, and Imma had made it a point to sing whenever he was near.

Never would Atarah forget the soul-deep weeping she had heard one evening, as finally that void filled—with grief.

Finally, six months after their deaths, Imma's songs inspired him to let himself mourn his parents.

After that, the healing could begin. Atarah had made it her personal challenge to follow up Imma's work on Tavi's heart by inspiring him to smile again. More often than not, she failed to win an *actual* smile…but she had become a master at making his eyes twinkle with otherwise hidden mirth.

She would sing his favorite this morning, from the ninety-second Psalm.

> How great are your works, Lord,
>   how profound your thoughts!
> Senseless people do not know,
>   fools do not understand,
>   that though the wicked spring up like grass
>   and all evildoers flourish,
>   they will be destroyed forever.

He looked over his shoulder as they entered the court-yard, his gaze snagging on hers for a split second. He had strange eyes—a bluish green, so striking against the tone of his skin and his dark hair. The other girls, when they were not dreaming of a betrothal with Abner, were swooning over those eyes.

He gave her no smile, of course. But oh, the twinkle. Atarah grinned back at him and followed her father toward the dais from which he would speak the morning prayer.

The students were a bit rowdy this morning, their voices a babble of excited speculation as she took her position beside

Abba. Everyone was anticipating the prophet's arrival as much as their own family was. She chuckled and leaned close to her father. "Good luck teaching them the Law today."

He breathed a laugh of his own. "I think perhaps it would be a good day to work on the new storehouse instead." He nodded toward the half-finished structure on the outskirts of their compound.

Yahweh Yireh had blessed them indeed this year—their crops had produced a bounty beyond any Atarah could remember, and the animals had been particularly fruitful too. They would have enough not only to get through the winter and spring before the next harvest, but to supply the needs of anyone in the community who lacked.

Abba lifted a hand, but silence did not reign. He shouted, but no one seemed to hear. So he turned to her with a roll of his eyes and an indulgent smile. "Daughter."

She stepped forward. Closed her eyes. Let the wind singing through the branches of the sycamores instill their melody in her spirit. And she sang.

As always, she began with a familiar melody, the one traditionally paired with the lyrics of the song. But rarely could she leave it at that. New notes always sprang into her mind, and she had learned long ago to let them.

Within moments, the crowd had hushed. Here and there, another voice would join in—the deep harmony of Abner's father's bass, the sweet soprano of the youngest students. They sang the traditional melodies, leaving her to run up a scale or give her notes wings like a bird.

Her heart pounded in her chest as the last lines spilled from her lips. This was living. This was praising. This was communing with El Roi, the God who saw her. She opened her eyes again, looking at the crowd not to see what they thought, but seeking one face.

There. Tavi stood at the back, as usual, hands still lifted toward heaven. They lowered as he opened his eyes. Looked her way.

Would he smile? Would he grant her that gift today? Maybe. Yes! There, the corners of his mouth lifted, the light in his eyes reached her even from here. The—

A shout pierced the morning calm, then what sounded like a thousand more, from all around the low walls of the compound. It was a sound she had never heard before but one that made terror dig claws into her spine.

They were under attack.

A NOTE FROM THE EDITORS

We hope you enjoy the Ordinary Women of the Bible series, created by the Books and Inspirational Media Division of Guideposts, a nonprofit organization that touches millions of lives every day through products and services that inspire, encourage, help you grow in your faith, and celebrate God's love in every aspect of your daily life.

Thank you for making a difference with your purchase of this book, which helps fund our many outreach programs to military personnel, prisons, hospitals, nursing homes, and educational institutions. To learn more, visit Guideposts Foundation.org.

We also maintain many useful and uplifting online resources. Visit Guideposts.org to read true stories of hope and inspiration, access OurPrayer network, sign up for free newsletters, download free e-books, join our Facebook community, and follow our stimulating blogs.

To learn about other Guideposts publications, including the bestselling devotional *Daily Guideposts*, go to ShopGuideposts.org, call (800) 932-2145, or write to Guideposts, PO Box 5815, Harlan, Iowa 51593.

Sign up for the
Guideposts Fiction Newsletter
and stay up to date on the books you love!

You'll get sneak peeks of new releases, recommendations from other Guideposts readers, and special offers just for you . . .

and it's FREE!

Just go to Guideposts.org/Newsletters today to sign up.

Guideposts®

Visit Guideposts.org/Shop
or call (800) 932-2145

Find more inspiring stories in these best-loved Guideposts fiction series!

Mysteries of Lancaster County

Follow the Classen sisters as they unravel clues and uncover hidden secrets in Mysteries of Lancaster County. As you get to know these women and their friends, you'll see how God brings each of them together for a fresh start in life.

Secrets of Wayfarers Inn

Retired schoolteachers find themselves owners of an old warehouse-turned-inn that is filled with hidden passages, buried secrets, and stunning surprises that will set them on a course to puzzling mysteries from the Underground Railroad.

Tearoom Mysteries Series

Mix one stately Victorian home, a charming lakeside town in Maine, and two adventurous cousins with a passion for tea and hospitality. Add a large scoop of intriguing mystery, and sprinkle generously with faith, family, and friends, and you have the recipe for *Tearoom Mysteries*.

Mysteries of Martha's Vineyard

Come to the shores of this quaint and historic island and dig in to a cozy mystery. When a recent widow inherits a lighthouse just off the coast of Massachusetts, she finds exciting adventures, new friends, and renewed hope.

To learn more about these books, visit Guideposts.org/Shop